THE
RAPTURE OF
CANAAN

ALSO BY SHERI REYNOLDS

Bitterroot Landing

THE
Rapture of Canaan

Sheri Reynolds

G. P. PUTNAM'S SONS
NEW YORK

This is a work of fiction.
The events, characters, and institutions portrayed are imaginary.
Their resemblance, if any, to real-life counterparts is entirely coincidental.

G. P. Putnam's Sons
Publishers Since 1838
200 Madison Avenue
New York, NY 10016

ISBN 0-399-14112-X

Book design by Chris Welch

Printed in the United States of America

For Mary Smith Cannon

Thanks to Joy Humphrey for critiquing this book through the mail, to Allyson Rainer for giving me page-by-page feedback, and to Amy Tudor for listening patiently to the sections I read aloud and still agreeing to edit it. Thanks also to my family for answering so many farming and pregnancy questions. And thanks to Candice Fuhrman, my agent, for keeping me going.

THE RAPTURE OF CANAAN

I'VE SPENT A LOT OF TIME WEAVING, BUT YOU'D never know it from my hands.

With threads, hair, and twisted fabric, I weave in fragments of myself, bits of other people. I weave in lies, and I weave in love, and in the end, it's hard to know if one keeps me warmer than the other.

And when I'm done, I lift the rug from the loom and study it in my fingers. When I back away five feet, it's bluer or more knotted than I'd remembered. And from twenty feet, it grins at me when all along, I'd thought it pouty. I ask myself, "Is that *my* rug?" But I like anything I make, the rug is never mine. I tell my eyes not to see so much at one time. I flip it over, and from the back, it weeps like someone lost.

Like all lies, loves, stories, it is imperfect, but I could walk on it. I could fold it over the edge of my bed and use it for a blanket or hang it on the wall. Instead, I wrap it over my shoulders, wear it like a shield, covering myself with a tapestry of views.

Tell me the story, Nanna," I used to beg my grandma, leaning against her in the porch swing, my head nuzzling into the space where her long arm connected to her shoulder, and she'd wrap that arm around me and rub my thigh as though it were a wrinkled napkin that she could straighten out if she worked on it long enough.

Afternoons in summer, with lima beans simmering just inside and the saltiness drifting out through the screen door, with curing tobacco sweetly ambering on the edge of a breeze and my Nanna holding onto me and waving the gnats away from my face, the ones that kept flying to the corners of my eyes, those were the afternoons that made me love my Nanna best, even though she admitted to being a liar.

"You don't want to hear that old story," she'd protest. "Herman shouldn'ta never put it in that sermon. You'd think the man would know better, with little children listening. . . ."

"Please tell it," I'd plead. "You tell it better than

Grandpa," and she'd pat my thigh a few times in the loving way that almost stings, but doesn't.

"I was just about your size, maybe a year or two older, living in Virginia with my mamma and pappa, in a big old house where we roomed in the upstairs and ran the grocery store in the downstairs."

"Where's Virginia?" I asked, taking her hand in mine and running my fingers along the routes of her veins that protruded like groundhog trails in the garden.

"North. Way up north. We owned the biggest house in the neighborhood, and all the families around loved my pappa because he'd give the children candy when they came in and he'd sell things on credit to people who didn't have much money.

"He had the biggest old heart in the world. When the men from the ironworks would come home on Fridays and blow all their money on liquor and then pass out on the street, he'd haul them inside. Had a little cot in the back, in a storeroom, and he'd let them sober up considerable before he'd send them home."

"Grandpa says drinking's a sin," I'd remind her.

"Your grandpa committed that one many a time before he got religion," she remarked. "Don't you tell him I said that. Anyway, my pappa was the gentlest man in the world, and I reckon that's why he let my mamma do whatever she wanted."

"Tell me what she looked like, Nanna."

"She had big eyes that she painted up and lips so pink that she left color on the edges of her cigarettes. Always had a cigarette hanging out of her mouth. And she didn't put up her hair the way other women did. Left it hanging down her back all the way to her tail," and Nanna'd reach behind me and tickle at the bones at the base of my spine, and I'd giggle.

"She was a *whore,*" I'd yell out the way I'd heard my grandpa yell out in church meeting.

"Your grandpa has a name for everything, but he ain't always right," Nanna'd insist. "Don't you tell him I said so."

"She was a *wicked woman,*" I'd yell again, and laugh and kick my feet that stuck out just past the edge of the swing.

"Weren't never wicked to me," Nanna'd say. "I wish to goodness Herman hadn't put that story in his sermon. Little child like you saying such things."

"I'm just teasing, Nanna," I promised, burying my face in her breast. "There's good whores. We learned in Sunday school. Like Mary who was Jesus' friend."

"She weren't no whore. She was a woman of passion."

"I might be a whore when I get big," I told Nanna to make her feel better, and she grabbed me right by the hair of my head and yanked me up.

"Don't you never let me hear you say that again," she said. "I will whip your ass righteously if I ever hear you say that again."

I held my mouth wide open at the sound of Nanna cursing, because while it was okay for men to say words like ass, it wasn't okay for women. But before I could tell her she'd have to say special prayers to be forgiven for defiling her lips, I was crying and Nanna was hugging me again.

———

4

That was the way things were with Nanna. For years and years, we'd sit together in the swing and she'd tell me the story, the same sad story in a hundred different ways. And when my legs grew long enough to dangle down near hers, and when I couldn't fit my head beneath her arm anymore and had to lean it against her shoulder instead, I began to finally understand the story differently, to understand it in the way Nanna might have—if she hadn't been the one who had to live it.

Leila," *I imagined her pappa calling.* "Come help me straighten out the paper sacks under the counter."

My Nanna, just past nine and already lanky like me, her hair pulled back into a tight ponytail like the one I wore, climbed out from her hiding place, a dark corner of the store where the edge of the grain bin almost met the edge of a cluttered shelf of plastic combs and soaps and yellowed magazines. She had to squeeze to get through. She'd been growing so fast that she worried that by the time she'd finished helping her pappa, she wouldn't be able to fit back inside to fetch her crayons and papers.

When I told myself this story, I always gave Nanna my worries, whatever they were.

"How much will you pay me?" she'd tease him, romping across the wooden slats of floor and behind the counter where he was waiting for a customer making her way to the register.

"How much will I *owe* you?"

"Hmmm," she pondered. Sometimes I saw her scratching her chin the way she still does when I ask her a question.

"How about two hard candies?" he offered, and kissed the top of her head.

"Let me think about it," she said, and went to work.

There were bags in three sizes. The smallest size held only a cup of washing powders or rice, but it'd hold a whole handful of Mary Janes. The next size was big enough for a bag of beans or a whole bottle of beer. But the big ones were Nanna's favorite. She could fit those bags over her head, cut out eyes and a mouth, and then decorate masks to wear to scare her mamma.

In my stories, the biggest bags were thick as skin. You couldn't even punch through them with your fist.

Nanna heard the delicate bells of the cash register and then "thirty-five cents" in her pappa's even voice as she made neat stacks beneath the counter.

"So how much?" her pappa asked again when the customer was gone.

"How about a line of paper dolls?" she'd bargain. She would have been good at that.

"Just for straightening out the bags?"

"Please?" she begged. Her pappa had shown her how to fold a grocery bag back and forth like an accordion in narrow, even strips, and then how to take scissors and cut out half a person so that when you opened it up, you found a whole line of children grasping hands. But little Nanna could never do it right. Her paper dolls had pointy heads or thick arms or feet like clubs.

"I reckon that's a fair trade," her pappa compromised. "But I won't be able to get to it till later."

"Thank you, thank you!" She danced around him. "I need some new dolls to color."

Just then a man walked in. I imagined the man with rough whiskers and a scruffy black dog following behind—even though Nanna couldn't remember all the details herself.

"Leila, go find your mamma and tell her to come here," her pappa instructed.

"Where is she?"

"Upstairs, I reckon. Or out back. Now run."

Nanna knew he didn't like for her to be in the store when drunks came around. He probably didn't need her mamma at all. He just wanted her out of the way. So she left, skipping out of the musky grocery and onto the street, waving to neighbors on their porches. Sometimes in my mind, I let Nanna stop to talk to a little boy on his tricycle, riding circles around the block. I gave him blond hair that jiggled as his wheels passed over the cobblestones.

Then Nanna would race into the house, up the stairs, pulling herself with the rail to improve her speed. She'd run through the airborne dust, spotlighted by the sun angling through the window, and wipe her face with the back of her hand to get the particles off, calling out for her mamma.

But there was never an answer.

Nanna'd look in every room, pausing only in her mamma's bedroom, in front of the vanity where her cosmetics and brush were left out. I imagined her staring in the mirror, touching her own cheek, and wishing it flushed the way her mamma's always looked. Then she'd throw down the brush she found in her hand and run out of that room too.

The next part of the story was always the same no matter how many times I told it.

Back down the steps and out the door, Nanna jiggled the handle of the gate. It was stubborn and wouldn't catch. So she pulled herself up on the wooden fence and peeked over the side. Her mamma was there, sure enough, sitting on the ground against the side of the house, sipping Coke through a straw right out the bottle. Beside her, a man Nanna recognized—the young man from the ironworks who sometimes helped her pappa unload shipments. At first, she was confused. Then she noticed the man's hand on the middle of her mamma's back, right at the place where her skirt began, at the place where her body was so shy that it curved inward.

I imagined Nanna staring at that sight for quite a while.

But she didn't call her mamma at all. She climbed down as quietly as she could and then ran, first towards the store to her pappa. But she couldn't go there. She started to go back upstairs, but remembered how empty it was, without her mamma or pappa, with just the dust hanging in the air.

So she bolted down the street past boys playing ball, past an old woman pruning her bushes, past the rug-maker's house and all the way into the cemetery where it was quiet and green and honeysuckled, where she could walk between graves and figure things out.

I knew how lonely Nanna must have been, but I thought maybe I'd like to live in a city someday—in spite of the drunks and noises. I figured if Nanna'd had a chance to stay there, nothing would have turned out the same. I wished we could have been little at the same time, best friends and next-door neighbors. I would have walked through the cemetery with her. I would have held her hand.

My grandpa Herman Langston was founder and preacher of The Church of Fire and Brimstone and God's Almighty Baptizing Wind. I think when he was trying to come up with a name for it, he just couldn't make up his mind, so he put all his ideas together and acted like a prophet, and nobody said a thing. Grandpa Herman was a big man with red hair and huge freckles that hid in his wrinkles. He wore his blood pressure like the glaze on a loaf of bread, sitting shiny on the surface. According to Nanna, when he was a young man, he used his fists on anybody who crossed him, and as far as I can tell, after he got religion, he did the same thing. Sunday after Sunday, I watched him standing in the pulpit, banging those fists down hard on the podium, saying, "There shall be *weeping* and *wailing* and *gnashing* of teeth, where the worm dieth *not* and the *fire is not quenched.*"

All around the church, penitents would be wringing their hands and crying, hollering out "Amen." My daddy, Liston Huff, would be on the shells of his knees, leaning his head against the pew and whispering loudly his private prayer to God and whoever else couldn't help hearing. My mamma, Maree Huff, would be sitting or standing beside him, her scoured hands held high in the air, her face turned up to the paneled ceiling, tears falling so hard she'd have to sit her shoes in the sun for the whole afternoon just to dry them out.

Beside them would be my brothers David and Everett, and later their wives Laura and Wanda, perfectly mimicking my parents. David was known for holding his bible against his forehead, banging his skin into the cover until he worked himself into a holy trance.

And at the other end of the pew, my oldest sister, Bethany, who was married before I was even born, sat with her husband Olin and their children Pammy and Mustard and her husband's oldest son James, who was just a year older than me.

But I sat with Nanna, in the pew behind them all. She'd give me a pencil and let me draw in her Sunday school quarterly once everybody'd got the spirit. I couldn't draw in my own because if Mamma saw the marks, she'd spank me good. Nanna'd give me rolls of Smarties, the little candy pills that stacked up in their plastic wrapper, green then yellow then pink then white, and it'd take me two hymns and one altar call just to get the wrapper open without making any noise. I always wondered where she got the candy but feared she'd stop supplying it if I asked.

Every two or three Sundays, Grandpa'd step out from behind his podium, his bible in one hand held up in the sky, his other hand over his heart.

"Here he goes again," Nanna'd whisper. "One of these days, he's going to fall over and die right in the middle of that story."

And I'd look up in time to hear him talk about liars and forgiveness.

"We've all sinned in the eyes of God. All of us," he'd say. "My own wife Leila, who you all know, my own wife turned her back on God. Turned her sinful eyes away from God and lied. Lied. Lied to the courts of this land, lied to the very people who were trying to bring a murderous whore to justice. But more sinful than any of that, she *lied* to her Heavenly Father, to her King."

"Yes, Lord," the people would call.

"Just a child. Just a wee child but old enough to know the difference in right and wrong. She saw her own mother engaging in sins of the flesh and *did not tell*. She did not tell her father. She did not tell God. She allowed it to happen."

"*Allowed* it to happen," my mamma would yell out.

"And on the day that her own mother pulled out a rifle and shot her father through the back so she could live in sin with a boy young enough to be her son, what did Leila do? Did she call out to God?"

"No, Lord," my brother Everett would answer.

"No. No, she did *not* call out to God," Grandpa Herman would continue, the tears sliding down his rough cheeks.

I'd look over at Nanna, who'd roll her eyes at me and then sneak me a wink.

"She did not call out to God. She crawled right in the bed next to her murderous mother and slept there. And when her mother handed her a little speech to say to the judge, she studied it, memorized it, memorized that *lie.*"

"Help her, Jesus," somebody cried, as if the things that had happened sixty years before were happening again.

"And she told that judge that her own pappa, the man who loved her more than any other earthly thing, had been beating her. She told that judge that her God-fearing pappa had pulled his belt from his pants and was striking her body when her mother pulled out that gun." Grandpa Herman grew quiet and sad, and a hush fell over the congregation as well.

"And why'd she do it, people? Why'd she lie before the greatest judge of them all?"

"To protect her mamma," Bethany hollered.

"To protect a *murderer*," Grandpa Herman corrected. "To protect a *whore*, a wicked, evil woman." Then he fell silent to give his words a chance to settle over the crowd.

"But God is good," Grandpa continued. "God will forgive. He'll baptize a sinner in his very blood and pull them out white as snow. We've got sinners among us, sinners who *need* God's blessing, God's forgiveness. Won't you come? Won't you pray to him now, say 'God, I've been a liar, a murderer, a whore.' Confess your sins to the one who will make you clean."

Then he'd pause and add, "Sister Imogene, play us a hymn," and Great-Aunt Imogene would hobble over to the piano that must have been older than she was.

Sunday after Sunday, we'd sing, we'd bow our heads, and I'd hold Nanna's hand while around me people were praying aloud, their voices competing for God's attention, growing louder and louder until I could talk to Nanna and nobody would know.

"Don't go up there," I'd beg her. "Stay here with me."

"I've got to go in a minute," she'd explain. "Lord knows, if I don't get on my knees after this kind of sermon, I won't never be welcome in my own house again."

"What do you do up there?" I'd ask her.

"Just bow my head and thank the Lord for you, and then I sing a little song or something. Don't matter what you do. Long as you go up there."

"I don't want you to leave me here," I'd say.

"Well, come on up with me. God knows, the whole congregation will be up there anyway before Herman lets us out."

So during the altar call, Nanna approached the altar, and whoops went up all over the church, and people cried, and I heard my own mamma hollering out *"Thank* you, Jesus." I went up there with her, and I could hear Grandpa proclaiming, "Lord, we thank you for the youth of this church, for the children who understand sin, understand their own hearts, the children with so much love inside them that they can offer it back to their own elders, who are sinners. Lord, I thank you for my sweet Ninah."

And I smiled to myself, thinking, "I ain't his sweet *nothing,*" and then I nudged Nanna and kept saying my ABCs, imagining them first upper case, then lower, thinking that periodic trips to the altar made a good impression. My whole family would appreciate me more, at least for the rest of that week.

I *don't think anybody knows exactly how Grandpa Herman* came up with his brand of Christianity. The church began years and years back, before my mamma was even born, when the church Nanna and Grandpa had been attending split into little pieces.

I used to imagine the building breaking apart, wondering how they decided who would get the back pews, who would get the front ones, who would get the altar. All I know is that Mossy Swamp Primitive Baptist Church broke into two other pieces so that when it was over, Mossy Swamp had a third of the congregation and two new churches developed: Mossy Swamp Pentecostal Holiness and The Church of Fire and Brimstone and God's Almighty Baptizing Wind. Grandpa Herman built Fire and Brimstone himself, in one of his own tobacco fields near the house. At the time, the congregation of Fire and Brimstone was basically his family, his parents and brothers and sisters and cousins, and Nanna's aunt and uncle, who she was sent to live with after her mamma went to prison, and all their children. But through the years, people joined up from marrying into the family and bringing their relatives, and by the time I was born, Fire and Brimstone already had eighty members. It was like having a big family reunion every Sunday, with Grandpa Herman leading it.

I guess you could say the church doctrine came from Grandpa Herman's own sensibilities. He used the Bible, of course, but only the parts he liked. He had a habit of altering the verses just a little to make them match his own beliefs. He had a good dose of Baptist in him, so we sang soulful hymns and got saved on a regular basis and baptized in the pond at the far edge of the property. But the Pentecostal part of him wouldn't allow us to watch TV or cut our hair, and he was always one to encourage speaking in tongues.

But there were other elements to Fire and Brimstone. I don't know if Grandpa got a copy of the laws from some other religion or if he just made them up, but he'd walk around saying things like, "He who invades another man's nets or fish traps or takes fish from another man's fishing preserve shall pay fifty dollars as compensation. Half to the man from whom they were stolen and half to The Church of Fire and Brimstone and God's Almighty Baptizing Wind. Amen." On Fridays, Grandpa was a judge, and any disagreements in the community were brought before him, where he'd make his decision, lead the arguing parties in prayer, and then make sure they were hugging when they left the church.

And the children were required to go to night classes where we memorized Grandpa Herman's laws. We'd sit in the tiny classroom with others about our same age, and a teacher would drill us again and again. "He who rapes a grapevine by taking more than his share of the fruit shall pay ten dollars in compensation, half to the man from whom the grapes were stolen and half to The Church of Fire and Brimstone."

"He who romps through another man's field and tramples the plants of his labor shall reseed and keep those plants until they bring forth the equal value and shall pay fifty dollars to The Church of Fire and Brimstone as penance.

"He who goes unto another man's wife and takes her for his own shall come before the church and confess such evils and shall pay five hundred dollars, half to the man from whom he's stolen and half to The Church of Fire and Brimstone. And if it happens more than once, he shall be cast out of his own community. But if he has left a wife and family, they may remain among the congregation."

The laws were written in thick booklets that only church-teachers and Grandpa Herman himself were allowed to read. The booklets were old and yellowed, and the pages looked as used as elbows.

There were other things about The Church of Fire and Brimstone that didn't show up in the religions of the children in my classes at school. We didn't believe in doctors—because they took the healing power of Christ into their own hands and used it to perpetuate the sinfulness of humanity—or so Grandpa Herman said. When schools first required that children be immunized, the church began teaching their children themselves until the state intervened and Grandpa Herman had to make the exception for vaccinations against measles and diphtheria.

As a child it all seemed so normal. My friends were my own cousins who wore dark dresses made for us by our mammas and nannas. We didn't associate much with other children in school because we had each other, and we'd been taught that regular Baptists or Methodists lived in sin, that any little girl with britches on her legs was going straight to Hell for trying to be a man, and that those children who learned their numbers off of television shows—even television shows especially made to help children learn—were being damned eternally, would be cast one day into the Great Lake of Fire for worshipping technology instead of the Blessed Redeemer. We didn't want to be friends with them anyway.

So during recess, I caught up with the other girls whose hair hung down their backs uneven, like horse tails, with the boys who wore dark pants all year around. And in the lunchroom, I could pick out other Fire and Brimstone children just by looking at the table, seeking out the paper bags in which we carried our food—because lunch boxes featured television characters, and we never ate school food since nobody could be sure who grew it.

Even the Holiness children, who also wore dresses, didn't cut their hair, and carried their lunches, were a threat to our salvation since the year that they'd held a Hallelujah-ween carnival for their children and invited our congregation to attend. Even though nobody was dressing up, Grandpa Herman rebuked them from the pulpit for condoning Satanic holidays, and after that, we cut off all association with the Holiness.

When I was a child, I saw our community as a special place where God's special children could be safe from the influence of the wicked world. Later, when I was older, I saw our community differently. I saw us like an island. Like an island sinking from the weight of fearful hearts.

———

Ninah." *Mamma shook me.* "Ninah!"

I couldn't wake up. In the summers, we worked in the fields all day, worked from daylight until dusk, walking miles and miles along narrow tobacco rows, popping the flowers off the tops of the plants with our fingers, popping the suckers that grew at the bottom of the stalk away with our toes, so that big leaves could grow bigger and the flower wouldn't suck out all the life. By the time supper came, we were so weary that even breathing felt like work. And that night, in spite of the muscles in my legs twitching and shaking, I had fallen asleep at the table. A piece of my hair had coiled into the gravy over my rice.

I jerked up straight, stretched open my eyes to see everyone looking at me. The table I was seated at held twenty, and there were three others just like it in the room. We all ate together, the entire extended family, and at that moment, all I knew was that a lot of eyes were watching mine. I didn't blink.

My brother David, who was just eight years older, reached out under the table with his foot and tapped at mine comfortingly.

"She's just tired, Maree," my daddy said. "Don't come down too hard on her."

"Did you say your prayers, young lady?" Mamma asked me. "Before you fell asleep?"

"I didn't mean to fall asleep," I answered.

"Don't talk back," Mamma warned, not harshly but firm. Mamma had great sunken eyes, and when she was angry, she squinted them so that the lines around them looked like just-plowed fields. I peered into the bowl of potatoes, still too groggy to be clear about what was going on. "And look at me when I'm talking to you," Mamma added.

I forced my head up.

"Maree," Nanna said. "This child didn't mean to doze off." She shook her head back and forth.

"And I'm not punishing her for sleeping," Mamma interjected. "I'm punishing her for not saying her prayers. At twelve years old, you'd think she'd have better sense. Did you say your prayers, Ninah?"

"No, ma'am," I answered.

"Then get up," she said. "And start cleaning the kitchen."

So while the rest of them ate, I scraped pots, heaping the leftovers onto a big plate for the dogs. By the time I'd finished washing the pots and draining the dirty water, the women were cleaning off the table, bringing me glasses and plates. They were chattering and singing, but in the background, I could hear Grandpa Herman talking to Daddy.

"Maree's right," he told him. "She's just keeping that girl in line. You got to toughen up, Liston. Loving your child and punishing your child ain't separate things. You know that."

And then I turned the water back on, running it clean and drowning out their voices.

About midway through the dishwashing, Nanna dipped her hands into the dishwater too, and our fingers kept hitting each other underwater, and we had to take turns rinsing off the forks and saucers. Whenever I wasn't careful, Nanna'd steal my dishcloth, yanking it right out of my hands, and I'd splash her a little. Pretty soon, she had me laughing, and then we were both singing along, reminiscing about the old rugged cross with everybody else.

That night before I went to bed, I kissed Daddy goodnight, and he said, "We just love you so much, Baby."

Then Mamma led me to bed, and when she pulled back my covers, there were cockleburrs and sandspurs scattered all over my sheets, scattered everywhere. I knew there would be.

Mamma got down beside me and we said our prayers

together, and she asked God to help me remember him, to help me have the strength to get through hard days and to show respect to my elders.

She helped me settle down on top of all those prickly nettles and when I made a face, she laughed, leaned over me, and kissed me on the forehead. "You know how much I love you, don't you?" she asked, and because I didn't want her to leave me yet, because I wanted to keep feeling her hair on my cheek, I said, "Tell me how much."

So she stayed awhile, beside my bed. She told me the story again of how I was an unexpected gift from God, a child she and Daddy hadn't planned and didn't know was coming. Then she said that maybe tomorrow I would get a special blessing for my night of discomfort and wouldn't feel so tired after working in the fields. And she left.

I couldn't sleep for a long time. The prickles were sticking in my back, and every time I moved, I got stuck in a new place. I knew I was supposed to remember the crown of thorns on Jesus' head, how much that must have hurt him. But I just kept thinking about suckering tobacco, about popping off baby leaves so they wouldn't take away the strength from the bigger ones. I imagined that when I woke up, I'd find little dots of blood on my gown and sheets. But of course, I didn't.

Maybe it was a blessing from God, but the next day wasn't so hard. I got assigned to a row in a particularly long field next to James, the son of Olin, my brother-in-law, and the stepson of Bethany, my oldest sister. His natural mother had died in childbirth, which happened sometimes since we didn't use doctors. All day long we stayed together. When he'd get behind, I'd slow down and wait for him, and when I hung back to pop flowers from the tops of very high plants, he'd wait for me—or else he'd step over and bend the stalk so that I could reach it.

The hired man on the other side who wasn't Fire and Brimstone moved very quickly, but then he'd been suckering and topping for years. We didn't mind that he stayed ahead because it was easier for us to talk that way.

"Did you get whipped?" James asked me, pausing and peeking at me through the leaves. Something about his eyebrows made him always look surprised.

"Nah," I told him. "Slept on nettles."

"Ugh," James said. "I'd rather just get whipped."

"I guess I deserved it," I muttered. I could see his big hands plucking through tussled green leaves, his dark head passing like a target in the spaces between plants. "If they'd been punishing me for falling asleep during supper, I probably would have gotten the strap. But since it was for forgetting my prayers, it was a bigger sin. I deserved it."

"No you didn't," he said. "But don't say I said so."

"I won't," I promised. And then I began singing, "I Am Bound For the Promised Land," and James joined in. We stepped out the beat hard in the soil and sang and panted our way down the row.

THE RAPTURE

God had mercy on our crops that year. Grandpa Herman said we must be doing a good job of confessing our sins because God wasn't plaguing us with too much rain or a drought. Our tobacco didn't even have blue mold. The leaves on each stalk were so wide and so firm that you could use them to fan your face. We decided to have a celebration in honor of God's abundance.

On the day when we emptied our first barn, the men barbecued a hog and the women hauled dishes of potato salad and baked beans out to the pack house in the back of a pickup truck.

We finished separating the leaves from the sticks and bailing it in burlap sheets, and then the biggest boys threw each bundle out the back door into a ton truck until the whole truck bed was heaped with huge, soft boulders of tobacco.

We had to wait a little while for the women to set up the food, but Grandpa Herman kept lifting the lid of the cooker and allowing the children to reach between ribs and pull off little strings of meat as snacks. Then we'd suck our fingers, anticipating the feast.

I thought the dinner prayer would never end. All the adults had something to thank God for, and everybody said thank-you for the exceptional crop—even though it seemed to me that one thank-you should be enough. But then we filled our paper plates with more food than we usually ate in a week. It was a regular Christmas at Fire and Brimstone—even though it was only August.

We ate on the pack house porch. Some people sat on the

steps, and others dangled their legs off the sides, and others stood behind a table we'd made by putting a sheet of plywood across two sawhorses. We ate until our bellies grew tight, and we washed it all down with iced tea, which was reserved for special occasions.

Afterwards, while the women scraped off the dishes and shared scraps with the dogs and chickens and pigs, the men stretched out on their backs in the sun and dozed. Resting on a work day was a real treat.

The pack house had a second floor where we stored stuff, and there was a door up there too, in the back, that opened up to nothing but warm air and white clouds. Mustard was the one who discovered that the ton truck was parked directly beneath the door, and he dared us to jump down onto the mounds of tobacco below.

When nobody would do it, Mustard said we were all chicken, and he backed up against the far wall, then sprinted across the room and right out the door, leaping through air and onto the cushiony bundles. Barley went next. Then Pammy and James. They giggled so hard they lost their wind and came wheezing back upstairs to do it again.

I was scared to jump and scared we might get in trouble, but I didn't want to be left out.

"Come on, Ninah," James hollered up from below, climbing out the back of the truck. "It's fun."

I didn't want to be the only one afraid, so I ran through too, dashing out of the dark pack house and into the light. Even after there was no more floor beneath me, I could feel my feet kicking. And even though I knew if I could just keep my eyes open, I'd be able to see more than I'd ever seen before, I squinted them tight and kept them closed even after I'd landed on the itchy pillows of leaves.

It wasn't as soft as it'd looked from above, but it didn't hurt exactly.

I clambered over the truck's ledge and went to find David. I wanted him to play with us like he used to, but he was asleep in the sun.

"Wake up," I said as I shook him.

"I ain't asleep," he muttered. "I'm just checking my eyelids for holes."

"David, come on," I called. But I couldn't get him to join us.

Then Grandpa Herman pushed himself from the opened tailgate of his pickup where he was sitting. "What are y'all doing?" he asked me, retucking his shirt as he spoke.

"Just jumping out the upstairs door into the truck," I admitted.

"On that tobacco?" he roared, and I was scared and only nodded.

But Grandpa Herman took me by the hand and walked around back with me. He just shook his head as he watched Barley fly down.

"You've done that enough now," Grandpa scolded. "You gonna mess it up. That might just look like 'baccer, but it's the clothes on your back and the food in your belly. No more jumping."

"Just one more time," Mustard begged. "Please?"

I couldn't believe Mustard had talked back to Grandpa. I knew he'd probably be beaten good. But Grandpa was in

the mood for a circus, I reckon, with the crops faring so
well, and he just laughed and said, "Come on down. This
is the last time though."

I stayed on the ground with Barley and Grandpa as each
of the other children ran shrieking out the door and landed.
Grandpa stood at the edge of the truck and helped everybody down, slapping the boys on their backs playfully and
kissing the girls on their foreheads.

"Don't you let me catch you doing that again," he said.
"The only reason you ain't in trouble now is cause this is
a holiday." Then he grinned at us all real big.

Because *The Church of Fire and Brimstone and God's Al-*
mighty Baptizing Wind wasn't recognized as a denomination
by a bigger group, there was always the problem of revivals.
Revivals happened twice a year, and visiting preachers
would come talk to us every night for a week and hopefully
bring souls closer to Christ. Grandpa Herman would look
into congregations from a hundred miles away, trying to
find somebody whose beliefs resembled ours. Then he'd
bring in a Baptist or Holiness preacher from a faraway
church who was willing to go over his sermons with Grandpa before shouting them at us. But afterwards Grandpa'd
call special church meetings for the entire next week to correct the flaws in the beliefs that the preacher had instilled.
We spent more time in church than most people spent sleeping, but Daddy said there was no better place to be.

The best times were when Grandpa Herman would be

away preaching revivals at other churches. When that happened, somebody had to go spend the night with Nanna so she wouldn't be afraid, and I always volunteered. Secretly, I knew that Nanna wasn't scared at all, but if she claimed to be, I got to move out for a whole week and sleep right in the bed beside Nanna on Grandpa Herman's pillow that smelled like dentures.

We made big jokes about Grandpa Herman's dentures because according to church beliefs, he shouldn't have them. If the Lord willed that he'd lose his teeth, he should live without them. But Grandpa Herman had some and nobody knew but Nanna and me. Or if they knew, they never mentioned it.

At Nanna's house, I only said my prayers when I felt like it. It wasn't like Nanna didn't want me to talk to Jesus, and I knew that she talked to him sometimes too. It was just that Nanna thought you should talk to Jesus when you felt like it—not because it was an obligation.

"Your old mamma's crazy as a nut," she'd say.

"Nanna," I'd protest. "How can you say that? She's your *girl*."

"Nah," Nanna'd argue. "She's Herman's girl. Spitting image of him. Except she ain't got the good sense that he's got. Herman's a *smart* man. That's how come he's got all this land with people working it for him all in the name of religion. Your poor old mamma can't think for herself."

"Yes she can," I disagreed. "She's got just what she wants."

"I reckon you're right there," Nanna'd say. Then she'd bring me hot chocolate, which I was never allowed to drink

at home, and she'd sit it on an end table beneath a handkerchief with little embroidered flowers that she kept in a
drawer except for nights when I slept over. She'd fix me a
plate of the cookies that we'd baked together, and we'd
dunk a cookie in our cups and see who could wait the longest to pull it out without breaking it off. But the truth was
that it tasted better if you lost.

The bedroom walls were painted white, and I asked Nanna
if she wouldn't like some pictures to put up, but she said she
liked to look at the shadow the tree outside made on the
walls after she turned the lights out. In bed, I liked to snuggle
up next to Nanna, who was skinny with so much extra skin
that it dripped a little on the sheets beside her. And she'd let
me touch the little blue place on her lip that she couldn't remember getting—like a tiny bruise that never went away.

"Tell me the real story," I'd beg her. "Tell me about the
day that it happened."

"Honey, that weren't a happy day for me," she'd explain.
"Herman's all but written it into the Bible and now I've got
you nagging me for details ever chance you get. It don't
make me *feel good* to talk about it."

I considered this for a while and decided I shouldn't
ask anymore. Then I felt guilty for bringing it up in the
first place.

"I'm sorry, little Nanna," I said, and rubbed her cheek. "I
just know that Grandpa don't tell it *right.*"

I heard her sigh, hard, and then she put her strong hand
on my hair and stroked it away from my face.

"Nothing much happened on the day she killed him,"
Nanna began. "I don't even remember it, to tell you the

truth. Don't remember what I'd been doing or anything because it was just a regular day. I'd probably been to school
and then come home and helped Mamma get supper ready
while Pappa closed up the store. I reckon we ate together.
I don't know.

"By that time, though, Mamma'd started slipping off with
the young man from the ironworks. His name was Weston
Ward, and he was a nice-looking man. As a matter of fact,
I used to stand outside the store with some of my
girlfriends, and we'd talk about him and giggle and wonder
what it would be like to be his wife. He had pretty arms,
full arms with lots of hair on them like an ape."

"Ugh," I moaned.

"They were *pretty* arms. And Mamma thought so too, I
guess, because while Pappa worked, she'd call him into the
house to help her move a piece of furniture or get him to
taste her soup. Sometimes he stayed in there for a while, and
I believe that Pappa knew it but just didn't know how to
handle it.

"And Mamma started to take long walks in the graveyard.
She'd come downstairs to the store and tell us she was going for a walk, and Pappa'd tell her to go ahead. A couple
of times I followed her there, and saw her meeting Weston.
And I know that's a sin, Ninah. It's a sin to love another
man when you're joined to one already. But I believe she
loved him. And I believe that it must be a wonderful feeling
to be loved so much by two men at the same time. I know
that's probably a sin for me to even think that way, but I
imagine having two men willing to give you the moon
would be a powerful temptation."

"It's not a sin for you to think that," I assured her. "I think that'd be nice too."

"But when a woman's joined to a man, she has to stick with *that* man, through thick and thin, good and bad. And my mamma didn't do that.

"On the day that Pappa died, all I know is that I was in the den, coloring a line of paper dolls I'd made myself. My pappa'd been giving me lessons for years, helping me make curls for girl dolls and showing me how to make their arms more narrow than their little hands. And I'd finally got the hang of it. So I was working in the den when I heard the gun go off."

"What'd you do?" I asked her, moving closer so that my head was right between her breasts and my feet were touching hers too. Her bony feet were cold as February.

"I sat where I was and hollered out for Pappa, but he didn't answer me. Then I listened for voices, but all I could hear was something moving around. So I hollered out for Mamma and she told me to stay where I was.

"So I colored and colored except I didn't change crayons. I colored every doll just as red as you please. Faces and dresses and hands and all. And then somebody knocked at the door, and it was Weston Ward. He asked me if he could come in, and I told him that I thought maybe Mamma and Pappa were hurt, and I asked him if he'd go look.

"They stayed in the bedroom for a while longer, and when they came out, Mamma was bloody and crying and told me that Pappa had shot himself."

"But he didn't, did he?"

"No, darling, but that's what Mamma told me. She told

Weston he needed to go find the police for her, and while she led him to the door, I ran back into the room where Pappa was."

"And he was dead," I said.

"Yes."

I could hear Nanna's voice change, and I thought she might be crying, but when I reached for her face it was dry. She even let me touch the skin in the moat beneath her eye. I held my fingers there to make sure I hadn't caused her tears.

"What'd it look like, Nanna," I chanced.

"Child," she said, reaching for my hand and pulling it down, "you don't want to know."

"Yes I do," I promised. "Cause I don't think you sinned at all," and then I started crying.

"She'd shot him in the back. He'd fallen down face first. There wasn't much to see because she'd put a blanket over him."

"Did you touch him?"

"Oh yes," she admitted.

"You pulled the sheet away?"

"Yes."

"And what was it like?" I asked because I couldn't stop.

"Like a fountain had sprung up out of his back," she explained. "And then gone dry."

"What'd you do?"

"Mamma pulled me away—or Weston pulled me away. I can't remember. I think they sent somebody else for the police and it was Weston who pulled me away.

"Mamma tried to tell the police that he'd killed himself because his business was failing, but she wasn't in her right mind by then. Anybody with any sense would know that a person can't shoot themselves in the back. They left her alone that night and took Pappa away."

"And you slept right in the bed with her?"

"Yes," Nanna said. "She cried all night long. Wailed out, and I knew she was really in mourning. I didn't understand all that was going on, but at the time, you see, I was too distraught to notice that he couldn't have shot himself there. I don't know if I would have figured it out if I'd been clearheaded.

"The next day, the police came to arrest her and took me to an orphans' home. After that, I could only talk to her when a lawyer picked me up and carried me to the jail with him. The two of them made up this story and wrote it down for me to memorize—about how Pappa'd been beating me real bad and Mamma'd killed him because she thought he was going to kill *me*."

"And you said it to the judge?" I asked her.

"I reckon I did. I don't hardly remember it. The judge didn't believe it though, and Mamma went to prison, and I got sent down here to live with your great-uncle and his family."

"What was it like in the orphans' home?"

"I can't remember, honey. And you've worn me out for the night. I don't have no story left in me."

"Okay, Nanna," I told her.

I didn't say my prayers that night, but before I fell

---

asleep, I made sure Nanna knew that I didn't think she committed a sin by lying to the judge. She didn't have any choice.

"Sin or no sin," Nanna said, "I've had nettles in my bed every night."

"Really?" I asked her, and slid my hand underneath her back.

"Not those kinds of nettles, honey," she replied.

That was the beginning of my understanding of metaphors. I thought about Nanna's nettles a lot, wondering how it could be that she felt prickles and stings to her skin when nothing was in her bed at all. But after a time, I came to realize that the nettles were all around her, inside and out. I dreamed of Mamma cutting me down the back, filling me up with sandspurs, and sewing me back together. Nettles every night and even in the day, slightly stabbing with every movement, every turn.

Then I started thinking about Grandpa Herman and figured he was the biggest nettle of all. One great big irritation in the bed with Nanna. I remembered his whiskers, seventy years tough, and knew how badly he must make her itch, how she must just want to leap out of that bed and sleep somewhere else.

To The Church of Fire and Brimstone and God's Almighty Baptizing Wind, metaphors were ways of saying the unpleasant. That's how they taught us everything they didn't want to say aloud.

In our after-supper classes, we'd recite, "He who carves a notch in another man's tree shall pay a hundred dollars. Half to the man whose tree he marked and half to The Church of Fire and Brimstone."

One night in the middle of this, my nephew Mustard, who was nine at the time and the youngest in our group, stopped Ben Harback, that night's teacher, to ask, "A hundred dollars just for sticking your knife in a tree?"

"Mustard!" his sister Pammy scolded under her breath. Pammy was eleven, a year younger than me, and mostly invisible.

"It just don't make sense," Mustard said. "A hundred dollars! That's a lot of money for one little notch in a tree."

"But it is not a lot of money for thieving, now is it?" Ben Harback asked Mustard, then looked at us all.

"Maybe not for stealing a baby pig or something," Mustard argued. "But for one little notch in a tree?"

I glimpsed at James, whose almond eyes were walnuts, and I couldn't tell if he was about to laugh or about to yell, but he was about to do something. The Saturday night classes weren't discussions. They were lectures and recitations. As far as I could remember, nobody'd ever asked a question before. We all knew Mustard was in terrible trouble and couldn't imagine why he didn't know. It would be more than nettles for disagreeing with the law book. Maybe even more than the strap. My ears felt hot. I put my hands onto the sides of the cold metal chair to cool them, wishing I could lay my ears there.

Ben Harback just stared at us all, his eyes cast down as

if he was looking at a tobacco leaf covered with a breed of worm he'd never seen before.

I thought about Mustard, all alone, the only brave voice, the rest of us sitting like eggs, just waiting.

"It's not about the notch or the tree," I whispered.

"What did you say, Ninah Huff?" Ben asked sharply.

"It's not about the notch or the tree either," I said louder. "It's about claiming something that doesn't belong to you." I couldn't tell whether I was getting us into trouble or getting us out of it, but it was a huge chore, no matter what it was, and my voice shook. "It's like if we told Grandpa Herman that we deserved to be paid for picking up leaves in the field when the field doesn't really belong to us at all and he already takes care of our needs."

"Yes," Ben sighed. "Thank you, Ninah."

But I knew my explanation wasn't quite right.

Mustard looked at me like he couldn't believe what I'd said, and then Ben attacked him directly.

"And you will understand one day too," he said to Mustard, "if you *listen* instead of speaking."

For the rest of that night at church, we all recited, obediently, and nobody else spoke out. But my ears were still hot, burning almost as fiercely as the inside of my chest, like nettles, and the whole time I prayed quietly that Mustard wouldn't have to spend the night in a grave to contemplate the wages of sin, prayed that I wouldn't.

Later that year, when the men loaded up bundles of tobacco on big ton trucks and hauled them off to the warehouse to be auctioned, when school started again and I climbed on the bus and found myself twenty miles away, at a big school where seventh-, eighth-, and ninth-graders teemed through the halls like ants and I couldn't pick out another Fire and Brimstone anywhere, later that year I had a change for the worse.

It started with the bleeding. I wouldn't have known what it was except that they showed us a film at school, and Nanna had mentioned it to me once, briefly. I still didn't want anyone to know. I hid my underpants in a box that first month, pair after pair until I was forced to sneak into Pammy's house and steal some of hers, the lining so white it made me cry.

Then there was my hair, so heavy that it hurt my neck to carry it, so heavy that when I leaned my head over the side of the tub on Saturdays to wash it, I couldn't pick my head back up until Mamma lifted it and squeezed the water out.

"Her head stinks," the girl sitting behind me in social studies would whisper to the girl to her left. "Why doesn't she wash it?"

And I'd turn around to see them waving their hands in front of their noses and smiling conspiratorially, but not at me.

When I washed my hair on Saturday, it was still wet on Sunday, and if it was braided, it didn't dry until Sunday night.

Then there was the problem with my chest, my nipples behaving like somebody had scared them, trying to crawl back inside of me just when everybody else's were showing off. It wasn't easy to undress for gym in front of all those girls who had bras. I couldn't do gym in a dress. I couldn't tell Mamma or Daddy because if they knew the school issued us shorts and T-shirts, they'd call up and make a scene. James had already warned me not to. In the few years since the school had required dressing out for gym class, the handful of Fire and Brimstone children had kept the secret. It was our only chance to prove that we had legs.

That was the year that Everett married Wanda, and they moved behind us into a cinderblock house between David and Laura's and Bethany and Olin's. I was the only child at home then, living in the house behind Grandpa and Nanna's. To the right of Grandpa and Nanna's, nine other houses filled with Fire and Brimstone relatives sat in a field like great mushrooms. All the houses were gray, and mostly they looked just alike. But to the left of Grandpa Herman's house, in the next field, the church emerged from the ground like a peasant's castle.

All I had to do was stand on the doorsteps, and I could yell out to anyone at all. If I filled my lungs enough and imagined them the color of Jesus' blood, I could call out so loudly, so clearly, that even the third cousins on the other side of the compound might hear. But it wasn't the same, being the only child in the house. It didn't matter that we were always together or that when I leaned out my bedroom window, I could see inside the other houses, the land all around us, the two new houses being built, the Fire and

Brimstone fields. It didn't really help that I could see the
barns, the pigpen, the chicken coop, the silo where we kept
the grains, and beyond, all the woods that belonged to us
too. It wasn't enough to make up for the lonely.

I missed the days when I was small enough to climb into
bed with Mamma and Daddy and stretch out on Daddy's
belly, tapping out hymns on his shiny front teeth while
Mamma played my back like a drum and we all sang
together.

Evenings when Mamma and Daddy sat out on the doorsteps talking to David and Laura, who were expecting a
child that next March, when I knew I was inside alone, I
crept into their bedroom, pulled back a blanket, and buried
my face in their sheets, sniffing for something that would fill
me up.

At *Fire and Brimstone, we all looked alike, and that made me*
lonely too. We didn't all have the same color eyes or the
same textured hair, but it really didn't matter. Our shadows
came in two varieties: male and female.

We were all lanky. We all dressed alike. We slept in the
same hard beds and washed with soaps made from the same
iron pot. All the men wore beards clipped close and work
boots that left the same muddy tracks. All the women pulled
their hair into buns and left their faces bare for the sun to
adorn as it would.

We may as well have been skeletons, unidentifiable. We
may as well have interchanged our bones.

I used to pray that God would stunt my growth and keep me little—so at least my frame wouldn't be confused with anyone else's.

Pammy was the relative closest to my size, and as we grew towards being lost in bodies all the same, I'd do my best to make my shadow different, even from hers. Afternoons as we marched through fields, I'd study our shapes bruised on the ground and pull myself up taller or fling out my arms to keep from getting confused about which shape belonged to her and which shape belonged to me.

It was the middle of October when David knocked at our door before daylight. I heard him downstairs, crying to Daddy about how Laura's unborn baby was demanding to get out. By the time I was dressed, Mamma and Nanna, Bethany and Wanda, the aunts and women cousins all sat in the living room inside David and Laura's house, praying and drinking hot water with honey. Laura was in bed. Nanna made her keep her feet up, forbid her to even stand to go to the bathroom. Pammy and I peeked in from the windows, listening to whispered words like "spotting" and watching Nanna remove soiled towels from between Laura's legs, watching Laura crying until Mamma crawled into bed beside her and held her head.

We crouched down in the bushes, and Pammy, who had a face like Grandpa Herman's, speckled as a trout, asked, "Will it die?"

"Yeah, it will die," I snapped at her. "If it comes out

now, it probably won't even have lungs yet. It won't be able to breathe."

"But God's wind's almighty," Pammy insisted. "It won't die if God doesn't let it."

"Even God won't be able to help it if it don't have lungs," I whispered back.

"Yes he will," Pammy sniffed. "God can do anything," and she stomped off, leaving me sitting behind the bush alone.

Pammy and I were in charge of the chicken coop. It was time for us to get the eggs, only an hour before the bus would come to pick us up and take us away for the day. I hurried to join her, running down the dirt road and feeling the morning air hit at my bare legs in the places where my socks had already slipped down.

By the time I caught up, Pammy was crying hard, and she looked at me and yelled, "You don't have no faith."

"I do too," I said.

We fed the chickens. She threw them the corn, and I threw them the laying mash that we kept in metal trash cans beneath an oak tree. While they were eating, we entered the lopsided doorway of their dark old pen that smelled hot and like a secret no matter how cold it was outside. We walked around opposite walls, lifting the eggs from the nests, wiping the ones streaked in manure onto the straw, and placing them in our baskets. Above us on the rafters, one old hen who had missed the breakfast call squawked out, scaring us both, and fluttered awkwardly down to the ground. Pammy jumped, and I hollered. The chicken ran out through the door, out into the sunlight.

———

I laughed to see Pammy jump, and she laughed to hear me holler, and we forgot, for a minute, about David and Laura's baby. On the way back to the houses, we were chattering and laughing about the big red hen. And then we remembered.

Passing by the barn, we picked up Mustard and James and our second cousins John and Barley, who'd been feeding the pigs.

"Wonder what Laura did?" Barley asked us.

"What do you mean?" I said.

"Grandpa Herman said she'd sinned. Said unconfessed sin was what made that new baby want to leave."

"That's not true," I hissed.

"That's what Grandpa Herman said," John insisted.

Hardly any women were at breakfast at all. Just Aunt Kate and Aunt Velma, who had cooked. Even the "good mornings" were somber, and we picked up our toast, eggs, and ham off the serving line, carrying it to the table without saying a word.

Most of the men were there, and midway through breakfast, Pammy called out, "Where's Grandpa Liston?" I hadn't seen my daddy since early. I didn't know where he could be.

"He's at the barn," Ben Harback answered, then paused to finish chewing what was already in his mouth. "Working on that baby's crib."

Nobody said a thing. I didn't look up, but if I had, I know I would have seen the other men giving him glances full of fury. It wasn't the kind of thing he should have said out loud. Ben Harback had come into the congregation several years earlier and claimed the beliefs almost as though he'd made them up himself. But he wasn't family, and he didn't know the unspoken rules, the ones you couldn't find in Grandpa Herman's booklet. He didn't know that when other people are in pain, you don't talk about it. You let them feel what they're feeling in private. You leave them alone.

Just before the bus came, I ran into David and Laura's house to kiss Mamma goodbye. She was in the room with Laura, and Bethany wouldn't get her for me.

"She'll be here when you get back," Bethany said.

"Will Laura be okay?" I asked her.

"She'll be fine," Bethany assured me, and shooed me out.

On the bus that morning, I sat with James. I had the seat facing the window though, and I didn't look his way. I stared out, through the fogged-up glass, watching Fire and Brimstone get smaller and smaller and trying to talk myself out of choking on something big and angry in my throat.

W*hen we got home from school that day, Nanna was the one* who gave us the news that Laura wouldn't be having a baby and wouldn't be feeling like talking for a time. David was with her, but everyone else was in the cemetery behind the church where they were laying it to rest. James asked if the children could go to the burial, and Nanna said yes.

I watched them all take off running with their books, their black shoes kicking up dirt behind them.

"I don't have to go, do I?" I asked Nanna.

"Won't bother me if you stay here. You can help me cut up taters."

I told Nanna I needed to do something first, and she didn't ask any questions. I dropped my books on the door-steps and ran the other way, towards the barn, to the place where Daddy'd been building the crib.

I swung open the barn door and slipped inside, to the very back where the saws and lumber and tools were kept. The crib was finished, small and perfect, sturdy legs and sanded boards, low so that Laura, who was short, could eas-ily reach in. He'd even carved a swirly design onto the headboard. And while I was sad about the baby that wouldn't be, I might have felt the most sadness for Daddy.

When I got back to the house, Nanna was standing out-side listening. There were raised voices coming up from the cemetery, almost like yelling. It didn't sound like preaching though. It sounded strange and uneven.

I took her hand and we hurried to the burial sight where Daddy was crying out, shaking his fist at Grandpa Herman and saying, "Don't you ever say a thing like that again."

"Liston, those aren't my words. They're God's words. 'The wages of sin is death,' " Grandpa Herman said calmly.

A few people in the midst nodded their heads in agree-ment, but Daddy shouted out again, "That's not what God meant!" and he stormed away, Mamma hurrying to hold onto him, hugging herself into his side against the cold.

Nobody *talked much about Laura and David's loss, but ev-*erybody grieved it, I guess. Even old Grandpa Herman finally kept his nasty opinions to himself, and the community healed over, quietly, with nobody picking at scabs.

But sometimes things hide beneath healed-up places. Flies lay eggs inside the gashes on cows and kittens, and then the wounds swell up, even after they're closed over, and unless somebody opens the wound again to release the worm, the thing inside keeps growing and burrowing its way out, painfully, blindly, persistently.

Maybe that's what happened to me. Even two weeks later in church, when Laura caught the spirit, stood up, began dancing around, chattering out a prayer that changed into a language nobody knew, even seeing her recovered and filled with God's strangeness, I hurt inside. It felt like something was trying to come out, something starving.

I was sitting between Nanna and James when it happened, too old to eat candy in church and too young not to wish for it. In front of me, Daddy was calling out his prayers and Mamma was crying again, her hands held up as if she thought God was going to fill them with kisses. Nanna kept her face straight ahead, pretending to listen though I suspected that in her mind she was retelling old stories in new ways. Beside me, James scraped the dirt from beneath his fingernails and flicked it onto the floor. I looked at his hands, almost as big as a man's, with his fingers widening at the tips like spatulas.

I felt the way you feel sometimes right before you go to sleep, when all you want to do is sleep, and then suddenly, when you're almost there, when your mind goes dizzy and it's almost like you don't have a body at all, you remember how long the night is, how you might not wake back up. And like a shock, you're sitting straight up, scared to do the thing you've done every day of your life.

And Laura began wailing out, stood up, and the congregation urged her on, their voices growing like mudslides. She shook and cried, her syllables tripping over themselves until she wasn't saying anything we knew, and the words she said sounded hard and maybe like curses in other languages.

"*Praise* be," Grandpa Herman yelled.

"Forgive me, Lord," I could hear my daddy saying, his back in front of me curled like an apostrophe, the bolts of his spine threatening his skin, and his head leaned against the next pew. "Forgive me for doubting your holy and righteous word."

"Thank you for your strength, my King," David called.

"Without you, I would be nothing," Laura chanted. "Without you, Oh Heavenly Prince, I would be lower than the ohlaba hebamashundi weya komo dhikam laticalama hebamashundi," and as she spoke, her voice went higher and higher, and her breathing got stronger, and then she was panting and squealing, crying, "Help me remember thy awesome and bewechya walabebeya komo hebamashundi," and I was embarrassed. Embarrassed to be hearing her voice, stretching up like violin strings, tighter and louder and screeching and punctuated with her frantic breathing. Embarrassed to know what her tongue must be doing inside her mouth, rolling all over itself like it couldn't help it. It sounded like something she should do somewhere else. Not in church.

And I was embarrassed to be sitting next to James, hearing it all, though we'd heard it all our lives. And I was embarrassed because Laura wasn't even ten years older than me, not even eight years older, and I didn't want that to happen to me. Not ever.

And I was embarrassed that God had never shared with me his language, had never given me special words, his almighty baptizing wind.

And I was embarrassed to think that I might find it in some other place.

Sometimes if we'd finished our chores and there was still a little bit of daytime left, the children could get permission to go horseback riding. We rode two or three to a horse even though there were usually enough horses to go around. It was easier to talk that way.

One afternoon we were out in the woods, with me and Mustard and James on one horse and Barley and Pammy and John on the other. It seemed like the girls always got sandwiched between the boys, and that day, I was protected by Mustard from the front and James from the back.

We'd already crossed the creek and had ridden to a hilly place with trees on either side so that I had to keep ducking to avoid being swatted by the tiniest branches. We'd gone farther on the horses than we usually went, and I was secretly hoping we'd end up at the pond where the boys went swimming sometimes but the girls were only allowed at baptisms since the water was rumored to be dangerous. I was hoping I'd get to explore.

"Let's take them to the top and run down fast," Barley called, and buried his heels in his horse's sides to make him go.

"Don't do it, Mustard," James warned from behind me.

But Mustard kicked the mare we were riding too, and she took off unexpectedly, making me hold tight onto Mustard, who was holding the reins, and making James grab onto me like I was sturdy as a pine, even though I wasn't.

When I shifted back, I was closer than I'd ever been to sitting in his lap, and after I'd gotten used to the feeling of traveling steep uphill, I kind of liked the new sensation of his nearness. I tried to tell myself that it was no different from sitting next to him in church, but it *was* different.

"Mustard, don't do it. The ground's too uneven," James hollered in my ear as we got closer to the top, and I yelled, "Ouch," even though his voice didn't bother me at all.

"It won't hurt them," Mustard said. "Hang on."

"Ninah, tell him to stop," James demanded, like I could make him listen.

But I didn't want him to stop. It wasn't that I wanted the horse to get hurt. I just didn't want to shift directions. I was too busy trying to memorize the way James' legs felt around my backside, hanging on, the way his arms felt buckled around my middle. I'd already forgotten about wanting to go to the pond.

From the top of the hill, Barley hollered out, and Pammy did, and John squealed as they held onto the galloping horse. We stopped and watched them soaring downwards, the horse's brown tail flicking as his front feet pounded the ground, then his back feet.

Then the horse stumbled over a hole, and all I could see was a tumbling of bodies, somersaulting clothes, and Pammy's red hair. But the horse neighed out, got up, and kept running. It was Pammy who grabbed his tail, and then we were watching her being pulled behind him, with Barley running hard to catch up and grab the reins. It looked like the horse's back hoofs were kicking Pammy in the belly even though later she said they weren't.

John was crying, so Mustard began walking our mare slowly down the slope. We could still hear Barley yelling "Whoa, boy, whoa" in the distance.

"Be careful," I warned Mustard.

"But hurry up," James said. "You got to get to him. I *told* you it was a bad idea."

Then we were down from our horse and checking on John.

"You okay?" I asked him. But he just moaned and showed us his scraped hands.

"Stop being a crybaby," Mustard yelled. "We gotta catch up with Barley and Pammy."

"Leave him alone," James screamed. "Go on ahead."

So Mustard climbed back on the mare and went trotting off.

"Come on, John," I said. John was a whiner, and I knew he probably wasn't hurt at all—probably not nearly so hurt as Pammy anyway.

I didn't offer John my hand, but James gave him his. He

helped him up and led the three of us through the ravine. And even though my thinking about John was more along the lines of Mustard's, I didn't say so. Not after seeing the way James was treating him.

On the far side of the creek, we met up with the others. Mustard was still on horseback, but Pammy was rubbing the fallen horse's head, and Barley was petting her neck. They were all laughing nervously.

"Don't you ever do that again," James scolded.

"It was kind of fun," Pammy said, but she was muddy, and I could see that her legs were shaking.

"Nobody got hurt," Barley laughed.

"*John* got hurt," James said.

And on the way back to the barn, we shifted positions on the horse. James held the reins, even though Mustard protested. I still sat in the middle, wishing there was some way we could go downhill so I'd have a reason to lean against him again.

Late fall and winter, when the crops were in, the men of our community took jobs laying bricks, building houses, painting, or reupholstering furniture. Fire and Brimstone men had a good reputation as strong workers who did twice what other men did during the day. They never went to work drunk or took a whole hour for lunch or knocked off early, so even Methodists or people without faith would hire them for the winter months.

But Saturdays were for hunting. Before day, the men

would rise, eat together, and head out to the woods, to the hundreds of uncut acres Fire and Brimstone owned. They'd take their dogs and guns and ride away in pickups, dropping off a man at every tree with a stand built into it, a crude treehouse where each man would sit and think about God while waiting for the dogs to run a deer down below.

Even the boys got to go. To me, deer-driving was one of the most mysterious habits of our community. I woke up early every Saturday too, looked out the window to see Mustard and James walking out with Olin, to see Barley leaving his house with his father, and John, who was younger and only had a BB gun, running to catch up. They'd laugh and puffs of smoke would appear in the cold air. They'd pat each other hard on the back and make their way into Grandpa Herman's house, stomping their boots on the steps. He'd hold the door for them all, welcoming them so happily with his forbidden denture-smile.

I wanted to go with them worse than anything.

Saturdays were expectant days. We listened for the shotgun blast, wondering who had fired, wondering if they'd killed a deer or planted another shell into the land, wondering how long it would be before the truck pulled up, a deer in the back, limp as a mop.

For the women, Saturdays were cleaning days, days for washing our clothes and our bodies, our floors and our windows. All we had to do on Saturday was wash and wait for the men.

One Saturday in November when the floors were already done, Mamma sent me out to the woodpile to collect a few pieces of firewood. I was on my way back into the house when I heard the pickups come bumping down the road. Mustard was in the back of the first truck, his red hair hidden beneath a knit hat but his red ears poking out obscenely. "James killed one," he hollered. "And they're getting ready to bloody him."

"James killed it," I yelled inside to Mamma. "Come on."

"Oh good," she called back, excited. "I'm getting my coat."

It was James' first deer. And whenever a man killed a deer for the first time, the other hunters collected the blood and entrails and poured them over his head. It was a family tradition, a rite of passage, and a man's special bath all rolled into one.

My daddy had built a place to skin and clean a deer just off the side of our house. He'd hung a noose, of sorts, from the rafters in the beams of the garage, and that's where they tied the deer up, upside down, so that they could rip it from top to bottom, and the head would hang low so they could saw it off more easily.

When we got there, James was beaming. Olin ruffled his dark hair, and Bethany put her arm around him. The women were coming from other houses, and the last of the pickups were pulling into the yard.

But when they pulled the deer out, it was a doe. I knew we had a law against killing female deer and couldn't understand why everybody was so jubilant. Grandpa Herman kept saying, "That was a good shot, son," and James kept grinning, saying things like "I just looked down and there she was, walking behind a blackberry bush."

I shuffled back to Nanna while they hung the deer up.

"It's a *doe*," I whispered to her.

"He won't kill a doe again," Nanna assured me. "It's his *first deer*," she added, as if that explained it.

I tried to remember whether other men had been allowed to kill a doe their first time. I figured they *must* have. But I'd never paid attention. It hadn't seemed to matter before that day.

"You got anything to catch the blood in, Liston?" Olin asked, and Daddy told me to fetch a five-gallon bucket.

We had one just outside the back door to catch rainwater, and I dumped the sludge out of the bottom and raced back.

By the time I returned, Everett and Olin had pulled the deer's legs apart, and Daddy had his knife stuck high in the deer's crotch. He was standing to the side, and as I placed the bucket beneath the deer, he pulled his sharp knife downward.

I should have moved, but I couldn't stop watching him open her up that way. About the time he reached the rib cage, the stomach and blood splashed out and into the bucket, stewed like vomit. I wasn't expecting it to come so forcefully, so soon, and I got caught in the spray.

I jumped back, but not in time to spare my face, my dress, or my shoes.

Ben Harback started laughing, and everyone looked at me. I found myself standing there, speckled with her blood, and with my arms held out to my side as if I didn't want my hands to touch myself.

"Child," my mamma said, "don't you have sense enough to know not to stand that close?" But then she was laughing too. Everyone was.

I backed out of the way, back to Nanna, who shook her head at me and slapped my bottom playfully. I looked down at my white socks all soiled.

"I'll have to do another load anyway," she said. "James' clothes will be a lot worse than yours."

Then we stood together and watched David pick up the bucket. James tried to run at first, half-playing but half-serious. Grandpa Herman caught him and told him to take it like a man, and then James walked into the circle and David dumped the hot blood over his head.

Everybody clapped for him, but nobody clapped as hard as Grandpa Herman. Drops fell from James' earlobes, trickled along his nose. He spit and spit and wiped his eyes.

While they were cutting the deer up, I changed clothes and took the bloody ones over to Nanna's. I took my underwear to her too, all those pairs I'd kept in the box. I stuffed them in the pockets of my dress, and she washed them with James' clothes.

That night the men cooked venison outside on the gas stove. It was cut up into small chunks and fried tender. But I couldn't eat it. Not that time. Even though it was James' first deer, I couldn't eat her.

That night Nanna returned my clothes to me, and all my underwear was clean and folded up neatly inside my dress. I could still see the stains on them though. They weren't white like Pammy's. They were dingy like the bottom of a sock.

James and Mustard and John and Barley had set out traps to
catch raccoons and squirrels and anything else that happened to fall prey. Though the next day was Sunday, the
boys were allowed to go check their traps after church and
after we'd eaten.

"Can I go with them?" I asked Mamma.

"Them woods ain't no place for a girl," she said.

"Please, Mamma," I begged. "I've finished all my
homework."

"Let her go, Maree. Ain't no reason why she can't run
along with them," Aunt Kate said.

"Ask your daddy," Mamma told me.

They were getting ready to leave already, and I told them
to wait for me. Barley moaned about it, but they waited.

Daddy was outside with the men, picking his teeth with
a stick he'd whittled down and slapping his knee over a joke
somebody had told.

"Can I go, Daddy?" I whispered in his ear. "I really want
to, and Mamma said I could if you didn't mind."

"I don't care," he told me. "Don't be gone long."

So I hustled off with the boys before Pammy found out
and wanted to come too.

"Girls can't hunt," John mocked.

"Well, you can't hunt either," I claimed. "Not with just
a little BB gun."

"I killed a bird with it," he said. "Killed *two* birds. And
I'm getting me a gun for my birthday. You wait and see."

"Even when you get a gun, you won't be able to shoot
it," Barley picked. "When you pull that trigger, it'll kick
back so hard your shoulder will be bruised for a week."

"Well, your shoulder bruises too," John whined.

We walked past the barn, and James stopped to stroke a mare's long nose. We walked past the pigpen and past the chicken coop and all the way back to the place where the field ended and the woods began.

"Where'd we put that first trap?" Mustard asked. "Weren't it right in there?" and pointed back down a path.

"Yeah, that's it," Barley agreed.

"Y'all go on in there and walk up the creek. I'll take Ninah with me and we'll check the traps from the other side and meet you in the middle," James said. "I want to show her where I killed my deer."

"Why do you want to show *her?*" John ridiculed.

"Because she ain't seen it yet and you have," James said.

"All right," Mustard conceded, and the three younger boys disappeared behind branches and brush.

James led me in another direction. "It's kind of growed up in here," he said, holding back limbs so they wouldn't slap me.

We walked for a long time, with him leading the way and me following, stepping over briars and over moss. As I crunched across lichen and then headed down near the creek through mud, I felt something churning in my chest like too much sorrow. I didn't want to *follow* James to a place I hadn't seen. I wanted to be the one showing him something. I didn't want to be the girl.

We found a place to cross the creek where a tree grew in the middle and we could step onto a root and then over to the other side. James offered me his hand, but I didn't take it.

"Not far now," he said after a while, and I watched his flannel shirt stretched tight across his back. I watched his dark hair curling up around his collar. He'd need a haircut soon. I followed his dark pants into the woods, deeper and deeper.

"You tired?" he asked me, looking back.

"No," I insisted.

"Well, why ain't you talking to me?" he asked. "You mad?"

I shrugged.

"Why are you mad?"

He stopped, and I stopped too, not wanting to get one bit closer.

"Cause you killed a *doe*," I said, "and she could have had ten baby boys for you to kill later, but now she can't because she's dead."

"They told me to," James argued. "They said, 'Shoot anything that comes your way.' It was the first one," he explained. "That rule don't apply to your first one."

"Well, it *should*," I fussed. "You shouldn't never kill a doe."

I was holding onto a skinny tree, shaking it in my hand. When I looked up at James again, I was surprised to see him so silenced. He didn't look like a big boy at all then. He looked little in his eyes.

"Want me to take you back?" he offered.

"No," I said.

"You sure?"

"I want to see it," I told him. "I want to see the place where you killed her."

He took my hand and led me through the woods into a clearing. On the other side, there was a tree with a stand in it.

"You were up there?" I asked him.

"Yeah."

So I walked over to the place where the little slats of board were nailed to the tree trunk and began climbing up.

When I was sitting on the narrow plank, with James right beside me, I said, "Show me where she was."

He pointed to a cluster of bushes over to the right. "She was right there," he said. "With her head down. And you see them branches over there, not in that first bush but the one behind it?"

I nodded.

"Well, I thought they were a rack," he explained. "I thought she was a buck. Otherwise I wouldn't have shot at her no matter what anybody said."

"Oh," I sighed, and looked into my lap, feeling like I might cry and hating myself for it. I told myself I should be relieved or even happy that James hadn't meant to kill a doe. But I was crying anyway. I didn't want James to see.

"Ninah?" he whispered. "Ninah?"

And when I looked at his face, all I saw were his lips, chapped and damp, his mouth open just a little and his chipped tooth right in front from the day we were playing in the pack house and he tripped on the stairs. I stared at his mouth until I had to close my eyes from the nearness of it, from the feeling of those chapped lips on the skin above my eyes.

I *was sitting in the porch swing beside Nanna, bundled up in* a blanket. Nanna didn't have a blanket of her own, but the end of my blanket stretched across her legs, so she wasn't too cold.

Pammy and Bethany sat outside with us for a while, watching the moon hover low in the clouds, the sky still streaked with hints of day. Bethany brushed out Pammy's hair, then braided it back neatly in spite of Pammy's protests. But then Pammy got whiny and wanted to go inside, so Bethany kissed Nanna goodnight, and they left.

"You need to get home and do your lessons," Nanna said.

"Don't have anything except a math quiz that I already studied for."

"When did you study?" she asked me.

"On the bus."

"That don't count," she said. "All that noise. You need to study it again."

"I'll go in a minute," I promised.

Nanna rubbed at my sock, pressed her bony thumb into my arch and moved it around and around beneath the blanket.

"Tell me the story of when you met Grandpa Herman," I begged her. What I really wanted to hear about was the first time they kissed, but I knew *that* story was off limits.

"Why do you want to hear that? I've told you a hundred times. Nobody else nags at me for stories."

"I like your stories," I said. "Tell me."

Nanna patted my foot, put it down, and picked up the other one, pressing into my heel. "I was just about your size," she began. "And stupider than a sunflower in the shade. And Herman came acourtin dressed in brand-new denim britches and a starched white shirt. Walked right up to Uncle Ernie's door carrying a handful of ragged azalea flowers he'd cut off his mamma's bush with his pocketknife."

"Was he grinning at you and winking?"

I smiled at her and she smiled back and said, "You've done heard this story, and I ain't telling it again tonight when you've got lessons to get. But don't think I don't know what's in your head, girl. I can see it in your eyes."

"Ma'am?" I asked her innocently.

"You're James' aunt, whether you like it or not. And he's your nephew, whether you like it or not. I can see you two looking at each other. And you better be careful, is all I got to say, because you're gonna get hurt if you ain't careful."

"I ain't *really* his aunt," I said.

"Not by blood, maybe. But by position. So you can forget that right now, do you hear me?"

"Yes, ma'am."

"Now get on home and study for that math test."

"It's just a quiz," I reminded her.

"Study," she repeated.

✒

When I got home, Everett and Wanda were sitting on the couch, talking to Mamma and Daddy. I could tell that

Wanda had been crying. Her eyes looked like pictures of boxers I'd seen, without the bruises. She and Everett were sitting close though, so I knew that the problem wasn't between them.

Daddy motioned me to his lap, and I sat down there with him in his chair, my skinny legs almost as long as his. I sat in Daddy's lap all the time—big as I was by then. But that day was the first time I paid attention to what his knees felt like against the backs of my thighs. I imagined what it would feel like to sit on James' lap and then whispered a little prayer for forgiveness.

"Honey," Daddy said to Wanda. "It's just going to take some getting used to."

"But I miss them so bad, though," Wanda stammered. She was fatter than the rest of us, but then she'd only been living at Fire and Brimstone for a couple of months. "I just don't understand why I can't go see them."

"Nobody's saying you can't see them," Mamma interjected. "Go if you want to. But you know that the minute you step foot in their house, you'll be breathing the air of their sinfulness."

"I know," she whimpered. "It's not that I don't like it here . . . ," and she buried her face in Everett's shirt.

Everett looked at us while she cried. Everett had a lot of muscles, and the muscles in his face were begging.

"Wanda," Mamma said, "you got to pull yourself together."

She looked up with her face all red and ugly and said, "I miss their bad manners and their jokes. I miss their drinking and fighting. I even miss laying in the bed on Sunday mornings and listening to Daddy snoring down the hall. I know it's a sin, to wish for those things. I know it is."

"What you have to do," Daddy told her, "is try to feel the way Jesus felt, dying on that cross for our sins. You have to think of your life as an example like Jesus'. Because one day your sinful people might look at you and see that they can step right off the broad road to destruction and onto the narrow path to righteousness, just like you've done."

"I pray about it," Wanda said.

"And we pray about it too," Everett assured her. "We pray for your family every day, just like you do. And don't that make us a stronger family here, joining our hearts in prayer?"

"Yeah." She tried to smile.

Daddy scratched my back while they talked. I bit my bottom lip and shamefully pretended his fingers belonged to James.

Mamma got out of her chair and went over to the couch and sat down on the other side of Wanda. "I know I can't be your mother, child," she said. "You've done got a mother of your own, and maybe one day, through your example, she'll see the state of her heart. But I want you to know that I'll be everything for you that I can."

And then Wanda leaned over and cried on Mamma for a while. Daddy winked at Everett to reassure him, and I saw that Daddy's eyes had tears in them too.

"Where you been, Peanut?" Everett asked me, trying to keep his voice steady and change the subject at the same time.

"On the porch with Nanna," I told him.

"Can you believe how this girl's growing?" Daddy asked him. "Bet she's shot up three inches this year."

"She 'bout old enough to go out on dates," Wanda sniffed, and Everett passed her his handkerchief.

"Not my baby," Daddy said.

"I don't *want* to go on a date," I said.

"Not til she's eighteen," Mamma teased—because most everybody in our community was married by seventeen or eighteen. "And then she can only take a date to church."

Later that night, before Wanda and Everett left, Mamma suggested that whenever Wanda got homesick, she should pinch herself with clothespins for distraction.

"Physical discomfort is one of the best ways to keep your mind on Heaven," Daddy agreed.

That night I carried a handful of clothespins to bed with me, since my mind was on everything *but* Heaven. I clamped them to the skin on the inside of my arms and on my stomach. I saved two for my nipples, and those hurt almost too much to bear.

That night I prayed that God would guide me, would help me forget about James' mouth and his hands that I couldn't stop imagining. I prayed that God would cleanse me with a dose of Jesus' pain and keep my body clean and sacred just for him.

And when I couldn't keep my mind on Jesus, I told myself the story of Nanna and Grandpa to keep from remembering the way kisses felt.

Leila watched him from the window of the bedroom she shared with her cousin Imogene. Herman Langston, spiffed up and brave, walking towards the back door. Whenever she thought he might look her way, she'd duck back behind the yellow curtains. But he wasn't looking. He didn't even know which room was hers. He kicked at acorns as he made his way to the house.

"What's he doing?" Imogene asked from the bed where she sat embroidering flowers on a tablecloth.

"Knocking. He's knocking on the door."

"Right now?"

"Yeah, he's knocking right now."

They sat quietly, straining their ears to hear what happened in the next room. Leila held her breath at the sound of her uncle Ernie's heavy feet plodding across the floor and then the squeak of the door opening.

"They're shaking hands," Leila whispered. "How's my hair look?"

"Fine," Imogene told her. "Rub at your cheeks though. Rub them hard to get some color."

"He's got flowers." Leila grinned.

"You're so lucky," Imogene whined.

They sat there and waited to hear Uncle Ernie's voice call to Leila, but it never happened.

"Can you see anything?" Imogene asked.

"He's still on the doorsteps, wait—he's leaving."

"What?"

"He's leaving." Leila stood at the window, staring out, not trying to hide, hoping he would see her.

"Lei-laaa," Uncle Ernie called from the other room.

"Sir?" she yelled back from the window, and when she did, Herman turned that way, looked and smiled, held up his hands.

She grinned back at him and waved.

"Can you come in here for a minute? And you too, Imogene."

"Be right there," Leila called back, still facing Herman, who was walking on, turning back shyly to catch her eye from time to time.

For the next hour, Uncle Ernie talked to the girls about courting. He said that Herman Langston could sit with Leila in church, if he was willing to go, but that there'd be no holding hands or touching of any kind. He said he'd already told Herman, and that once he'd proven his intentions for Leila, he might be able to accompany her on walks.

Back in their bedroom, Imogene shrieked and giggled, and Leila blushed. It wasn't until later that she saw the pink azalea flowers lined up across the outside of the windowsill.

<hr />

The church and its classrooms were sacred places. Anything done there had to be done with the spirit of God in mind. Once when Mustard was little and church was dismissed, he hopped up off the pew and dashed outside. Bethany yanked Olin up, unhooked his belt before he even knew what was happening, and followed Mustard out onto the church stoop where she blistered his backside in front of God and everybody, beat him until he wet his pants, just for running in the sanctuary.

But in the fellowship hall, a rectangular building situated just behind the holy structure and surrounded by some scraggly pine trees, we could be ourselves. That's where we ate, when the whole church ate together, and that's where we had our youth retreats.

A couple of times each year, the Fire and Brimstone young adults would host retreats for the Fire and Brimstone youth. On those occasions, all the children would bring blankets and pillows from their houses, and we'd praise God from twilight to daybreak if we felt like it, studying scripture and singing songs and talking about everyday situations we faced that the adults didn't have to.

David and Laura and Everett and Wanda and Ben Harback and some others who weren't yet shackled with children of their own would lead us in workshops about how to deal with the children on the bus who made fun of us, about how to know when we should tell our elders about unholy books we might be reading in school. We did fun things— like building a bonfire and destroying fashion magazines that somebody brought in from town just for the occasion.

We had boiled peanuts and popcorn. We could talk about anything there.

But that all happened later, after Grandpa Herman had given his sermon.

Each time, Grandpa Herman would come in early. We'd all eat supper together, and then he'd lecture us while we sat at the wooden tables in front of him. Then he'd tell us to put our heads on the table, with every head bowed and every eye closed.

Obediently, we'd follow his instructions.

Then he'd ask us to raise our hands if we wanted to go to Hell. He'd say, "Unless you've been saved and baptized in the precious blood of Jesus, each and every one of you will be going to Hell."

And then he'd tell us stories about how Jesus was coming back, any day, probably within the next five years, and that we needed to be ready to greet him. He said that unless we'd been baptized, when the rapture happened, we'd be left behind. We'd wake up one day and call out "good morning" to our parents and hear no reply. We'd look for them only to find their clothes left in the bed.

He said that we'd run out of food. That big bugs would chase us around and sting us with their tails, and that though we might be sickened unto death, we could not die.

He said we'd turn on the faucet in the bathroom and find only blood running out and would have nothing to drink.

He said evil multitudes would come unto us and cut off our limbs, and that we wouldn't die. We'd sit there, with no legs to run with, and be stung and stung again by the beasts.

And then he'd say, "But you don't have to be left behind. You can go straight to Heaven with all of God's special children if you'll only open your hearts to Jesus, ask him for forgiveness and welcome him into your hearts."

And then he'd tell us to raise our hands again if we feared going to Hell. Whoever raised their hand would be taken away to the church where Grandpa Herman would lead them to salvation.

It happened the same way each time. The youngest children invited to the youth retreats would get saved right away. I'd raised my hand years earlier, but each time

Grandpa Herman gave his after-the-rapture speech, I found it hard to catch my breath, hard to focus on God's love and not God's meanness and spite. I thought that really I wasn't saved at all.

Grandpa Herman said that when you were truly saved, you felt like you could fly. But I never felt that way. Not about Jesus.

And each time I knew that I must not really be saved, that I must not have opened my heart to him. I tried to figure out how you go about opening your heart. I tried not to think about being left behind, but in the nights, I kept slipping out of bed, checking the faucet to make sure it wasn't bleeding.

On that occasion, it was John who went away with Grandpa Herman and came back testifying. We listened to Grandpa Herman's words coming out of John's eight-year-old mouth, and it made me feel sick all over.

But then we broke into groups, and my group had just me and James and Pammy and Lorrie Evens and Joshua Langston, both older cousins who lived on the other side of the compound. David and Laura were our leaders and they talked to us about "Teenage Temptations," about how at our age, we might be tempted to put on lipstick at school or smart-mouth a teacher in hopes of winning the affections of a boy or girl in our class. But they said it was important for us to wait until all those urges passed and until we had secured our hearts in Jesus. They said we would find a mate among God's special children if we didn't show off, and to come and talk to them if we had problems because it hadn't been too long since they were our age.

Then they took questions, and Lorrie asked about kissing, and I could see David and Laura both thinking that next time, Lorrie would have to move up with the high-schoolers that Everett and Wanda taught. Laura told her it was "inappropriate," and Lorrie shut up.

Then Pammy asked if it was a sin if we accidentally let our knee socks fall down and a strange boy saw our legs. David told her it wasn't one, but that she should keep her socks up, and Lorrie suggested that she could get rubber bands to hold them at the top.

I didn't ask anything at all, but I worried that the next year when Pammy went to junior high and had to dress out for gym, she'd tell.

It was almost midnight by the time Ben Harback released the younger children. Then they began playing Red-Rover, and he started the popcorn, and pretty soon, the older groups were let out too.

Pammy and I made up a little cushiony bed, and then we sat up talking for a while. Some of the smaller children fell asleep, and across the room, Ben Harback and David sat with some boys telling jokes, and Lorrie Evans was in the corner talking to Wanda and Laura and pretending to be all grown-up.

Me and Pammy sat on our pallet and pulled a thick white blanket over us, up to the neck. Mustard came and stretched out beside Pammy, and she said, "You can't sleep here. You have to sleep with the boys."

Mustard said, "I don't want to sleep here anyway. I want Ninah to tell us a story."

And then James sat down beside me, and Barley sat at the

foot of the bed, and Mustard smacked Barley with his pillow, and Barley hit him back, and everybody laughed.

"Everything okay over there?" Ben Harback called.

"Yeah," Barley hollered. "Ninah's gonna tell us a story."

"Shhhh," Laura whispered loudly. "Some people are sleeping. Y'all keep it down."

"Go ahead, Ninah," James said. "Tell us a good one."

"Hmmm," I thought. "Okay. I'll tell you about the time that Nanna and Grandpa Herman lost their shoes."

Barley settled down and pulled the tail end of our blanket over his legs. Pammy moved over to make room for Mustard, and James moved in closer to me.

"See, back in the days when Nanna and Grandpa first started courtin, he'd come by her house early in the morning and pick her up for school. And that was how they dated. Just walking to school together.

"One day Grandpa Herman picked her up, and they set out on the dirt road towards the schoolhouse two miles away."

"I'm glad we've got buses now," Barley said.

"Me too," Pammy echoed.

"Anyway, it was a sunny day, in April maybe, and the sap was running in the trees so the whole place smelled like pine, fresh and warm."

James, who was sitting next to me Indian-style, had started to shiver, and I moved in closer to Pammy so that our sides were touching and offered him part of the blanket.

"Thanks," he said.

"What happened next?" Mustard asked, sleepy.

"Grandpa Herman told Nanna that they should take off

their shoes and not wear them that day. That they should hide their shoes somewhere and pick them up on the way home."

"Could you go to school without shoes?" Barley asked.

"You could way back then," Pammy answered, and yawned.

"So they stopped on the side of the road. And Grandpa Herman peeled off his shoes, but Nanna was shy about her feet. Grandpa Herman said, 'Look,' and did a little dance for Nanna with his white skin shining.

"And then he sat back down beside Nanna and started unlacing her boots."

"Nuh-uh," Pammy said.

"Yes he did," I promised. "He reached down and untied her shoes and then he pulled them off her feet one at a time. And then he reached up and took her socks and pulled them down too, slowly, down her legs."

"Really?" Mustard said.

"Yeah. But he didn't touch her skin."

About that time I felt a poke and realized it was James' hand, resting on my leg. I pulled in my breath quick and kept talking.

"He folded her socks up neatly and stuck them back inside her shoes, and then Grandpa helped Nanna up. They felt the prickles underneath their toes of baby blades of grass just breaking through the soil."

"So what'd they do with their shoes?" Barley asked.

"Wait a minute. I'm getting to that," I told him.

I looked around, and Laura and Wanda were still talking to Lorrie. David and Everett and Ben were still giggling in the corner. Nobody was looking our way at all. James' fingers fumbled lightly at my leg, at the skin behind my knee that's softer than newborn biddies. I slid down a little, and my dress slid up, and then he was massaging the place where my knee changed to thigh.

"They took their shoes and stuck them in a drainage pipe that ran underneath a dirt road. The pipe had a lot of dirt packed over it, but it was like a bridge, separating two sides of a creek. Except the creek had dried up. Anyway, that's where they left their shoes for the day, and they danced all the way to school, feeling dusty sand powder up around their toes and leaving footprints side by side for anyone to see."

James' eyes were only half open. His mouth was half open too. Pammy, laying right beside me, didn't notice a thing. I was very still.

"But that day at school, it started raining. It rained from the time they got there until just before they left. And when Grandpa Herman met Nanna on the school steps after the last bell, they knew they were in trouble deep."

He reached up quickly, to the middle of my thigh, shifting his body as he did it so that anybody who was looking would just see the blanket change positions from his movement.

The heat rushed up my body and into my face. I licked my lips and kept talking, trying not to breathe out loud.

"They got their feet and legs all muddy walking back to the pipe," I told them. "Nanna had splats of mud above her knees that she had to flick off with her fingernails. But then when they got to the place they'd left their shoes, they were gone. Washed away by the creek that had come back to life in the storm."

"What'd they do?"

"They had to go home and tell their parents about their sins," I said.

And then James reached up again, almost too high, just barely escaping the edge of my underpants, and his hand there felt like a thousand ladybugs crawling. For a second, I thought I might lift right off the bed, zip up into the air, and float across the room. I felt like a pine tree in spring. I knew if I opened my mouth again, there was a chance I'd speak in tongues.

"And then?" Barley posed.

I cleared my throat, and James slid his hand back down to my knee, and I quivered all over without meaning to.

"And then they couldn't walk to school together for the rest of that year. Except they did it anyway. Grandpa Herman would wait for Nanna half a mile down the road, and then Imogene would walk ahead of them and holler back to Nanna if she saw anybody else coming so that Grandpa Herman could duck into the woods.

"And they didn't even care that they had to wear old shoes that were too tight and left marks across their feet because they were in love and it didn't matter."

"That's a good story," James said.

"Y'all should go to bed, maybe," I sighed, and rolled over to face Pammy.

THE RAPTURE

That night I dreamed of Jesus on the cross, on a cross in the field behind The Church of Fire and Brimstone and God's Almighty Baptizing Wind. I dreamed I was standing at my bedroom window, and Jesus was on the cross, holding a handful of azaleas for me.

I dreamed I went outside in just my gown, and walked up to him. He was too nearly dead to speak, but all he had in his eyes was love for me. And I walked up to the wound in his side where he'd been stuck with a sword. I put my mouth on that wound and began drinking from it, swallowing his blood.

And then the wound in his side became a mouth, kissing me back, and I could slip my tongue into the wound, feel the inside of his skin with my tongue, circle it there, tasting him.

But when I looked back at Jesus, he'd turned into James.

I sat up and peered around the dark room. Bodies lay everywhere, sleeping against walls and beneath tables. I didn't know where James might be.

I got up and walked to the door, outside, pulled the door quietly and settled on the steps.

It was cold. I stayed there a long time, and then Everett came outside too.

"Ninah?" he whispered, and I jumped.

"Hey," I said.

"What's the matter?"

"I had a bad dream," I told him. "A real, real bad one." And he sat down beside me and pulled me under his arm.

"Wonder how in the world you could have a bad dream at a youth retreat?" he asked me.

"I don't know."

"Is something on your chest?"

All I could think about were the clothespins I should have with me. If I had the clothespins on my chest, I'd be thinking about Jesus' pain and not the unholy things parading through my mind.

"What if I'm not saved?" I asked him.

"What do you mean? You got saved years ago."

"I know," I told him. "But sometimes I don't feel like I believe enough."

"You don't believe? What don't you believe?"

"I *believe,*" I corrected myself. "It's just that sometimes I don't feel the way I think a saved person should feel. I try really hard to concentrate on Jesus, but other things get in the way when I don't even mean for them to."

"It's okay, Peanut," Everett said.

His beard was nestling against my ear, tiny hairs stuck out farther than the rest of it, and even though James didn't even have a beard yet, I kept thinking of him.

"Why don't we just pray about it? And you can ask God to come into your heart again, with all sincerity, and then you'll know you're saved."

"Okay," I agreed, and we prayed. Everett prayed aloud for my salvation, but I prayed quietly, promising God that if he'd just let me go to Heaven when the rapture happened, I'd give up kisses until I was married. I promised I'd never let James touch my legs or even hold my hands, if God would just save a place for me in the sky.

When we were done, Everett kissed my head and helped me find my way back to bed.

But it didn't help. I still imagined that I'd wake up the next morning, and everyone would have been resurrected except me. I saw myself in the unpeopled room, shuffling through blankets and clothes until I came to the place where James had been sleeping. James with his curly dark hair and slant-eyes. I saw myself lifting his shirt and his pants, sniffing them and settling down at the place where he'd slept, and covering my face with his socks—as if they could protect me from the giant stinging insects.

I *decided to concentrate on Jesus' pain as hard as I could.* I put sandspurs in my own bed and pecan shells in my shoes to remind me with every step of how Jesus had suffered. I cut out a picture of Jesus on the cross and taped it to the inside of my underwear for protection—because if I was saving myself for Jesus, I knew I'd better get him there fast.

I was trying not to hobble on the day I helped Grandpa Herman prepare the place where Dot, our mare, would drop her baby. Nanna was out there too, scratching the girl's mane and rubbing her belly. I'd been cleaning the stall, shoveling manure into a bucket and then raking the dirt neatly in honor of the colt we were expecting.

Grandpa Herman brought out a fresh bale of hay and cut the twine that held it with his knife. He scattered the fresh hay, then leaned up against the fence and breathed in deep.

It was a good smell to me too, the combination of horse and straw. I finished raking the front of the stall, leaned up against the trough where Dot's salt block rested, rounded on one side from her big tongue, and waited for instructions on what to do next.

Grandpa Herman looked over at me slyly, like he'd figured out something I hadn't. "What you limping for, Ninah?" he asked me.

"I ain't limping," I said.

"Well, yes you are. I've been watching you all morning. Is something wrong with your shoes?"

"No, sir."

"Maybe your feet's just growing so fast that your shoes is hurting you. Come here and let me see them."

"They fit," I answered, walking towards him all the while.

I had to lift my foot up onto the fence where Grandpa studied it. He tilted my boot one way, then the other, then began unlacing it.

"What are you doing?" Nanna asked him, and came over to where we were standing.

"The child's shoe's hurting her, Leila," he said. "I'm just trying to see what's wrong with it."

Grandpa Herman pulled off the first boot, then looked at it, looked in it and saw the thick hulls inside. He shook them out into the straw, and I thought I would cry, partly because he'd found the shells and partly because he'd sprinkled the sharp things over the horse's bed.

Nanna walked up behind me and put her arms around me. "Who told you to walk on hulls?" she asked.

"Nobody," I said.

"You saying you decided to walk on pecan shells all on your own?" Grandpa Herman asked, and I nodded.

"You're telling me that Liston and Maree don't even *know* you got shoes full of shells?"

"No, sir," I said again.

"Well, tell me right now what you've done wrong that's so bad you willing to walk on shells when nobody is making you?"

"Nothing," I promised. "I just wanted to know Jesus' pain, just a little touch of what it felt like."

Grandpa Herman laughed outright, laughed big and hard at me, shook his head at Nanna, said, "I swear," which nobody was supposed to say, and then leaned over and kissed me on my socked foot. "Well, you go right ahead," he said, and laughing, he walked off.

Nanna didn't let go of me. She held on even as Grandpa Herman shuffled towards the houses. He turned back once, still laughing, and said, "Next time you get in trouble, girl, you can't use this as your punishment. It ain't like a savings and loan, you know?"

I thought Nanna might fuss at me for walking on shells, but she didn't. Instead, she showed me how to massage the horse's belly, how to coax it to relax. She put my hands right at the place where the colt had dropped so low, and I thought I could feel its curled-up outline in its sack.

Nanna reached right down to the mare's private parts and rubbed her there too, stretching her and showing me how to prepare her pelt to give when the time came. I memorized her wrinkled fingers and how they moved.

"Why you walking on hulls, Baby?" Nanna finally asked me.

"I don't know," I told her.

"You still feeling the flutters over James?"

"I guess so," I admitted.

"Oh Lord, I thought it might be too late."

"What should I do, Nanna? I'm sleeping on nettles," I told her. "I'm praying almost all the time. Do you think a fast would help? Like maybe if I didn't eat until supper every day?"

"Have you been holding his hand?" she asked me.

"Only one time," I said, and shamefully closed my eyes.

"Well, a fast ain't what you need," she said. "No child your age ought to be skipping meals."

"What should I do, Nanna?"

"Lord, I don't know," she said. She sat down on the hay, and I sat down beside her, and she lifted my chin with the cup of her hand.

"They natural feelings," she whispered.

"But he's my nephew."

"Sort of," she agreed. "Is James your same age?"

"A year older."

"Oh, Lordy," she said, and then she cackled out. "And you done held his hand!"

"One time right after he killed his first deer," I told her. I wanted to tell her so much more. But Grandpa Herman had held my foot, and I felt like I might have betrayed her somehow, and I couldn't mention the other kinds of touching.

"Well, you try to stay away from him a little while," she said. "And I'll see what I can do."

———

"What do you mean?"

"I don't know. Just try to stay away from him for a while."

❧

I *was peeling onions and chopping them up with Pammy that* day, getting ready for supper. The great pot of stew was cooking, and all the adults were sitting around, drinking hot water with honey and talking about the mare.

"I expect she'll be having it tonight," Grandpa Herman said.

"We'll keep an eye on her," Mamma said, and Daddy walked over and put his arm around Mamma's waist.

"Be glad to," Daddy added.

Nanna went over to Grandpa Herman and straightened his little bit of hair on top that had fluttered off to one side. He reached up and stroked her arm, and they stood that way for a time.

"I been thinking about Ninah and James," Nanna said. "They're near about courtin age and seem fond of each other."

Everybody hushed up to listen to her.

"They're about the same size," she went on, confidently, even though Bethany's eyes looked like they might jump out her head and do a little jig on the table. "And I believe we'd do good if we joined together as a community and encouraged them to spend time together and see whether or not they'd make good partners."

"Leila," my daddy said, "they're . . . ," and he tried to figure out how we were related. "They're cousins, or . . ."

"Ninah's his *aunt,*" Bethany leaped in.

"But not by blood," Nanna went on. "Certainly by position, but not by blood. And it just seems to me that if we want to keep this community together, there's no better way to do it than to bring together two children who've grown up with the same strong values and sense of place."

I knew that wasn't what Nanna believed. It stunned me to hear her say it. She's lying, I thought to myself, but then I remembered that she supposedly had a history of it.

"Now, Leila," Grandpa Herman began, and I looked up from the chopping block for the first time, my eyes pouring water, and through the blinking onion-haze, I could see Nanna pinch Grandpa Herman's shoulder hard. I could see him try to wiggle away.

"Of course, we don't want them together if they don't want to be," Nanna continued. "So I was wondering how it would work if they became prayer partners. It'd just give them some time to spend alone with God, to ask for his guidance, and then they could see whether or not they'd make good mates."

"That don't sound like a bad idea to me," Grandpa Herman finally conceded. "It's true that James and Ninah have grown up like brothers and sisters, but that kind of love might be a good place to begin a marriage in several years. And they both seem like they got their heads on straight. Ninah's so worried she's going to sin that she's taking measures against it all on her own."

Out the window, I could see James and Barley and Mustard at the woodpile, swinging axes and splitting firewood. James had taken off his coat and rolled the sleeves of his flannel shirt up to his elbows. Out there working like a man and missing it all.

"Oh, Ninah," Pammy whispered. "You're going to have to marry *James*." She said it like it was a curse. "In the night, he has gas, and in the mornings, you can't even stand to walk in him and Mustard's *room*."

I looked at her but didn't say anything.

"I don't know, Herman," Daddy said. "Seems like they're just too young."

"They are young," Grandpa agreed. "But it makes more sense to get them thinking about it early than to have James go weak-kneed over some little Baptist in his class. Some little *Baptist*." He smiled and made a motion to his chest like all Baptist girls got bigger breasts, and the men laughed. The women pretended not to notice.

I ran cold water over my hands, shook them off, dried them, and left the room.

Mamma followed me out, towards the bathroom. When I walked in, she came right in behind me, and I was still crying from the onions, but she thought it was something else.

"It's okay, Baby," she said, and hugged me. "You got years to make up your mind who you want to marry. And it's good to have a prayer partner to share your thoughts and worship with."

I hugged her back, wondering why it was that I'd left that room. A part of me wanted to cry for real. A part of me wanted to thank Nanna, and another part of me wanted to yell at her. A part of me wanted to rejoice and rip from my underpants the Jesus who'd been scratching me for over a week.

By supper time, it was settled. Every evening when the adults had prayer time and the children played or got their lessons, James and I would meet someplace and say prayers of our own. Grandpa Herman made a list on his napkin of things we could begin to pray for, listing the names of the sick and afflicted, the names of neighbors with lost souls including Wanda's relatives, the names of those among us with losses and hopes and heavy hearts.

After we'd eaten, all the men took James out back and talked to him about his responsibilities. I wondered what he was thinking, worried that he didn't like me at all, that he already had a Baptist girl of his own and that he was just practicing on me. I wondered if Pammy would tell him how it all happened.

And when Nanna looked over at me later and winked, I didn't know what to do with my face.

That night the mare got sick, so sick. She'd shake her weak head and blow snot out her nose, and she had foam coming out her mouth and stringy, yellow-green spit. I stayed at the barn with Daddy and Mamma, trying to help Dot have her baby, but she was sicker even than that. We had kerosene lanterns hung at either corner of the stall, but I held the flashlight on her private parts while Mamma rubbed her back and Daddy tried to help her drop the sack.

"Ninah, you all right?" Daddy asked me. "You can go to the house if you want to."

"She'll be fine," Mamma assured him. "She's old enough to help out."

But I wasn't so sure. I wondered if James had seen an animal give birth before. I wondered if they'd send James away if he was out there—the way the men always sent me inside when they cut the pigs.

The baby wouldn't come out all the way. It was hung up inside her, and she was bleeding bad. Daddy reached his long arms up into the horse and tried to pull, but it still wouldn't come. I took a towel and wiped at the dangling saliva. Dot stared at me like she wasn't even seeing me, her big eyes lost in the dark and the pain.

"Is this the way it always happens?" I asked, but neither of them heard me.

And after Daddy had the sack on the ground, in the bloody straw, Mamma tried to get Dot to respond, but she could hardly move, and the blood poured out of her like pee.

The colt was wet and sticky, with bony legs that trembled when she tried to stand up. Daddy was crying, helping the baby out, and Mamma was crying, rubbing at Dot's face.

"She's going to bleed to death, Liston," Mamma said. And then, "Ninah, get some towels."

But before we could get the bleeding stopped, Dot's head thudded hard into the straw. Mamma tried to wake her up, slapping at her neck and then rubbing her face, saying, "Come on, girl. Come on."

Her eyes filmed over like a fish.

Then I looked at Daddy, who was holding the newborn in his arms, the spindly legs sticking out in every direction, and Daddy was kissing its little head, and saying, "It's okay."

We took the tiny horse into our house, and Mamma sponged it off with warm water while Daddy ran back to the barn to look for some kind of formula.

"I'll have to get some tomorrow from the supply store," he said. "If we strain some milk, do you reckon it will live through the night?" and Mamma said maybe, so I warmed up milk and poured it through cheesecloth.

"We ain't got the right kind of bottle," Daddy said.

"A baby bottle will do for now," Mamma told him, and he went over to Clyde Langston's where they'd just had a baby to borrow one.

That new horse sucked and sucked. Daddy laughed and cried and put his hand on Mamma's shoulder, and Mamma smiled and told me to go to bed.

"What will you do with it?" I asked her.

"We'll stay up with it for a while," Mamma said, "to make sure it's all right."

"Are we keeping it in the house?"

"It don't have nobody else to keep it safe," Daddy told me.

"What about Dot?"

"We'll bury her in the morning, I reckon," Daddy said. "But you got school. So get on to bed."

"Say your prayers," Mamma reminded me.

And I did say my prayers. I prayed and prayed to stop seeing Dot that way, dying on the straw with the hulls from my shoes scattered beneath her.

There was a girl in my class at school named Ajita Patel. She wasn't Holiness or Baptist or Methodist or even Christian. She was foreign, but she didn't speak with an accent, and when we were doing chapters in social studies on other cultures, the teacher asked Ajita to give a special presentation.

She came to school that day wearing the cutest pants I'd ever seen, green ones with tiny pink flowers printed all over them. And they got tight at the ankles, and at the top where the elastic went, they had strings to pull them tight around her waist, and at the bottom of each string was a tiny bell so that when she moved, she tinkled and chimed just a little. She had on a white shirt tucked into those pants, and her hair was pulled back in a French braid, the kind my mamma didn't know how to do, and at the bottom where her velvety black braid touched the middle of her back, she had a ribbon made out of the same fabric as her pants. She had silver rings through her ears, and even though she was smaller than I was, she looked so much older.

Ajita stood up and told us about India, about how she was born there in a village but then moved away when her father got a job in the United States. She said that in her country, they had hundreds of gods and everybody worshipped a special one in their houses. She told us about one god who had an elephant's head and a boy's body and showed us a statue.

We passed the small statue around the room, and when it came to me, I touched it.

She said that in India, the people worshipped cows, and that they'd never, ever kill a cow to eat.

I thought about all our cows, in the pasture behind the barn, how we raised them and drank their milk and sometimes slaughtered them to cut into pieces and wrap in freezer paper and keep for special occasions and for when the men didn't kill a deer.

She said that every year, a doctor would come to the village and all the children would gather underneath a tree and get shots.

I knew that shots were bad. We had to take them in order to go to school, but we got them in a building in town, where the walls were all painted white and nurses in uniforms would say, "Owie, owie, owie, owie," and then stab at your arm while they were talking. And afterwards, Grandpa Herman had to say special prayers over you, and your mamma and daddy had to fast until the knot in your arm went away to atone for all the unnatural chemicals which were the products of man's sinfulness.

She said that in the United States, they worked hard to bring other Indian families over because in India, people were starving and couldn't get jobs. And when a bunch of cousins and aunts and uncles immigrated, her family took them into their home and helped them adjust and find a place to live nearby and get jobs.

That part didn't sound so different from my family.

But I wondered how it could be that Ajita Patel was so proud not to be a Christian. She was a nice girl, who always did her lessons and made good grades on her tests. She didn't chew gum or talk during class. In the lunchroom, she sat next to me sometimes, and even though I didn't talk to her, she'd smile at me and I'd smile back, knowing that surely it couldn't be a sin to smile.

But then I got to thinking that it wasn't fair for Ajita Patel to perish eternally just because she was born in another country where they didn't celebrate Jesus.

The next night when James and I came together as prayer partners, we met with Mamma and Daddy and Bethany and Olin and Nanna and Grandpa Herman. The adults didn't usually come together, but since we were in training, they decided it would be good for us to have an example. We didn't even have to pray that night. We were there to watch.

Grandpa Herman told us we were spiritual warriors waging a battle for souls, and then he asked us if we knew anybody we'd like to pray for. I mentioned Ajita Patel, saying that she wasn't a Believer.

"What'd you say her name was?" Grandpa Herman asked.

"Ajita Patel. She was born in India. Do you think she'll go to Hell just because she was born in the wrong country?"

"Ajita Patel is *headed* for Hell if she doesn't know Jesus Christ as her Personal Savior and Lord," Grandpa said. And that was the end of it.

James cut his eyes at me. He knew Rajesh Patel. I knew

that he talked to him sometimes too—because I'd seen them walking together between classes, but I never told on him.

"Who else should we pray for?" Daddy asked, and people threw out names.

"And don't forget Ben Harback," Olin said.

I wondered why we needed to pray for Ben.

"Does Ben have a heavy heart?" Nanna asked.

"He's having some trouble keeping his eyes on the cross," Grandpa Herman whispered. "He's been driving off after dark sometimes, and I believe he's got his eyes on that little backslidden Holiness Corinthian from over at Mossy Swamp."

"Well, should we pray that he can convert Corinthian?" Bethany asked. "Or should we pray that he redirects his vision?"

"I believe in Ben's case that we should pray for the latter," Daddy said.

And then they bowed their heads around the room, and joined hands with their prayer partners, and they began emptying their hearts to Jesus, aloud, shaking and quivering with the intensity of it.

James looked at me, and I looked at James, and then looked back down, trying to imagine us opening up that way before God.

They went on for a long, long time. Sometimes they'd fall silent, and then somebody would remember somebody they'd forgotten to pray for and start in again, and soon the whole room was full of speaking and crying and spitting out all their anguishes to God.

"Guide us, O Lord," Grandpa Herman said. "And help us know how to help Ben if the time comes that he needs us. Lead our hearts in the ways you would have them to go."

"Help the children like Ninah," Bethany called out. "Help them when sin walks into their classrooms, proudly, and other children's words make them question your holy beliefs."

"And Lord, we just ask you to bless Ninah and James," Nanna said. "Teach them to love gently, to confide in each other, and to save themselves for your glory until they're old enough to understand the responsibilities of adulthood."

"*A*men," Daddy said.

"And help James and Ninah to know that they can tell you anything, precious Lamb. Help them to grow through you," Mamma begged.

I'd grown up hearing people pray for me aloud. It never made me very comfortable—when right in the middle of the supper prayer somebody would say, "Ninah's had a cold all week. Help her see that you're just teaching her about Jesus' pain through this illness," or "Ninah's having trouble learning the state capitals, Lord, and give her little brain the room to retain the knowledge she needs."

I never liked it, but it was so completely ordinary that I was used to it. Besides, most of the time it *wasn't* me they were praying for. They prayed over *everybody*, so it'd be just as likely to hear them ask for special blessings for Mustard or Joshua Langston.

But that night when they were praying for me and James together, it felt different.

Afterwards, Grandpa Herman told us that we could hold hands in prayer if we felt the need, but we weren't to hold hands at any other time. James nodded obediently, and since it was an unusual circumstance for the prayer partners to meet together in the first place, since usually the prayer partners met separately, all around the compound, James asked them where the two of us would gather.

"I reckon you can go into a room in one of your houses," Grandpa Herman said, and Daddy nodded.

"Y'all can have the living room and we'll take the bedroom," Mamma said.

"Or we could do the same thing," Olin offered.

As everyone was leaving, James looked at me and smiled, and my heart fell into my pelvis, like it'd been doing so often.

It had to be the strangest feeling in the world—knowing they were giving us permission to spend time alone together, knowing they were trusting us when I couldn't even trust myself.

And I surely couldn't trust James.

I wasn't sure if what I felt was a thrill or a fear, but it was bigger than anything I'd ever known. I couldn't stop remembering his hand on my leg, his big man's hand on my long, long leg. And I couldn't stop reciting in my head, "Ajita Patel is going to Hell. Ajita Patel is headed for Hell." But I didn't believe it.

I wondered if she'd felt a man-sized hand on her thigh

yet, slipping beneath her soft green pants. And it excited me to think that probably she hadn't.

All that winter James and I came together as prayer partners, and all that winter he never touched me. He held my hands, of course, and his grip was always sweaty. And we'd sit together and list things to pray for, and then we'd pray, but mostly silently.

Afterwards we'd discuss which of us would go to the gym at the beginning of lunch and wash out our gym suits. The gym teacher, who understood that it wasn't our fault that we couldn't wash those clothes at home, kept detergent there for us and a special place to hang them up. Some days he'd wash out my suit, and some days I'd wash out his.

But he didn't touch me.

Some nights he could have. We prayed in the living room of Mamma and Daddy's house, and if he'd wanted to, he could have kissed me at the beginning of prayer time, when Mamma and Daddy had just gotten started.

And sometimes, I'd hear Mamma and Daddy crying out and panting, and I'd wonder if they were really praying at all. That secret blushing that goes on inside your skin would fill me up, fill me red and sweet, like exotic fruit from India, and I'd grip James' hand tighter, hoping he'd feel it too. But he didn't.

It made me sad—not just because he didn't put his hand on my leg, not even on my foot. It made me sad because when I saw him, I felt ashamed. We didn't play anymore or cut up on the school bus. He still sat next to me in Sunday morning services, but he held his head straight up and listened to Grandpa Herman. I still felt like drawing in the Sunday school quarterly—and would have if Nanna had given it to me. Grandpa Herman even started calling on James to pray aloud in church, and he did it like someone seasoned. On Sunday afternoons, he sat with the men and laughed at their stories and paid me no attention at all.

And it made me angry with Nanna for interfering. I remembered how nice it had been when it was sneaky and deliberate, when we were still children and looked at each other out the sides of our eyes and saw all the pleasures of the whole world looking back.

Sometimes when we were praying, I'd open my eyes and watch James' face, his square jaw left loose so that his bottom lip fell down just a bit, just enough for me to look into the darkness that was his mouth and imagine my whole body hiding there, warm beneath his tongue.

T*hat next spring as it got closer to time to plant the garden,* Grandpa Herman decided that the children would be the ones to get the soil ready. So after school, we'd go out and work in the dirt. James and Mustard and Barley would take turns with the hand tiller, and I'd pick up sticks and roots, along with Pammy and John, and carry them over to the edge of the field where we'd burn them later.

It was a big field, and while we worked hard, we played

too, kicking clumps of dirt at each other and drawing figures in the soil.

It was out in the field where I talked to James.

Barley was taking his turn with the tiller, and James and I both had armloads of old tobacco stalks to carry to the far end of the field. Pammy and John were working opposite us, on their way back to pick up more, and Mustard was helping Barley.

"Listen," I said, "if you don't like being my prayer partner, you can just tell Grandpa Herman to find you another one."

"Why would I want to do that?" he asked.

"Well—in case you don't like me," I told him.

"I like you fine," he said.

"You do?"

"Yeah," he said, and stopped and wiped his face off with his sleeve and spit. "Why would you think I don't like you?"

"I don't know."

"You're the one who didn't want to be my prayer partner."

"Me?"

"Yeah. Pammy told me that when you found out you had to hold my hands, you cried like a girl."

"I wasn't crying," I insisted. "I was cutting up onions."

"Oh."

"The whole reason they put us together in the first place was because I told Nanna"—and I paused—"I told Nanna that I liked you and to help me figure out a way," and I paused again. "Well, just a way to see you more."

"Oh," he said again, and tried not to smile but did it anyway. "Really? Nanna did it?"

"And ever since—well, you ain't acted like you wanted to be with me."

"I wanted to be with you," he said. "I just thought you were—I don't know—like *them.*"

"What do you mean?"

"You know, like a Believer, in everything."

"You mean you're not?"

"I didn't say that," he said stubbornly, and started walking again.

"You're not a Believer?" I yelled out, and then I started laughing out loud.

He looked back at me and said, "I am too a Believer. But I don't think for a minute that Rajesh Patel is going to Hell. Or his sister either. And if you think that, you're just . . . full of *shit.*"

"I don't think that," I said, running to catch up with him, laughing so hard my lungs felt like they might explode from the happiness. "I can't believe you said that *word.*"

Then James crumpled beneath his face. "I didn't mean to. I didn't mean it. We have to pray," he said desperately. He looked like someone just realizing that he'd taken his last breath.

"I don't *care,*" I assured him.

"Well, *I* care," he said. "And of course Rajesh is going to Hell. He sure can't go to Heaven. Where else could he go? We have to pray."

James fell on his knees right there, pleading with God for forgiveness. I knelt on the ground beside him, listening to him swear that he was a Believer. But I didn't pray with him. The wind was blowing his curls everywhere. He had the most beautiful curls I'd ever seen. It was all I could do to keep from rolling with laughter on that hard earth.

That night when James and I met together in prayer, we prayed like never before. We prayed out loud.

James said, "Heavenly Father, help David and Laura to conceive a child in your image," because they'd been trying since their last loss and weren't having any luck.

And I said, "Thank you, Lord, for Nanna, who's always there to help us and love us and who still sleeps on nettles for past sins. Please bless her."

James added, "And help Ben Harback make a decision about whether he wants a life inside this community or outside of it. And help the Patels to come to know you, Lord."

And I said nervously, "Help me and James to know your love, to be able to share with each other your love."

And James gripped my hands hard and said, "Let me love Ninah for you, oh Jesus. Let me be the one to show her your love."

I could feel my hands shaking. I wasn't sure if he'd asked for the same thing I'd asked for, but I thought his request might be a tiny bit different.

The next day when we got off the school bus, we all went straight to the field, dropping our books at the end of the row. We were almost finished preparing the soil, and we were just in time. It was the second week of March and the seeds needed planting.

But we'd only been working for twenty minutes or so when Daddy trampled across the cleared ground in our direction.

"Hey, Uncle Liston," Barley called out, and Daddy nodded his head.

Daddy was always either smiling or praying or crying. His face was hardly ever as blank as I saw it then. I knew something was wrong immediately.

"How much y'all got left to do?" he asked.

"Ought to finish it up this afternoon," James said.

"Well, how 'bout you boys come with me and leave the field to the girls," Daddy replied. "We need to dig a grave before dark."

My stomach tried to flip over, but I wouldn't let it. I took the tiller from James and walked off, not wanting to hear what came out of Daddy's mouth next, but unable to make my ears cooperate.

"Is somebody dead?" Mustard asked.

"No," Daddy said. "No. The community's taken a vow of silence until supper time. Herman will talk to us then. So don't open your mouths again, okay?"

We all nodded back.

I didn't want to think about what had happened. I worried that Nanna was sick. I worried that James was in trouble or I was. I knew I needed to keep my mind on Jesus and everything would work out. But I couldn't.

Up on the hill beside the church, I could see the men with their shovels. I imagined James' hands callused and blistered from so much digging.

It was so quiet that I thought I could hear things moving beneath the ground.

I thought about human voices, the way they shout and whisper and break, the way they shade each other and dip. I wondered what Jesus' voice had sounded like, if it was scratchy or booming or stammering or smooth.

I thought about my own voice, lean and low, the way it sounded when I answered a question at school, too loud and always a surprise. I thought about the way my voice sounded in prayers, like a single bell that rings just once but echoes on and on and holds itself in the air and then falls. Or how it hides behind other voices and hopes no one will notice.

I knew that boys' voices changed, but that day, I realized my own voice had. Before I'd gotten so old, it'd sounded the same way always—sassy and clear. But by that time, my voice had deepened, slipped down towards Hell on its way up to Heaven. I knew that my voice had been holding back a holler, that it wanted to break wide open like the sky or the ground. But my voice was heavy, a flute without holes, wooden, imperfect, and thick.

❧

That evening we ate without words, everyone saying their private prayers over their servings of corn bread and venison stew. I was glad to see everyone there, glad to see that Nanna, though somber, seemed as healthy as she had the day before. No one was dead. So someone had sinned. Terribly.

I knew better than to look around during the evening meal and kept my eyes on my plate for fear of being accused of insolence.

Towards the end of the supper, a baby started crying, hard. Normally no one would even have noticed. Someone would have picked it up and cooed and hushed it with their familiar mothering hum. But not that night. The baby cried on and on, and when Freda Langston finally picked it up, Grandpa Herman broke the quiet.

"A tiny child," he huffed, "before it is even old enough to speak is selfish. Selfish. Born a manipulator. Before it has even learned to walk, a baby sins. Knows how to get its way. Cries out, demanding to be comforted. And so we come into this world sinners. Sinners who *cannot* to save our lives live perfectly.

"It's the curse of Eve," he continued, standing by that time and as red-faced as I'd ever seen him, "that we sin. That we disobey God outright. That we live for our bodies, *feed* our bodies, *comfort* our bodies, and forget about our *souls*.

"Our *souls*, people. We need to be feeding our souls.

"And every time we open these mouths, to satisfy the wants of the body through word or food or drink, we turn our backs on Jesus.

"If it wasn't for the curse of Eve, we wouldn't *need* this food. We'd be perfect spiritual beings nurtured solely by the love of God," and then Grandpa Herman picked up his plate and threw it at the door so that it hit the wall and shattered, the pieces falling onto the floor like a leftover song.

We all sat upright, our spines aching to be obedient, our eyes cast downward, and my heart glad that it wasn't *my* baby that had prompted his sermon. I hoped that in his bed that night, Nanna would smother him with a pillow. But only for a moment.

"One of those among us, Ben Harback, has been found guilty of imbibing in forbidden drink. He came onto these holy grounds this morning with his breath tainted and his eyes reddened by Satan's own sweet piss.

"He has admitted to his crime. He has asked to be forgiven. And praise God, the one above is capable of granting him that forgiveness. For the scriptures read that 'If we confess our sins, he is faithful and just to forgive us our sins, and to cleanse us from all unrighteousness.' Where *is* that in the Bible, Ben Harback?"

"First John, chapter one, verse nine," Ben muttered.

"On behalf of The Church of Fire and Brimstone and God's Almighty Baptizing Wind, you are hereby ordered, Ben Harback, to single-handedly teach the children the laws of Jesus Christ and the laws of this community for the next year. If it be God's holy will, you will rededicate your commitment to Christ and to this community through your preparation and service. Clearly it will do you good to return to your studies of the laws."

"Yes, sir," Ben answered from the corner where he was sitting. I looked up for the first time to see him shamefully alone, without food or water. I wondered what Grandpa would do if I went to sit with him.

"But the Bible also teaches us that 'the wages of sin is death; but the gift of God is eternal life through Jesus Christ our Lord.' And *where* in the Bible is *that*, Ben Harback?"

He cleared his throat and mumbled, "Romans six: twenty-three, sir."

"Speak *up*," Grandpa demanded.

"Romans six: twenty-three," Ben repeated.

"That's correct," Grandpa patronized. "And in order to remember those wages of sin, your grave has been prepared, Ben Harback, where you will lay this night and contemplate the wages of sin, where you will pray without ceasing for God's delivery of your piteous soul.

"Now clean up these tables," he said to the rest of us, "and report to the cemetery in exactly one half an hour where Ben's funeral will be held."

Around the room, people moved for Grandpa Herman, and a slow chorus of whispers began until Grandpa yelled out, "In *silence.*"

Ben climbed into his grave willingly. It was still cold in open air, and I couldn't imagine how cold it must be deep in the earth. Grandpa Herman led us in a song, and we stood around the grave holding hands, singing to God for the renewal of Ben's soul.

And then we formed two lines on either side of the grave where there were mounds of dirt, and everybody had to throw in one shovelful.

Of course his hands were free. He could protect his face or move around. The dirt we threw in was just a symbol of his death to the world, in hopes that when the sun came up, he'd be born again, resurrected like Jesus and pure.

And then in the brisk night air, Grandpa Herman gave another sermon, about God's forgiveness, and I think he brought up Nanna again and how she'd been a liar and had been spared death. He said that if it was God's will, Ben Harback would be spared too, and that he'd come back into our community as a soul-winner for Jesus.

I stood beside Nanna as he spoke. I didn't have to ask her what she thought of Grandpa's punishment. I already knew.

I wondered how she could love such a man, with his mind so twisted and his vision of himself as just beneath an angel.

I wasn't the only one who considered such things.

As we were walking home late that night, Mustard said, "That's just crazy. Having to sleep in a grave just for drinking a little bit of alcohol."

"He was drunk," James said, stone-faced. "It's a bad example."

"Yeah," Pammy agreed. "I know now that I'll never get drunk. Not that I was planning to."

"But sleeping in a *grave,*" Mustard said.

And later at home, when I was supposed to be asleep already, I crept to Mamma and Daddy's bedroom door to eavesdrop on their conversation.

"That man will break," Daddy said.

"He'll be fine," Mamma assured. "God will sustain him."

"Don't you ever wonder why your daddy gets to be the one who makes the rules around here?" Daddy fussed. "Don't it seem like we could talk it over as a congregation. I know drinking's a vice, but Maree, my God, that man might die of pneumonia. He made a simple mistake. Who hasn't?"

"I don't want to hear this, Liston."

"But you've *got* to think about it sometimes, don't you? The things he says. The things he's teaching our children."

"Our children have grown into good, God-fearing people," Mamma insisted. "You go look outside this community and see where you can find a family with four children who grow up to obey the commandments of the Lord."

"I ain't talking bad about the Bible," Daddy said. "But what if that'd been David? What if David had fallen and taken a drink? Would you feel the same way if *he* was the one in the grave?"

"One of the benefits of our children *growing up* in this community," Mamma jeered, "is that we don't have to worry about them doing something like that."

"Honey," Daddy said, "it's not the end of the world that the boy took a drink."

"And the boy will be better off tomorrow, when he's repented."

That night I looked out at the cemetery for a long time before I fell asleep. I kept watching to see if Ben Harback would climb out and leave. I thought that if I was in his position, I'd be out of that grave and out of Fire and Brimstone before the sun came up.

I'd been staring a long time before I saw Nanna sitting on the ground not far from the place where the dirt still sat in mounds on the earth. I wondered if she was counseling him, if she was feeling sins of her own and wanted to repent. I don't know if she stayed there all night. I didn't want to know.

The chicken coop at Fire and Brimstone had been falling down for as long as I could remember. The boards were so weathered that you could scrape off the outside layer with your fingernail, and after every big storm, somebody had to get a ladder and nail down the rusting sheets of tin that served as a roof. But we'd repaired the chicken coop so many times that the nails could be pulled out of the soft boards with the tips of the smallest fingers.

Pammy and I had been begging for a new chicken house for years. The grown-ups kept laughing at us, saying Fire and Brimstone had better uses for its lumber and how much shelter could chickens need?

But every time it rained, I'd look at Pammy and she'd look at me, and we'd know exactly what the other was imagining. Chickens huddled together, trying to dodge the water that blew in between the cracks of their walls, their skinny chicken legs no thicker than reeds bogging down as they scratched for worms in their muddy floor.

The rest of the family prayed for crops, but for years, me and Pammy had been praying for the chickens. They were our responsibility.

One afternoon when it'd just stopped raining, I badgered Grandpa Herman about it again.

He was half-hidden under the hood of the tractor, fiddling with a wire while Barley cranked it, then shut it off at his command.

"Goodness gracious, Ninah," he said to me, though he spoke to the motor, "the way you worry about them chickens, you'd think they'd lay golden eggs."

They *might* lay gold eggs if we treated them better," I tried. "There's holes in the walls and holes in the roof. The roost is broken on one side, and . . ."

"James," Grandpa hollered. "Go get some of them leftover boards from behind Clyde's place and fix the chicken pen before Ninah has a stroke."

James, who'd been helping Daddy change the oil in the pickup, wiped his hands and headed my way.

"Thank you, Grandpa," I said—even though I didn't want the chicken coop patched. I wanted it renovated.

"And get that girl a hammer, and put her to work too."

"Yes, sir," James agreed, then turned to me and winked, and laughed because he'd winked at me in front of Grandpa, but Grandpa's head was still under the tractor's hood.

———

Y'*all crazy about these chickens,"* James said later, hammering a one-foot square of plywood over a gap in the structure. "These holes ain't nothing but windows for the chickens, and now you're covering them up."

"Windows have glass," I argued. "You see glass in any of

these holes?" I was working beside him, and doing twice as much as he was. But I didn't care if he was lazy. I didn't care much at all.

"You and Pammy are the ones who used to say the holes were windows. Pammy used to claim that when you came to feed them, they'd be looking out and waving."

"They do sometimes," I played.

"And weren't it just last year that y'all tried to get Nanna to make curtains for them."

"No we didn't."

"Did too."

"It weren't last year though," I laughed.

We moved around to the back. James found an old stool and climbed on it to reach some high places, but I hammered a two-by-four at the very bottom. I was still thinking of ways to keep the ground inside dry, and since the earth was muddy already, I could beat the board into the dirt without even needing nails. It seemed so backwards to be sturdying the foundation when the building was already standing.

"That ain't gonna work," James said from above.

"Why not?"

"Just won't," he said. "And look, you're dragging the tail of your dress in the mud."

"So?"

"That ain't no way for a girl to look," he said. "Get up. I'll fix it in a minute."

"No," I said, and kept working until I got the board just the way I wanted it. And then James banged his thumb, choked back a curse, and wrapped his lips around the hurting place.

"Look what you made me do," he said.

"Weren't my fault," I laughed.

"Was too," he said. "You talked back. A woman ain't supposed to talk back, so a girl surely ain't."

For a second, I wanted to knock the stool right from under his self-righteous feet. Then I reminded myself not to fight evil with evil.

And then I did it anyway. I stood up and pushed the stool he was standing on over. He fell into the bushes that surrounded the chicken coop. The branches cracked beneath him, and then he rolled onto the ground.

He landed on a big stob, and his side was bleeding. As little dabs of blood blotted through his shirt, I got real worried about what I'd done.

"James," I said, and I knelt beside him. "Here, let me see."

But when I pushed up his shirt, he slapped my hand away. "What'd you do that for?" he asked.

"I don't know." I just sat there, looking at him as he examined his scrape, studied his shirt, and fingered the little tear.

"Well, you shouldn't talk to me like that," I began. "Cause you don't own me. And you won't never own me. I know more about this chicken coop than you ever will—" and I stammered and started to cry. "Cause I care about it, and you don't."

He looked at me like I'd gone mad.

"And that's not all, either. You can't tell me what to do because I know just as much as you, and I can hammer a nail better than you can. And it don't bother you for your britches to get muddy, so why does it matter if my dress does?"

"Well, that's what the Bible says," James declared. "A woman ain't supposed to do the work of a man." He was holding his side close, like he was holding in his ribs, and I was worried that I'd hurt him bad, but I didn't back down.

"Well, if I'm a woman, then whatever I'm doing is woman's work. Don't that make sense to you?"

"I reckon."

"And do you really see anything wrong with the way I hammered that board? Look at it."

He looked but didn't have a thing to say.

"I hope you ain't hurt," I said. "Let me see it."

James pulled up his shirt, and there wasn't much to it. Just a little scraped place edged in blue.

"I'll say I'm sorry if you will," I offered.

"For what?"

"For thinking I'm not as good as you and ought to do what you say."

"That's not what I meant," he said.

"It's what you said."

"Well, it ain't what I meant."

We finished patching the henhouse before time for supper, and in the afternoon grayness, we stood together facing the feeble building, our backs turned to anyone who might walk our way. We pretended to admire our work, our hands joined.

"I know you got more sense than most men at Fire and

Brimstone," James whispered. "I didn't mean to hurt your feelings."

And though I knew James could change his mind quicker than rain could turn to mist, I decided to believe him.

I really wanted to believe him.

T*ell me a story,*" *I said to Nanna.*

"What story you want to hear this time?" she sighed, pretending to be aggravated.

I was staying home sick from school, my face all stopped up from the pollen that had fallen, dusting our doorsteps greeny-yellow like hay cut too soon. Mamma was out in the garden with the other women, tending the plants that had just sprouted up. Some of the men had already quit their winter jobs to begin working on the tobacco beds. The young plants were still protected by polyethylene sheets, but they needed irrigating and then pulling up and setting out into the vast fields.

It was always Nanna we stayed with when we were sick. But no one claimed to be sick at Fire and Brimstone unless it was real. Though Grandpa Herman was the one who meted out most of the punishments, Nanna was the one who believed in education. She didn't have much of an education herself, but she discouraged us from faking sick by giving each child who stayed home from school a bowl of prunes every thirty minutes until we went to the bathroom. It didn't matter whether you'd broken your arm or stumbled onto the flu. You ate the prunes.

Nanna believed a good cleaning out would make anyone well. I thought it must be a belief that she picked up from Grandpa. By the time the prunes went through you, you'd eaten three or four bowls, at least, and it seemed to me a fate almost as bad as sleeping in a grave.

I was on my second bowl when I asked her to tell me about Grandpa Herman's sins.

"Ninah," she said. "Why in the world would you want to hear about another person's downfalls?"

"He just seems so perfect," I said. "And he can't be. I just wanted to hear about something he did wrong."

"I think that's an abomination," Nanna said, and left the room.

"Well, he talks about *your* sins," I hollered. "Almost every Sunday." I could hear her in the bedroom, shoving things around, pulling on a stubborn drawer, then forcing it back in.

When she came back out, she had a jewelry box, and she sat down beside me and opened it up.

"Do you see this pin?" she asked, holding up a ribbon attached to a medal so old that it looked like a penny that had been scraped and softened from switching to a million different pockets.

"Yes," I said.

"Herman got this pin from serving in the war," she told me. "Do you know what kinds of things happen in a war?"

"Yes, ma'am."

"Now I just want you to think for a minute about being in one. I want you to think about the things you'd see, the friends you'd bury. I want you to think about what it'd feel like to choose between shooting a man or coming home a coward. Or think about what you'd do when you came face-to-face with a person your same size—just from different parts of the world with different kinds of plans for it—what you'd feel like if you had to pick up a gun and shoot someone."

I thought instantly of Ajita Patel.

"Grandpa Herman shot somebody?" I asked her incredulously.

"Course he did," she said. "He was in the war. And I want you to think about how you'd feel if you went off to war, freezing cold and without your family and barely living, how you'd feel if you got a letter in the mail that only came once every few weeks telling you that our own child was dead, had been dead for a month, and you didn't know it."

"Did that happen to Grandpa?"

"Yes," Nanna said. "It did. And I want you to think about who you'd talk to, all them lonely nights scared to death that the enemy was going to attack you if you closed your eyes. I want you to tell me who you'd trust."

"God, I reckon," I said, ashamed.

"I reckon you're *right*," she said. "When there's nothing else there, that's who you turn to."

She pulled out a photograph of some men in uniforms, all standing together with their arms around each other's shoulders.

"That one there," she said, pointing, "is Herman."

"That's Grandpa?" I squealed.

"Handsome, ain't he? And the man on either side was dead before he come home."

I didn't know what to say. Nanna put the photograph back, closed the jewelry box, and walked off to her room.

When she came back, she had another bowl of prunes. I whined and stretched out on the sofa. She came to the end where my head was, and I lifted it up, and she settled beneath me, pulling my hair out of the way and throwing it across the arm of the couch behind me.

She began feeding me the prunes, one at a time, and I let her.

"Your grandpa saw a lot of things he didn't like," she told me. "When he came home, he was ruined through and through. It weren't nothing but the grace of God that made him whole again.

"There weren't a thing in this world he could do except start over. Now the truth is that Herman weren't a man of God before that war. He was a drinker and a carouser, and I loved him just the same. He fought and he gambled and he lied as bad as I ever did. But that war changed him. Made him scared. Made him want to hold onto ever thing he had with a grip so hard it could strangle a person if he weren't careful.

"When he got back, he got involved with the church, started making a family as quick as he could to replace the one boy we had before he left. And I admit, it weren't the easiest adjustment I ever made. A year before he left these United States, I married him and committed my heart to him forever, and I'm not the least bit sorry for it."

She popped another prune into my mouth even though I wasn't finished with the one she'd put in there before.

"We'd been back together for about a year when the church split up, and Herman went about beginning Fire and Brimstone just like a drill sergeant. He organized it and planned it and worked for it for a long time. And he finally got everything that mattered to him in a space big enough for him to wrap his arms around.

"He did it out of love, Ninah. Love and need. He prayed about it and promised God if he'd give him a place where he didn't have to know fear and didn't have to remember and keep living with the things he'd seen, he'd run it just the way he thinks God runs Heaven."

"Do you think God runs Heaven like this?" I asked her.

"I doubt it," she said, forcing another prune between my lips even after I turned my head away. "But Herman is doing the best he knows. He's still holding onto what he's got, and I believe he's still scared that someday, somebody could come in here and split us apart and he'd be by himself again."

"I didn't know that," I told her.

"He's not a perfect man," she began, and then the screen door slammed and Grandpa walked in.

"Leila," he said. "Do you know if we got any brake fluid?"

"It's in the barn," she told him. "At the back—on the second shelf, I believe."

"You sick, Baby?" he asked me.

"Pollen headache," I said.

"Ummm," he muttered. Then, "Get me a glass of water, Leila. My boots are too muddy to walk in there."

I lifted my head up to let Nanna free. She sat the prunes in my lap.

"She'll be better tomorrow," Nanna promised, shuffling off to the faucet.

"I'll bet she will." Grandpa Herman laughed.

While she was gone, he reached over to the bowl of prunes and started stuffing his mouth.

"How many bowls has she fed you?" he whispered.

"Three," I said.

"God bless you," he said. "Let me help you out." And he ate some more.

When Nanna got back, Grandpa drank his water and announced, "I got to get back out there. The brakes is squealing on that tractor," and he leaned down and kissed Nanna on the head and winked at me.

"You see," Nanna said when he was gone. "That's love."

⌐

David and Laura lost another baby before April was over. I wouldn't have known except that Mamma pulled me aside to tell me before James and I met to pray one night. She said nobody had mentioned it because they wanted to give the baby time to settle in Laura's womb before it became public knowledge.

David was outside tying off some grapevines he'd planted next to the house. I went over to where he was working and stood there until he saw me.

"Hey, Peanut," he said.

"Hey," I told him. But I couldn't think of what to say next. He was looking at me like he was expecting me to say something, and all I could do was notice that his sideburns were beginning to get gray hairs in them. Aging came early at Fire and Brimstone, but David was only twenty-two.

"Something on your mind?" he asked, and stood up, brushed off his hands on his pants.

"I just ... I just wanted to say that I'm sorry about the ... I'm sorry you and Laura won't be having a baby. I know how much you want to build the family."

He nodded his head up and down, opened his mouth like he was going to say something, and then shook his head and walked away, leaving me standing by his new vines.

I bent my knees a little and breathed hard.

When he got to the edge of the house, he turned back and said, "Thank you, Ninah."

It made me crazy how James went back and forth between believing what he'd been taught and believing his own instincts. I knew I did the same thing, but James did it worse. He was like oil and vinegar poured into the same bottle, one minute shaken together and the next minute separated. Cloudy, then clear, then cloudy again.

"Do you think we should be trying to convert the Patels?" James asked me one night.

"No," I said.

"Why not?"

"They've got their own gods," I told him. "Suppose it was me and you living in India. Do you think we'd appreciate it if somebody walked in our house with a little elephant-headed statue and told us we should worship it?"

"That's different," James insisted.

"Nuh-uh," I pressed. "It's exactly the same."

"But if they don't know Jesus, they can't go to Heaven."

"Maybe they have a Heaven of their own."

"Ninah, don't say that. You know that the only way to Heaven is through Jesus Christ. You *know* that."

"I don't *know* what I know anymore." I shrugged. "But it just don't make sense for them to perish in the Lake of Fire when they haven't even *heard about* the Lake of Fire. Now does that make sense to you?"

"But if we tell them, then they'll know about it."

"But if we tell them and they don't believe it, then they really *might* burn forever. The way I see it, they're better off if they've never heard."

James and I had already begun to sin together, but we'd talked it over and decided that it wasn't really such a big sin. We didn't use the entire time for praying to pray. We prayed for a while, and then we talked, and then we prayed to be forgiven for talking. That was that.

We discussed Grandpa Herman and Nanna. The Patels. The things we learned at school that contradicted the things we learned at home.

I was the one who talked James into it. It wasn't very hard. I just suggested that we could serve the Lord by discussing his beliefs as easily as we could serve him by praying.

He always disagreed with me whenever I said outright that I thought Grandpa Herman was too strict. But underneath it all, I think James questioned him too. After Ben Harback slept in the grave, I mentioned that nobody else made people do that—not the Baptists or the Holinesses. I told him that maybe Grandpa Herman was more worried about keeping the rest of his community under his thumb than about Ben's soul, and James nodded.

One night he said to me, "Do you think if we prayed hard enough, that Jesus would speak to us through each other?"

We were sitting on Mamma and Daddy's brown couch with the green-and-white afghan thrown over the back. I leaned my head into the afghan and asked James what he meant.

"Like, do you think that Jesus would say something to you that's just for you, not for anybody else? Not for the whole world. Just for you. Do you think he might say it through my mouth?"

I bit my bottom lip and considered it. "Like if I was having trouble talking to Mamma, not that I am, but if I was— would Jesus give you advice for me?"

"Yeah," James said, excited.

"Maybe," I said. "I don't know."

"Maybe we should pray for that. Because wouldn't that be good? If you could be Jesus for me and I could be Jesus for you? Wouldn't that be the best thing?"

"Would that mean speaking in tongues?" I asked. "Cause I'm not sure I'm ready for that."

James leaned his head back beside mine. "I don't think so," he said.

———

We *prayed for it a lot. We met for prayers every night after* Ben had gone over the commandments with us, every night after we'd recited, "If a man calls a woman a harlot without substantial proof of her sins, he shall pay a hundred dollars, half to that woman's husband or father and half to The Church of Fire and Brimstone and God's Almighty Baptizing Wind."

"If a man leaves the Church Bread, the Holy Body of Christ, in the place where a mouse can eat it, that man shall pay fifty dollars to The Church of Fire and Brimstone."

"If a boy pollutes an animal, that animal shall be killed and the boy's father shall pay two hundred dollars to The Church of Fire and Brimstone."

None of the laws we recited mentioned the real punishments. Not the fasting or the nettles or the strap or the sleeping in graves. Just the money.

And money was a strange concept at Fire and Brimstone. James and I talked about that too—about how odd it was that Grandpa Herman handled all the money. The money from the crops, the money the men made at their outside jobs, the sin money. Grandpa Herman was the sole banker for our community. He collected it all, and then redistributed it to each family according to their need.

But he didn't distribute much. Only enough to pay for a few sins each year.

"Wonder what he does with all that money?" I asked James.

"Puts it back into the farm, I guess,' he answered. "He's not exactly wearing gold rings on his fingers or anything, Ninah."

"I know. But think about it. We grow our own food. We make our own clothes. Wonder where all that money goes?"

"Pays for tractors and pickups and new houses. And material to make clothes with."

"Do you think we're rich?" I asked him. "If we were rich, we wouldn't even know it."

"I doubt we're rich," James said.

And sometimes we discussed particular laws. Like the one concerning the pollution of animals.

"How could anyone pollute an animal?" I asked him.

"I don't know." James blushed.

"What does that mean? Polluting animals? Like if you smoked and you blew it in their faces?"

"I don't think that's what it means."

"And why would the animal need killing? That would mean it's partly the animal's fault, right?"

"I guess so," he said.

I started laughing. "Well, when's the last time you walked by a cow and it said, 'Oh James, will you smoke a cigarette so you can blow it in my face? Or will you pee in my water so I can drink it and be polluted?'" I was giggling so hard I had to cover my mouth with my hand. You can get away with a lot of things during prayer time, shouting or crying or speaking in tongues. But giggles don't usually happen when you're on your knees.

"Ninah," James said. "Come on, Ninah. Let's pray."

"But I'm still thinking about it," I tittered. "Maybe what you'd have to do is pick up a bunch of bubble-gum wrappers off the bus and collect them until you have whole pockets full. And then the next time you're at the barn and a billy-goat calls out, 'James, pollute me,' you'd throw them over his head. And maybe they'd still have some gum *in* them so they'd stick to his hair and then he'd be polluted."

"Ninah!" James said again, seriously. "We don't have much time left."

"It's funny," I said. "It's crazy the things that wind up in that booklet."

He grabbed my hands, pulled me off the couch and onto my knees, on the rug before him.

"Heavenly Father," he began, "please bless our community, surround us with your light, and help us to keep our minds on you." We'd gotten pretty vague at that point.

"Please bless the sick and afflicted, and please give us freedom and power and boldness and wisdom and love and understanding and the very Holy Ghost of God."

That was something he'd picked up from hearing Everett pray. Everett was good at listing, and he'd taken to listing the same things every time Grandpa Herman called on him.

"And God," James said, "we've been talking to you for weeks now, asking you to speak through us. So I'm begging you now to give Ninah the special words you want me to hear."

He paused, and I listened. I listened to hear whatever

God was telling me. I tried to come up with the right thing, but just got confused and said nothing at all.

After a while, James said, "Okay, God. We'll keep trying. Please make us worthy and ready to receive your love. Amen."

"Amen," I echoed.

One Saturday night late that spring, *only a few weeks before* school let out and suckers hadn't even grown on the tobacco so we weren't too tired from our working yet, the children all met in the church classroom to go over the laws.

Ben Harback had been reciting with us, night after night, but that particular night, he didn't show up.

"Ben's late," Barley said finally.

"Real late," Pammy added.

"Do you reckon we should tell somebody?" Barley wondered.

"Nah," Mustard said. "Give him a little more time. He'll be in trouble big if Great-Grandpa finds out he's late for class."

"My fingers hurt so much from shelling them early peas," Pammy complained. "I think early peas have tougher shells than late ones." She was trying to make small talk to pass the time, but nobody was in the mood.

"They're exactly the same," I chided. "Your finger's just ain't used to it yet."

"I think I'm going to get Grandpa," Barley said.

"No, don't," Mustard insisted. "Ben'll get in trouble."

"We could sing," Pammy suggested. "How about 'When the Roll Is Called Up Yonder I'll Be There'?"

"I don't feel like singing," I said.

James looked at the clock and rolled his eyes. "If Ben don't get here soon, we're gonna be late for prayer partners," he said to me.

"It'd be okay, I guess. It ain't our fault."

"No, it won't be okay. I feel the power tonight. I need to pray with you, Ninah."

"He *needs* to pray with you, Ninah," Barley taunted. "He *needs* to."

"Ugh," Mustard whined. "You mean you really *like* saying prayers?"

"He *needs* to," Barley said again, slapping Mustard on the thigh, and they both laughed so hard I blushed for James.

But James ignored them.

"Come on, Ninah," he said. "I think it's time."

"Where can we go?"

"You can do it in the bathroom," Barley teased. "If you got to pray that bad, you shouldn't be picky." And they cracked up again.

James grabbed my hand and pulled me up.

"Holler for us when Ben gets here," I told Pammy.

We didn't go to the bathroom. We went to the choir loft, just behind the pulpit where Grandpa Herman gave his sermons. James led me through the little swinging door, and we knelt on the second row where the men stood.

"Lord, I've been listening to you," James said. "I've been praying and praying about this, and I know you've given Ninah something to say to me."

We paused, and I listened, but what I heard was the sound of James' last words hanging near the ceiling.

"I'm here, God," I said. "I'm listening. I've been praying for this too. I want to be the one to give James your special instructions for his life. Please speak through me."

But nothing happened. Nothing at all except I could feel his hands sweating and trembling. I pulled myself closer to him to hold him steady.

We waited in silence for a while, and then James said, "Lord, maybe I'm confused. Maybe I'm the one who's summoned to be your holy conduit for Ninah. Give me your words, Precious Lamb."

He was speaking so honestly, so totally sincerely, and I wanted to keep my heart open to God, but I was trying too hard not to laugh, imagining James as a holy conduit. And then I felt his knees next to mine, so close, and I recognized his breath, warm and tinted with something that smelled like grass, and I wanted to be his holy conduit too, whatever that was.

And then his mouth was next to mine, and he was speaking into my mouth, and I hoped it might be Jesus, so I didn't pull away.

"Lord, I'm not sure what you're telling me," he whispered right down my throat. "I'm not sure that I'm feeling you right, but I want to, Jesus," and then he kissed me like a waterfall, and I kept my mouth wide open until he called out, "Ninah, this can't be right. We have to pray."

So I said, "God, I think we're getting mixed signals. You have to lead us cause we're in the choir loft and Ben Harback's late, and we don't know what to do."

———

"Give us the strength to wait until we're ready, Jesus," James mouthed.

I couldn't stop looking at his mouth.

"Please help us, Lord."

And then I leaned into him and kissed him on the throat and at the place where his soft shirt rested against his neck.

"Ninah," he said. "We have to pray. We have to *pray!*"

"That's what we're doing," I said, and ran my lips across his eyelid.

And then God spoke. Really fast. And then I knew him like I'd never known him before.

———

L*ater, I couldn't stop looking at James. It was the only thing* that made the burning okay. We were the ones who finally told Grandpa that Ben Harback hadn't arrived. We walked right by the classroom where the others were still waiting, walked out into the night that whirred with crickets and cicadas, walked right up to Grandpa's door where I knocked and James said, "Ben didn't come. Ninah and I left because we need to go home and pray."

Nanna was there, and she looked at me, and I looked back at her for too long.

James took my hand, in front of them both, and led me to my house, where Mamma and Daddy greeted us and told us to mention Everett to God because he had a special need.

We didn't remember Everett. We didn't remember much.

I couldn't stop looking at James, who had something in him as sweet as I imagined wine to be.

———

If Ajita Patel was right and we came back to this earth again and again, throughout eternity, I knew James must be Jesus himself. And he had chosen me.

―

Ben Harback didn't show up that night, not in the classroom where Pammy and Mustard and Barley and the others waited until Grandpa Herman burst in on them, all red-faced and panting and made them copy down the first six chapters of Revelations. He didn't show up at Great-Aunt Imogene's house either, where he slept in an extra room. He didn't come home at all.

But I saw him that next afternoon. We were working on our language arts modules, and I was at the grammar station, next to the window, working with Ajita Patel on semicolons, when I looked outside and saw him in the bus parking lot slouching between two buses, talking to Corinthian Lovell.

Corinthian was several years older than me, but she'd been held back so many times that we'd lost count. She had blond hair that fell just down to the shoulders, and she made a habit of frosting her eyes with colors that didn't appear in nature. She was from a backslidden Holiness family where the girls still wore dresses all the time, but her family didn't abide by the real laws, and Corinthian wore tight skirts cut up to the middle of her thighs. I wondered if her mamma knew about her lips, bright red, or if she painted them on each morning after she left.

Corinthian rode my bus from the junior high back to the

elementary school in the country, but she switched buses there and went off towards Mossy Swamp while our bus kept going towards Fire and Brimstone. I wondered if she'd be on the bus that afternoon or if she'd sneak off with Ben.

"Ninah?" Ajita whispered.

"Hmmm?"

"Do you have an extra pencil? I'm out of lead."

I looked down at her pencil, the kind that looked like a pen except it had an eraser that you pumped downwards to get sharpness.

"Not that kind," I told her, "I have a regular one."

"That's fine," Ajita assured me, and smiled.

So I gave her my extra pencil, feeling a little embarrassed because it had bite marks around the eraser, and went back to work. Those were the first words I'd ever said to Ajita Patel. I wondered if it made us friends.

Even after I got back to my grammar, I couldn't stop wondering if maybe in secret, Ben Harback prayed with Corinthian the way that I prayed with James. Because if that was the case, whether she was a backslidden Holiness or not didn't matter. That kind of praying was outside the realm of judgment.

When the last bell rang that afternoon and Ajita returned the pencil to me, she said, "I can get you one of those plastic pencils. We have a whole box of them in my dad's office. They're kind of nice to write with."

"Okay," I said. "Thanks."

James *was waiting for me outside the building. We'd discovered* that if we sat on the bus together, the other children didn't pick on us as much—or maybe it just didn't matter.

"Come on," he said. "We're not going to get a good seat."

I hurried away with him and was almost at the bus before I realized I'd left my math book in the language arts room. "I forgot my book," I said. "I'll be right back."

I was already running when James hollered out, "You don't have time. You'll miss the bus."

I dashed down the empty halls into the classroom, picked up the book, and ran back. The bus door was already closed, and the engine was cranked when I banged on the door, and the driver gave me a nasty look and opened it.

All the seats near the front were taken. A fat boy from the special education classes sat next to James, who looked at me apologetically and shrugged as I walked past him.

"Sit down," the driver yelled, and then the bus moved and I staggered forward.

There were no empty seats except at the very back where Corinthian sat with her bag thrown into the vacant space next to her.

She pretended not to see me, looking down at her finger-nails which were painted exactly the same shade as her lips, and I stood there looking at the seat and waiting.

"Sit down," the driver hollered again, and I picked up her bag and plopped onto the vinyl cushion.

Some of the kids nearby tittered and whispered, and Co-rinthian rolled her eyes, tossed back her hair, and continued to ignore me.

At the back of the bus, things were different. That's why James and I usually rushed to get a seat at the front.

Some bad girls just ahead of me, who dressed like Corinthian but were my age, started singing a song.

I got a boy with a foot-long pecker. I'm gonna let him put
it in.
I know Mamma taught me better, but screwing boys just
ain't no sin.
I ain't gonna tell my mamma, for she would just smack
me hard.
I'm gonna screw him in her bedroom, on her sofa, in her
yard.

Then they'd look back, waiting for me to react.

"Hey, Corinthian," one of them said. "You like your new seatmate?" And they both broke out into giggles again.

From the front of the bus, James kept looking back, checking on me, and I'd wave at him to make him think everything was okay.

"I think your brother's worried about you," she said to me finally. "I think he's worried about your *soul.*"

"He's not my brother," I answered. "He's my boyfriend." I liked the way it sounded when it came out.

"Ain't you Fire and Brimstone?"

"Yeah," I said. "So?"

"I didn't think they'd let you have boyfriends at Fire and Brimstone."

"Well, I got one," I bragged, acting tough.

"Does your mamma know?"

"Yeah. She don't care."

"That ain't what I heard," Corinthian spat. "I heard at Fire and Brimstone, you can't even touch each other until you're married."

"Just cause that's the rule don't mean everybody obeys it," I said suggestively.

"You for real?" she laughed. "You and your boyfriend doing it?"

"That's private."

"You ain't doing it," Corinthian insisted. "You don't even know what it's like."

"I might," I answered.

"I know about Fire and Brimstone," she said. "Y'all crazy out there, staying up all night in church and stuff. You wouldn't have time to do it if you wanted to."

"Are you gonna marry Ben Harback?" I asked her.

"Fuck no," she said.

"I think he loves you," I told her, shaking off the shiver her language was giving me.

"Ben's crazy. Talking about God all the time. I ain't interested in that."

"Well, why are you sneaking off with him then?"

"I don't know," she said. "He's kind of cute."

She was looking at me by that time, like maybe she'd forgotten who I was and how I looked and where I lived. I looked at her lips too, wondering how it would feel to smooth color over them, wondering if it kept them warmer in the winter or kept them from breaking open.

"When you wash your mouth off, does that color stain up the rag?" I said before I even thought about it.

"What?"

"The lipstick. Does it leave marks on the washrag?"

"I don't know," she answered, looking at me like I was the stupidest person she'd ever seen. "So do you know Ben?"

"Yeah."

"Does he have a girl—out there at Fire and Brimstone?"

"No."

"He stayed in our barn last night," she bragged. "He hates y'all."

"Well, why don't he leave then?"

"You *can't* just leave. Everybody knows that. Y'all'd come find him and assassinate him or pull him back by his ears."

"That's not true," I defended.

"Plus, he's got this thing about Jesus or something. I can't figure it out. They let you *fuck* at Fire and Brimstone?"

I blushed. "Not before you're married," I said.

❧

When we got to the elementary school, I moved up to the front of the bus with James before everybody else got on.

"What were you talking to her for?"

"I didn't say all that much," I said, and looked down at my math book, at my pencil case on top. Inside it was the pencil Ajita had used.

"Corinthian's dirty," James mocked.

———

"That's a stupid thing to say," I told him. "She's just a person."

"She's a wicked woman," James announced. "All you gotta do is look at her to see that."

I opened up the pencil case and took out the one Ajita had borrowed. I opened a notebook and began writing my name over and over, pretending to do homework but really just feeling that pencil in my hand, imagining how it must have felt in Ajita's hand. It felt like a secret even though it probably didn't count as one. But it was something I knew that James didn't. I thought that if Ajita had germs on her fingers, then they were on mine by that time, and it was a funny kind of sharing that I craved.

When we got home, there was another vow of silence, but nobody had to dig a grave.

And when we went in for supper, there was no food at all. The tables were set, and we took our seats behind empty plates, all white, and I kept staring at the plate, at the edge of my reflection in the plate.

Grandpa Herman gave another sermon, an angry one about Hell. But I didn't listen. All during that hungry supper, I looked into the empty plate, staring at my lips and thinking about how much better they'd show up in the ceramic shine if they were painted red.

I thought about Corinthian and imagined her as my great-grandmother, who wasn't a wicked woman and didn't know a single thing that I hadn't learned already. The only difference in me and her was that she was brave and had money to buy lipstick, and I didn't.

———

I didn't feel guilty either. Not for imagining myself painted up while Grandpa Herman called Ben Harback before the congregation and officially condemned him.

I wanted to talk to James. I wanted to explain to him how Corinthian probably just needed to be loved, to tell him that if she was really seeking the pleasures of the flesh, she'd surely look for someone more wild than poor Ben Harback.

The one thing we did have for supper was water, and I sipped at mine until it was gone.

"Did you or did you not engage in pleasures of the flesh with the young woman from Mossy Swamp?" Grandpa hollered.

"I did."

"Did you or did you not know her biblically?"

"I did," Ben said.

Around the room, I could hear the air racing out of all the lungs, as if everybody in that room realized at one time that they'd taken into their lungs Ben Harback's air. All around the room, people held their breath.

"Fornication," Grandpa said, "is grounds for being thrown out of this community. Is that what you want, Ben Harback?"

"No, sir," Ben mumbled.

"Fornication is grounds for being tossed sidelong off the streets of Jasper, through the Pearly Gates, and into the Great Lake of Fire. Are you aware of that, Ben?"

"Yes, sir," he said.

"Did you force this young woman?" Grandpa asked.

"No, sir."

"Do you intend to marry her?"

"I'd like to marry her," Ben began. "But she ain't a Believer."

"But are *you* a Believer?"

"Yes."

"And you consider your behavior to be the behavior of a *Believer?*"

"I've sinned," Ben cried. "I've sinned awful. But I don't want to be cast out of this community, Preacher Herman. There ain't no place else a man can be this close to the Lord, and I want to be close to him. I'm just a weak man. . . ."

"A weak and despicable man," Grandpa added.

"But I want to make my heart right. I really do."

I peeked over at James, who sat at the other side of the table. He was staring blankly into his plate. I tried and tried to will him to look at me, but he didn't. Inside, I felt the worst lonely I'd ever known.

"I haven't decided what to do with you yet, Ben," Grandpa Herman said. "I don't want my community tainted with the sourness of your soul. I have asked God to guide me in my decision, and he hasn't gotten back to me. If you want to remain among us, then I'll pray for an answer. In the meantime, you're sentenced to the cellar, where the door will be bolted and no man, woman, or child shall look upon your sinful face."

I didn't know which cellar he was talking about. I didn't even know we had a cellar, but I figured if we did, it was bound to be full of rats.

"Liston," Grandpa said. "See this man to the cellar."

Daddy got up, and Ben followed him out.

"In order to remember the importance of discipline and purity, no one will eat this day," Grandpa said. "Dismissed."

We stood up, and the women began collecting dishes, carrying them back to the kitchen. I tried to get James' attention, but then he called out to Grandpa.

"What is it, son?" Grandpa said, exhausted.

"Could I just talk to you for a minute?" James asked.

My heart jumped into my throat, and I couldn't swallow it down. I could feel it beating in my neck, and I imagined my neck like a lizard's, pulsing.

"Ninah," Mamma called. "Come wash these dishes."

I went into the kitchen where somebody was drawing the water already. The steam rose up hot from the bubbles.

I thought we'd just be washing the glasses, since nobody used the plates or forks. But I was wrong. We washed them all.

When the dishes were done and Mamma put her arm around me and led me out of the fellowship hall, Daddy was standing there with Grandpa Herman. They stopped us before we went down the steps.

"Ninah," Daddy asked me, "did you sit with Corinthian Lovell on the bus today?"

"Yes, sir," I said quietly.

"Ninah!" Mamma exclaimed, pulling her arm from around me and looking at me like I'd killed a preacher. "Corinthian is the object of Ben's sins."

"Why did you blemish yourself that way?" Grandpa scolded.

"There weren't no seats on the bus left," I told them. "I forgot my math book and had to run back inside, and when I got back, I didn't have any place left to sit."

"That's understandable," Grandpa said. "But did you *speak* to her?"

Both Mamma and Daddy looked at me hopefully, and when I said, "Yes," they both shook their heads.

"What did you talk about?" Daddy asked.

"She wanted to know about our community. That's all."

"So you talked to her about God?" Mamma asked.

"Yes, ma'am. And about Fire and Brimstone too. She was asking about the rules. She wanted to know about what we did in church, and I told her. I thought maybe she wanted to join," I lied.

"So you were testifying?" Daddy tried to understand.

"Yes, sir." I looked down.

"But you knew she was a child of Satan, did you not?" Grandpa asked.

I didn't say anything at all.

"Did you or did you not know that Corinthian Lovell was a wicked girl?" he continued in the same tone he'd just used with Ben.

"Yes, sir."

"Well, for that, I think you have earned the strap," Grandpa said. "You are neither old enough nor wise enough to take on the responsibilities of conversion. Do I have your permission, Liston?"

Daddy closed his eyes and nodded.

"Maree?"

"My blessing," Mamma said, and walked off.

I hoped he wouldn't wait until the next meal and do it publicly. If I was going to be whipped, I wanted it to at least be a private humiliation.

I guess you could say I was lucky.

"Come on," Grandpa said, and he yanked me by the shoulder and led me towards the church.

Behind me, I heard the fellowship hall door slam, then Nanna asking Daddy what I'd done.

He led me up to the front, to the table in front of the altar where the communion bread and grape juice sat on days when we took Christ's body.

"Bend over," he said, "and lift your dress."

I'd had the strap before, but not since I was little. I wondered if he made all the women lift their dresses. I tried to remember if any woman in the congregation had ever gotten the strap, but it seemed like they just fasted or slept on nettles.

When my dress was lifted and I was tensed up already, he said, "Slip down your underpants," and I almost died, but I did it.

And then he whacked me again and again, swinging that belt so hard that I could hear it sneering at me as it sliced the air. I didn't cry though. All that time, I hoped that there wasn't something about the skin on your bottom that changed when you fornicated. Or some little smell. Some way for Grandpa to know.

But I didn't consider anything I'd done to be fornicating. There was no way a big word like that could describe anything as nice as knowing Jesus all the way through.

When he was done, he pulled my underpants up and my dress back down in one swift movement, and then he pulled me to the floor and prayed with me, telling God how he was proud to have me in his family and congregation, and not to let me slip into sin anymore.

But I didn't pray. I kept wondering how James could have done such a thing. I tried to figure out whether Jesus would have told if he'd been in James' position. I decided that Jesus would never snitch.

On the way out of the church, Grandpa Herman said, "Sometimes I hate having to be the one to carry out these punishments."

I walked back to my house seething. I wanted to smack James so hard he landed in the Lake of Fire. But only for a second.

I was late getting to prayer partners, and when I got there, James was waiting on the couch. But Mamma and Daddy were in there with him too, and they asked James to sit tight while they talked to me.

I went with them into their bedroom where Daddy said, "He didn't hurt you, did he, Baby?"

And Mamma interrupted to say, "That isn't what I'm concerned about, Liston."

"I'm sorry," I said to them both. "I sinned, and I've asked God to forgive me."

And then Mamma hugged me close and I could smell her skin, faintly eucalyptus and warm. "I am so proud of you,

Ninah," she said. "For being such a strong girl and admitting to your mistakes. You won't talk with that girl ever again, will you?"

"No, ma'am," I said, but not loud enough to block out the sound of Mamma's stomach growling.

"Then go on out to James," she said, and slapped me on my backside, forgetting, I guess, that Grandpa had just hit me there, but Daddy remembered and gritted his teeth out loud.

"I've got to run get my bible. I left it in the bathroom. I'll be right back," she said to Daddy, and hurried off.

"He didn't hurt you, did he?" Daddy whispered once she was gone.

"Not too bad," I said.

"I'm sorry," Daddy muttered. "Now get on out there with that boy."

I made the walk down the hall take longer than it should have. With every step, I asked Jesus to help me not kill James.

When I got in the living room, he was sitting there, his head drooped down, his hands together between his open knees. He looked up when I approached.

"Thanks a lot," I said sarcastically.

"Ninah," he began.

"No, shut up. I'm not done talking to you," I snapped, and then I had to pause to think of what I wanted to say. I was standing directly in front of him, hovering over him, and it felt good to have him sitting there so pathetic and so much lower.

"You know that I didn't do anything at all on that

bus," I said. "I didn't do *nothing*. And you know that I'm not like Corinthian, and that I don't want to be. And you *know* why I sat back there. I mean, it wasn't like I *chose* to sit with Corinthian Lovell, James, so why'd you get me in trouble?"

"I don't know," he said, and his voice broke, the way it did sometimes so that it sounded like he might yodel.

"I never told on *you*," I said. "And you're friends with Rajesh Patel."

"We ain't *friends*."

"Well, I'm not *friends* with Corinthian either. But I still got the strap tonight just for talking to her."

"I'm sorry," he said.

"Well, if you're so sorry, why can't you at least look at me?" I asked him.

"I don't know," he said, peeking up for just a moment and then looking back down.

"I thought you loved me," I said, and then I started to cry.

"Ninah," he said. "Don't."

"Leave me alone," I told him. "I thought you *loved* me."

❦

Justice comes to everyone, I guess. I don't know how it can be that you can wish somebody evil and then feel so bad when it knocks them behind the knees and flattens them on the floor.

I'd been hoping and praying for James to get in trouble. I didn't want it enough to cause it though. He could have danced naked on the school bus, and I wouldn't have told. But that didn't mean I wasn't wishing.

I'd been saying prayers with James for a week, but we'd reverted back to the old way, where we didn't talk and didn't pray out loud and looked forward to the time when we could unclasp hands and go do our studying. I'd half forgiven him by then, but not completely, even though he'd said he was sorry every day and tried to kiss me once before I pushed him back.

Then the last day of school, after Ajita Patel had given me one of those foreign pencils and told me that she hoped we'd be assigned to the same classes next year, Pammy told me about James' sin on the ride back to Fire and Brimstone.

She was sitting next to me, her books stacked neatly in her lap, and she whispered into my ear, "James has to sleep on nettles for a *week*."

"Why?"

"He polluted his bed," she said slowly, so quietly that it took a minute for me to process her words.

"What does that mean?" I asked her.

"I'm not sure," she said. "He soiled it. And Mamma found out and told Daddy, and Daddy got real mad."

All of a sudden, I figured it out. I remembered the film from school about the things that happen to girls' bodies and the things that happen to boys'.

"*Polluted* it?" I asked again.

"I think he pooped," Pammy said, and then covered her mouth to keep from laughing.

"But that's an accident, right? He probably couldn't *help* it."

"It's still a sin," Pammy said. "And now he has to sleep on pine needles and cockleburrs and thorns."

"Thorns?"

"Yeah, a whole bunch of them. Daddy went out in the woods and cut them down."

"That's awful," I said.

And later that night when James and I met in the living room, I said, "I heard you have to sleep on thorns."

"Yeah."

"That hurts," I uttered, but it sounded so stupid that I shut up.

"Are you still mad at me?"

"No. I guess not."

"Good," he said. "Do you want to go for a walk?"

"Will we get in trouble?"

"Everybody's praying for the next hour. I reckon we can pray outside as good as we can pray inside."

So we left. We went out to a tobacco field where the plants were just thigh high and walked in a few rows so that we wouldn't be visible to anybody skipping prayers that night.

"I'm sorry you have to sleep on nettles," I said, and I meant it.

"It's like there's all this stuff in me," he said. "And it needs to come out. But every time it does, it's a sin. I can't figure it out."

"That'd be hard," I agreed.

"Girls don't have it."

"But if we're created in God's image, then it doesn't make sense that it would be a sin."

"It's the curse of Eve," he whispered.

"I don't know. I'm not sure it's really a curse."

"Yes it is," he proclaimed. "You just don't know."

"Tell me," I said, and he started to, but then he stopped.

"Ninah, we can't. We have to pray."

"Okay," I agreed. "That's fine with me."

And so James asked again for Jesus to lead us and help us and to speak through us.

But every time he said that part about the speaking-through, it happened. Jesus just whirlwinded around inside me until he got so big that he started slipping out, and I think it happened the same way with James. Jesus just filled us up, so full we had to share it. It wasn't fornication. Not there, with the tobacco leaves lisping in the warm wind, not with the moon overhead like a spotlight so that God could see from way up above.

Later, I told James that if it helped, he wouldn't have to sleep on nettles ever again.

Later, I told James that it must be God's will, because otherwise, we wouldn't be able to sneak away and get back inside before prayer partners were over.

Later, I told James I loved him like the air, always moving, but constant as a hope.

He brushed off my back each time, and his hands felt like a remedy to all the badness I'd ever known.

✦

Grandpa Herman didn't decide what to do with Ben Harback for forty days, which Grandpa said was a sign. When he came out of the mysterious cellar that I couldn't even find on the property, he looked like a rib, having eaten nothing except rice for so many days, and the sunlight hurt his eyes so bad that he squinted almost all the time. I figured that by that time, Corinthian had forgotten him for sure, and it made me ill.

We were already gathering tobacco, walking row after row and popping off the four leaves on the bottom of every plant so that by the time we got back to that particular field, the higher leaves would have grown.

The day after Ben Harback reemerged, he was in the fields, but he was so weak that he fell behind, and Mustard had to help him keep up. James had moved on to bigger things than cropping tobacco by that time. He was driving the tractor, pulling the wooden drag where we tossed the leaves behind him.

"You okay, Ben?" I asked him that afternoon. Because he hadn't been in the sun all summer, his skin was pale as a cotton boll and not as absorbant. He was already lobstering in that heat.

"I'll be all right, I reckon," he said.

"Cause you can sit on that drag if you ain't feeling good. Me and Mustard will cover for you, and James won't tell."

"I'll make do," he insisted.

He'd been underground so long that his voice sounded funny, like he had water in his lungs, and when James stopped at the end of a row to wait for us to crop the last few leaves and then turn the tractor around to go back down the next, I stopped him.

"Ben's sick," I told him.

"Why do you say that?"

"Look at him. He's about to fall down."

"He'll be okay," James said, and drove on, riding high, like king of the field.

We took a break in the middle of the afternoon, and Ben climbed weakly onto the drag with the rest of us, and James drove us back to the barn where a bunch of women were putting the tobacco leaves onto the conveyor belt and Nanna was straightening them before they went through the stringer where they got stitched to the old wooden sticks.

During summer, we were allowed to drink Coca-Colas in bottles and eat Nekots out of their plastic wrappers on breaks. It was the only relief we got from the sun and the work.

We took twenty minutes to catch our breath. Even the men who were hanging the sticks in the barn got to come out and talk.

"You all right, Ben?" Nanna asked him.

"Yeah, I'm fine," he said.

"We're glad to have you back with us," David added.

"Glad to be here," Ben said. "It's been lonely down under. I reckon I shouldn't say that, since I had God to converse with, but I missed you people."

"We missed you too," Daddy said.

Before we left to go back to the fields where the strong people worked, where James drove a tractor and David did, where all the older children worked cropping tobacco and the younger ones followed them picking up dropped leaves, and the littlest ones not even old enough for school sat at the edges of rows and played with their toy tractors, I pulled Nanna aside and said, "Ben Harback's gonna pass out."

"You reckon?" Nanna asked.

"He's pale and he can't keep up and he needs to go to bed."

"I told Herman not to put him in this field before he got a good meal," she said, walking back.

Nanna motioned Ben to the side of the barn and was talking with him when Grandpa Herman drove up in his shiny pickup and Ben hurried back to rejoin the croppers.

We went back out in the sun, plucking off our leaves and laying them onto the drags in big armfuls. We hadn't been working long before Ben threw up. I heard him gagging and didn't want to look, but I didn't want him to get in trouble by falling behind. So I kept crossing over to his row and Mustard helped too while Ben choked and wiped his face.

"I can do it," Ben panted after a few minutes. "Y'all get back to your rows. I'll get mine."

"It's okay," Mustard tried. "Take it easy."

"I can *do* it," he bellowed. "Leave me alone." He leaned over, cropped a handful of leaves, and tossed them on the drag next to the ones I'd just put there. A clump of vomit fell off his shirt and landed on the trailer.

I had to talk myself out of getting sick. I had to force myself not to think about it.

Me and Mustard let him keep going, and I prayed for my own weak stomach instead of for Ben.

We were halfway down the next set of rows when Mustard hollered out, "Hey, Ben's fell down."

James didn't hear him and kept driving slowly along.

"Hey," Mustard called again. "Ben's down."

I ran over to Ben, and some others rustled through tobacco stalks to where he'd collapsed. Somebody stopped James and he turned off the tractor.

"He ain't hardly breathing," Pammy declared.

"He's breathing," I said. "Don't exaggerate." But I was worried. His face was sunburned to the point that it looked like you could wipe his skin off with your fingers, but beneath that redness, it seemed like the blood had drained away. It was the scariest color I'd seen, doughy pink and almost runny.

"Let's get him up there," Barley said, and picked Ben up from under the arms. Mustard got his legs.

We all hopped onto the drag, trying to balance our weight in the middle so that it didn't tip up or down, and Mustard sat up on the tractor's tire shield to keep it from being so heavy.

I wiped at Ben's face with a tobacco leaf. It was all I had.

James drove back to the barn going so fast that the nickels and dimes in the engine sounded like steady quarters. Dust clouded around us as we hit bumps in the road. Dust particles muddied in our sweat.

"Slap him, Ninah," Pammy said. "Wake him up."

So I did. I hit him on both sides of the face and then once really hard in the middle of the chest, all the time asking God to preserve him.

"Ben," Pammy shouted. "Ben!" She yelled it in my ear, but I didn't fuss.

When we got to the barn, Nanna ran over to us, and Grandpa Herman pulled the truck up, and Everett and Olin lifted the still-unconscious Ben into the back. Nanna leaped in, and then Grandpa drove away.

"Get back to work," David said. "Everybody back in the fields."

So we went.

James asked me if I thought Ben would be okay, and I said I hoped so. James asked me where he was staying, and I told him that I figured he was in Nanna's spare bedroom. James asked me if I thought God was punishing Ben, and I told him that God didn't need to because Grandpa Herman took care of that better than anybody else I knew.

"Sometimes when you say things like that, I wonder how God would even be willing to speak through you," James smarted.

"Well, it's the truth," I said. "Leaving a man in a cellar for forty days. I don't see how you could call it anything else but cruel."

We were out behind the barn. James and Barley and Mustard were in charge of watching the fires that burned beneath the leaves, making sure they didn't get too hot and ignite the curing tobacco during the night. Because James was still working, I got to go outside for prayer partners.

Nobody was concerned about it. Barley and Mustard were there too. But they'd fallen asleep already, in the soft sand beneath the shed where the tobacco stringer was parked next to the barn door.

And we were on the far side of the barn, closest to the woods, stretched out on our backs and looking up at dark sky pocked with clouds. We couldn't even see the moon.

"Do you ever worry that what we do sometimes during prayers could be considered . . . fornicating?" James asked.

"No," I lied. "What we're doing is different. It's just a part of a prayer. Besides, it isn't *you* I'm doing it with. It's *Jesus.*"

"Yeah."

"I don't think we should mention it to anybody though," I added.

"No," James agreed. "They wouldn't understand. Sometimes I worry that we're fornicating though."

I felt an awful pinching in my stomach when he said that. I knew that if James really started believing he was sinning, he'd tell. I didn't know what Grandpa'd do to us if he found out. I suspected it would be far worse than anything that had happened to Ben—since Ben came into the community late in life, but we'd grown up there.

"What Ben did is different," James coaxed himself. "That's nothing like what we do."

"No."

"I mean, if Ben had been following God's instructions, he wouldn't never have gotten caught—do you think?"

"No," I said again.

"Me neither."

I rolled over onto my side then, facing James, and I put my hand on his shirt and ran my fingers along the middle of his chest. He was skinny. We both were.

"But if you're Jesus to me," James figured, "then when I'm loving Jesus through you, that means I'm really loving a *man*. Do you reckon that makes me—you know—funny?"

"Jesus ain't a man," I giggled quietly. "He's a spirit. He's a God. That's not anything *like* loving a man."

"You're right," James said, rolling over to face me, and then I flattened back out on my back.

He ran his hands across my abdomen, across those bones that poked up at the place where my hips began.

"They feel like noses," James whispered.

"If you're really worried about it," I said quietly, my voice getting lower and earthing, "then maybe we should ask Jesus for a sign."

"What kind of sign?"

"I don't know. We could pray about it and see what happens."

So we prayed together, then quietly alone, and the whole time I was scurrying through my mind, trying to think of a way to make James certain that what we were doing wasn't a sin.

Finally, I thought of something that might work.

"Lord," I said aloud, "I think you're trying to give me something for James. I'm not sure what it is yet, so please make it clear to me."

"Thank you, Jesus, for speaking to Ninah," James prayed.

"The ring?" I pretended to ask God. "You want me to put the ring on his finger?"

"What ring?" James muttered.

"Look," I said to him with as much sincerity as I could muster. "Jesus gave me a ring for you, to put on your finger. He's *marrying us*, James."

I took his hand in mine, reached for his middle finger, and then slipped the invisible ring down over the knuckle.

"Can you feel it?" I asked him. "It's gold with little diamonds all around."

"I can feel it," James laughed, and then he started crying. "Oh God, Ninah, can you believe it? Wait, I have to ask God if there's something for you."

While he prayed, I felt low and wicked, and I expected at any minute to hear a trumpet in the sky, God calling his children home to get them away from someone as evil as me. I felt lower than river sludge, but I wasn't about to back down.

"Thank you, Christ," James said. "Thank you for your sign."

"What'd he say?" I asked.

"He gave me a ring for you too. Give me your hand."

And he worked his fingers down mine, pausing for a second, then pushing until he fit it in place.

"It's got rubies in it," he said. "I saw it."

"Really?" I asked him.

"Yes!" James laughed and cried and shook with relief. "I'm so *glad*," he said. "You're my wife. At least before

God, you're my wife. Oh, Ninah, I'm so glad you prayed for a sign."

"I hope nobody can see the rings except us."

"They *can't*," James followed. "He told me."

"Really?"

"Yeah. We're the only ones who know they're there."

And then James was on top of me again, but it was different—because I knew it was James and not Jesus. I didn't feel glowing and holy afterwards. I felt like I was made from mud.

I *didn't know what to do. In my bed that night and for nights* afterwards, I stared up at the ceiling and prayed for a tornado to come down and suck me up and throw me in a river somewhere far away. I prayed for the ceiling to fall right in on me and flatten my face and scar me up so that nobody, not James, not Jesus, not anybody at all would ever want to touch me again.

I had bad dreams about being whipped in front of the altar. I had bad dreams that James was whipping me, then rolling me over and being Jesus for me, except he wasn't Jesus. He was Satan. Either Satan or Grandpa Herman.

I woke up sweating, and kept climbing out of bed, creeping to the bathroom where I stood before the faucet. But I couldn't even turn it on to make sure it ran water and not blood. Because all I deserved was blood.

But I didn't see any blood. Not anywhere. Not in the

faucet and not in the toilet after I peed. Not in my underpants. Not on my sheets. No blood at all.

I thought maybe the rapture had come already and we'd all missed it, the entire Fire and Brimstone community. I knew I had to be living in the years of plague and revelation. There was plenty of food, but I couldn't eat. I'd seen no stinging beasts, but I jumped for fear of them at every corner.

I knew it was my fault. I'd taken something beautiful like our prayers and turned them into something horrible—just so I could keep feeling good. And I *didn't* feel good. Not at all.

Nanna said, "Honey, what's eating at you?"

And I wanted to say it was a little baby Jesus, eating me up from the inside, eating me like cake. But what I really said was "Nothing."

"Something's on your heart, ain't it?" Nanna asked.

And I fell into her arms and cried like I'd been left behind. As she held me, I thought for sure that that'd be the last time I'd ever feel my Nanna, so soft in spite of her bones.

"Is it about James?"

"Yes," I wailed. "He's different now."

"He's just growing up, child. And you are too. I know he's spending more time with the men, but he hasn't forgotten you. That's how men are."

"Can I stay here for a while?" I asked Nanna. "I don't want to go home." It was a Saturday, and I was supposed to be helping Mamma clean.

"Yes," Nanna said. "I'll run over to your house and tell Maree you're helping me with my floors. Go ahead and get the broom."

So I spent the afternoon with Nanna, while Mamma cleaned alone and the men fished. But I couldn't talk. I cried and my nose poured so hard that I could have mopped the floor with snot, but Nanna didn't make me work. She brought me a bowl of prunes instead, and each one doubled in my mouth.

I *did not sleep on a single nettle. I thought about it. But then* I decided that I wasn't even comfortable when I was awake, so why should I be miserable when I was asleep? I was going to Hell anyway, no matter how many thorns I covered up with, so I didn't even bother.

James was happier than I'd ever known him. All he wanted to do was kiss on me during prayer partners. He didn't even try to be cautious about it because as far as he was concerned, we were husband and wife during that hour every evening.

Before, there'd been something graceful about his tentativeness. But all that was gone. Before, all he'd had to do was brush against the skin on the inside of my legs and it was like a glorious electrocution inside. But after we had the rings, the rings that weren't even real, James seemed clumsy and forceful, and I hated it.

But from time to time, I'd forget how bad things were. Sometimes, when he put his mouth on just the right part of my ear, I'd think that maybe God *had* been speaking to me, that maybe I wasn't making the rings up, that if James said God had given him a ring for me, then maybe it was at least partly true.

Then I started wondering if maybe how you made God answer was by giving him the first part of the sentence you wanted him to say.

I thought I was a liar, but I wasn't certain.

One Sunday in church, sitting between Nanna and James like I always did, with Grandpa Herman right in the middle of his terrible story about how Nanna was a liar who had lied to God by not telling about her mamma's affair with Weston Ward and an accomplice to murder because she didn't stop her daddy from being killed, I decided to speak in tongues.

It wasn't something I'd been planning. And it wasn't something that God told me to do either. It just happened, all of a sudden, like a rooster that crows in the middle of the day for no apparent reason.

I stood right up and spoke out. I said something like, "Lord, please open my heart and fill me up with your beauty and love. Lord, I'm asking you for your precious gift."

In front of me, Mamma and Daddy, David and Laura, Everett and Wanda, Bethany and Olin all opened up their

mouths and started praying out loud, so loud that I felt like
I needed to shout.

"Lord, I'm here. Take me and fill me up," I said again.

"Praise God," Grandpa Herman called.

"Help her, *Sweet* Jesus," Olin yelled.

All around me, I could feel a heat, and I wasn't sure if
I was going to pass out or not.

"Lord, I want to know you inside and out," I hollered.
"I want to know your hebamashundi welaka oma
hebamashundi."

The only word I knew for sure that I'd heard people
speak in tongues was hebamashundi, so I let that one move
my lips again and again.

Then I knew I was going to pass out. I was almost certain. I felt sick and weak and carried away. As far as I could
tell, God wasn't leading me anywhere. I was making the
words up as I went, and they seized up in my mouth and
spilled like lies all over the hard wood floor.

"Help me, Jesus," I tried. "Help me not get caught in
your welamaka oma hebamashundi," and then I began to
whisper or maybe to cry.

Around the church, there was the sound of whoops and
Amens and clapping and the strange words that I was making up, making up, and everything was dark on either side
of me, but right up front, where Grandpa Herman stood,
beckoning me with his arms, it was bright for a second, and
then that was gone too and I was sitting back down, out of
breath, convulsing inside.

I couldn't look at Nanna or James. I couldn't sing aloud

with the congregation though I moved my heavy tongue through the song.

> *Jesus can't come in until we throw old Satan out.*
> *And I want Jesus in me—cause that's what I'm about.*
> *So beat me till I'm weary, and whip me till I'm blue*
> *And make a space, Sweet Savior, for no one else but you.*

It was the longest day in church I've ever known. I couldn't break the trance I'd induced myself. I walked around for days whispering under my breath "hebamashundi, hebamashundi."

My mind was slow those days. I worked in the fields and sang with everybody else, but later I couldn't remember it. I went to supper and picked at my food, but by the time I went to bed, I couldn't recall what we'd had. I went to prayer partners with James and obliged him as much as I could, and I guess I even talked to him, though I can't imagine what I said.

Ben Harback, who had recovered from his sickness, finally broke in two. He just came in mad to breakfast one morning and told Grandpa that he was sick and tired of his bullshit, and that he intended to leave and tell the whole world about what Fire and Brimstone had done to him. Grandpa Herman ceremoniously kicked him out, and as Ben was leaving, he yelled things that made the women cover their ears. But I didn't cover mine. It didn't even shock me.

And then we had a week of preachings every night after prayer partners, all titled "Vitamins Against Evil" to help the rest of the congregation not fall into Satan's hands like Ben had done. I sat beside Nanna each night, but I didn't talk to her, and when she put her hands on my legs to pat them during the sermons, I hardly felt it. We didn't get into our beds until long past midnight and had to be in the fields when the sun came up, which meant we ate breakfast in the dark.

I knew that I was probably having a baby, and that probably it was James' baby and not Jesus'. But I didn't have the energy to do anything about it, to even think about it. So I didn't.

"Hebamashundi," I whispered to each leaf of tobacco as I popped it off the stalk. "Hebamashundi," I mouthed to the hornworms I shook off before I tossed the tobacco onto the drags.

My eyes locked into a blurry, unblinking place. When we'd finished a field, I'd stand at the edge, looking over the stripped stalks with only their tops left and thinking that we'd made ruffles by popping the leaves away. We'd taken the tobacco's clothes and left it with only ruffles to hide beneath.

The whole time James would pray, I'd say it over and over to God. "Hebamashundi, hebamashundi," like it was a password into a secret gate that I really needed to get through.

At nights, I didn't talk to Jesus. I imagined him. I closed my eyes and saw him on the cross, holding azaleas for me, dying for me, bleeding for me, *instead of* me, and I was jealous of Jesus, who could die when things got tough. It seemed like he got a lucky break.

Do you think that somebody like Ben Harback, who has sinned so terribly and so many times, can still enter the kingdom of Heaven?" I asked Mamma one day as we were putting clothes on the line. I was beginning to worry about my soul and my belly. I'd finally admitted that you can only stay in a trance for so long before you have to wake up and rejoin the world, before you forget how.

"If he does enough penance," Mamma said. "And if he asks Jesus to come back into his heart."

"You mean Jesus will *leave* your heart sometimes?" I said, and handed her a pair of Daddy's pants. The wet clothes were draped over my arms, weighing me down so much I kept moving to keep from being planted there.

"Oh yes," Mamma said. "Your body is a temple for the Lord. And if it gets to looking like a pigsty in there, the Lord will just find him another home."

"But I thought God was always with you," I said.

"It's a cooperative effort," Mamma explained. "God will always be with you, but first you have to get the conditions right. You have to invite him in and mean it. What are you worrying about this for?"

"Cause I don't want Ben to go to Hell just because he sinned," I claimed.

"Well, you worry about your soul and let Ben worry about his, okay?" And then without waiting for me to answer, she started singing "The Old Rugged Cross."

I didn't join in though. I didn't even remember that I was supposed to until she turned back and said, "Is something the matter, Baby?"

"No, ma'am," I promised, and began the second verse.

Then I got to thinking that maybe it was *Jesus' baby*—because if we really hadn't been sinning and had only been knowing Jesus through each other, then it couldn't be anything *but* Jesus'.

I counted back and discovered that the baby almost had to be planted inside of me before James and I had exchanged the invisible rings, the rings that only James and Jesus could see.

If God had given a virgin a baby before, he could do it again. I thought I must be a virgin. I had to be. Because in order to not be a virgin, you either had to be married or had to be wicked, and I was halfway convinced that I wasn't either of those even though I had a few doubts.

I couldn't imagine why God would want to curse a person like me—because I worked hard and obeyed my parents and prayed and didn't sass at grown-ups hardly at all. So I decided that maybe it wasn't a curse.

And then I comforted myself with the knowledge that unless a baby's *supposed* to stay planted in your womb, it falls out. It had happened to Laura over and over, and Grandpa said the baby had left her because of sins. So if I was really so wicked and evil, the baby would have left me too.

And I knew that I came to Mamma and Daddy when they weren't even meaning to beget me, and they'd always said that I was the special child, the one God intended for them to have even though they didn't plan it. So if I was carrying a child of my own, that had to mean that it was God's special plan, and God had surprised people before, and they'd survived.

I decided I'd better tell James about it. I thought that if I made it sound like we were getting a special gift, maybe he wouldn't be upset.

"What?" he nearly shouted. We were in the living room again, with Mamma and Daddy just down the hall in the bedroom.

"Shhh," I begged. "I think I'm having Jesus' baby."

"What do you mean you're having Jesus' baby?"

I tried to act excited, but my voice jerked a little. "I'm, you know, with child."

"Ninah, you can't be."

"I am," I said.

"Oh shit."

"James, don't say that."

"Oh hell, fire, and damnation," he cursed. "Ninah, they're gonna kill us."

"Even if it's Jesus' baby?" I started to cry. I wanted him to put his arm around me, but he didn't.

"It's *my* baby, Ninah. Not Jesus'."

"But if I was knowing Jesus through you, then you were just the vehicle," I tried.

"Oh, for God's sake, Ninah."

I don't know what surprised me more, hearing James' reaction or realizing that all that time, he didn't think Jesus was acting through him at all.

"You mean you don't think it was Jesus—when we touched?"

"No," he said. "It was me and you, sinning like crazy."

"But even at first?"

"It was me and you," he said again, shaking his head. "The Devil comes to man in the shape of a woman. I knew that. But I didn't think it'd be *you*." And he walked out.

⟜

I sat on the doorsteps next to Mamma, *pulling the silks from* corn. At the bottom of the steps, Daddy leaned over a bushel basket, shucking one ear after the other, yanking off the green husks and passing the naked corn to us to clean.

Mamma could pull off a silk without even breaking it, but I always pulled too hard, from the wrong angle, and ended up having to dig out the silks with my fingernail.

As I worked, I thought about what James had said, and I fumed. I wasn't the Devil. The Devil wasn't inside me. I was almost sure.

Daddy tossed husks to the ground and with them, the crown of silks curled up and darkened like little-girl hair turned brown.

I always thought of corn as female before it was shucked.

Undressed, it turned hard and regular, the kernels lined up like soldiers. Underneath, it didn't look the way I always thought it should.

I didn't think I was the Devil, but I wondered if beneath my skin, I was so different I wouldn't even recognize myself.

I hated James that night. Nobody had ever said anything so cruel to me before.

And if what we'd done was a sin, then it'd come from inside us both. Not just me. And not because I was the woman.

I studied Daddy's hands as he passed ears to me. The silks hung from his fingers like temptations that wouldn't fall away no matter how hard he shook them.

I looked at Mamma's hands as she coaxed the shiny threads from between kernels, determined to remove every last clinging menace.

I left silks on my ears on purpose—little secret ones that wouldn't be noticed right away. And I must have been the Devil, at least a tiny bit, because I was on fire from the inside, hot and smoldering and thinking terrible things about James.

I handled the corn so hard I punctured kernels with my fingers. I thought being the Devil wouldn't be so bad if I could just burn James up.

$\rule{1.5cm}{0.4pt}$

By the time I saw him again, I didn't feel quite the same way. He said he was sorry, but it was the weight of his hand on my thigh, the way his thumb stroked easy that reminded me how much I loved him too. He was so scared, and I wished I was powerful enough to protect him. I wished I had wings like a bird so I could hide him underneath. If I was a bird, I'd peck him five or six times hard on the head and then let him under my wing.

"We gotta run away," his voice quaked.

"Where would we go?"

"To the beach?"

"We can't do that," I pleaded, even though a part of me wanted to race for the road. "They'd find us. We don't have any money."

James wept. He started crying hard, and I hadn't seen him cry since he was little. It looked so funny, big sobs sputtering out of an almost full-size man's throat. They weren't the kind of tears people had in church, where they just fell freely and ran down faces like rain on a windshield. They were squeezed out through squinted eyes, and accompanied by a sound like his lungs were colliding into one another. I didn't know what to do. It scared me for him to cry, but I tried not to let him know.

"Do you have any idea what they did to Ben Harback for fornicating?" James asked me.

"Locked him in the cellar for forty days," I told him.

"They did more than that. They cut him. And the reason he had to stay underground for forty days was because he had to heal up before he could walk around again. And that day in the field, that day when he passed out, he was already sick and in pain."

"No," I said.

"It's true. And if we stay here, that's gonna be me, Ninah," and he broke down again.

"Least you don't have a history of sin," I tried to comfort.

"Don't matter," he stammered. "Don't make one bit of difference."

"If you knew we weren't being Jesus for each other, then why'd you keep doing it?" I asked him, not accusingly, and I ran my fingers through his soft dark hair.

"I didn't think God would let it happen," he said. "Cause God was with us the whole time. I didn't know something so awful could come from something so nice."

I started to tell him that it wasn't awful, but then I thought about what might happen to us. At the very least, we'd be sleeping in graves until the frost.

But I was glad to know that he thought God was there. All along. Right with us all that time.

"We'll run away," I told him. "I'll come up with a plan."

"We can't."

"Yes, we can," I assured him, and I put my hands into the tops of his trousers, and that's when I felt it. Barbed wire. Wrapped around him again and again.

"Where'd you get it?" I asked him.

"The barn," he said. "There's more in there."

"Come here," I said. "One more time." And I pulled him to me so that I could feel it too, the sharp wires x-ing into my skin, poking little holes into each of us each time he pushed.

"Harder," I told him.

"It hurts," he choked, and paused to wipe his eyes.

"Harder," I insisted. "To know Jesus' pain." It was difficult to know for sure where all the tears were coming from.

⟵

That next morning at breakfast, I couldn't eat. Just the smells of the food were too strong, corn bread so thick and hot and oniony. I put a piece in my mouth and chewed and chewed as it got bigger. I had to swallow everything twice, and even then it didn't want to stay.

James wasn't eating either. He wasn't even trying. I watched him staring at his fork still resting beside his plate, his eyes studying it like a holy relic he couldn't imagine touching.

"James, you feel all right?" Bethany asked him, and he looked up from the table quickly to nod.

His eyes looked surprised—like somebody stung by a bee. I wondered if mine looked that way too.

⟵

In the fields that day, I figured it all out. On Thursday when James went with the men to the tobacco auction, I'd hide between the big burlap heaps of tobacco on the back of the ton truck. And then James would distract them when they first got to the warehouse, and I'd jump off and dive under the truck until the men walked inside.

I'd meet James outside the warehouse, next to the high-

way, and we'd run into the woods and then follow the
road along until a trucker came by. We'd thumb a ride
into town.

We'd go to Ajita Patel's house and call Corinthian
Lovell, who would help us, I was almost sure. I'd cut my
hair, and she'd paint up my lips, and we'd cut off James'
pants into shorts so he wouldn't be recognizable as a
Fire and Brimstone. Then maybe she could call Ben Harback and he'd take us to the beach an hour away where
we'd disappear.

We'd get jobs in a store or maybe as lifeguards or something. We'd find a barn somewhere and sleep there until we
made some money. Or we'd call the gym teacher from
school and see if she'd loan us enough money to get by for
a week until we found a job.

We'd find somebody who had a garden and sneak in after
dark and pick tomatoes and cucumbers to eat until we could
afford to buy food of our own. And later, we'd sneak back
into that garden and replant it. Either that, or we'd leave
them a fruit basket on their doorsteps at Christmas,
anonymously.

I wondered if people at the beach planted gardens.

The more I thought about it, the happier I got. We could
just leave. Contrary to what anybody might think, me and
James could just run away and be done with Fire and Brimstone forever.

But it didn't happen like that.

We finished filling a barn that day, in spite of the heat and
stickiness that teamed up against us. We were so tired we
could have skipped supper and gone straight to bed, but we

didn't. I sat at the table and ate, though James only pretended to.

Then when it was time for prayer partners, I staggered out to the barn to meet James, who was tending the fires with Barley and Mustard. I was going to tell him about our plans if I could get him far enough away from the other boys. And even though I was scared, I was a little excited.

By the time I got to the barn, I was hollering out. Then I saw Mustard stretched out on a drag and Barley laying on his back on the stringer, already asleep even though it was barely dark. Barley rolled over and said, "Ninah, shhh."

"Y'all make him do all the work," I fussed.

"It's his *turn*," Barley said.

"Huh?" Mustard jumped up quick, his eyes springing open. "What?"

"Go back to sleep," I told him, "It's just me."

I peeked into the barn, calling James, but I didn't see him. I thought maybe he'd gone out back to wait for me at the place where we prayed when he tended fires.

But he wasn't there either.

"Did you find him?" Barley asked. He was up, but groggy, and walking behind me.

"No," I said.

"Huh," Barley pondered. "Is it late?"

"Quarter to nine."

"Well, he's got to be around here. We were just talking to him not long ago. We just layed down. He can't be gone far."

"Maybe he had to use the bathroom," I said, and walked back to the barn shed and waited.

There were a couple of lanterns hanging from the rafters, and I stooped in the sand beneath the light, picked up a tiny stick and twiddled it in the doodlebug hole, around and around, waiting to see if the bug was at home.

"If he don't come soon, I'll be your prayer partner," Barley offered. I couldn't tell if he was teasing or not.

"He'll come," I said.

Looking through the rickety barn door, I could see the low burners blazing orange, spread out all along the ground, heating up the tobacco inside. It was very dark except for the orange glow given off by the squat fires, and I could see the shadows of tobacco hanging from the rafters, from the wooden bars stretched from wall to wall, layered like hair. It reminded me of what Hell must be like, looking into that hot door, and I wanted to back away.

It was a funny feeling that shook me, one I can't exactly describe. I thought I might throw up or pass out, and so I walked away from the light and away from the barn's heat. But I tripped over a tobacco stick and stumbled into the drag where Mustard had been sleeping.

"Hey, Ninah. You okay?" he asked, then yawned.

"Yeah. I think I got too hot," I answered, and I tried to sound ordinary, but my voice was marbled with panic. I was almost sure James had left Fire and Brimstone without me.

If I couldn't be with James, I wanted to be alone, but Mustard didn't know that. He hopped down and stood with me, away from the light.

"It's too hot to even breathe," he muttered.

"Yeah," I agreed.

"James probably snuck off to the pond to cool down."

"You think so?" I asked hopefully.

"He told me this morning he wanted to finish that barn early enough for us to have time to go swimming. I guess after me and Barley fell asleep, he just went on his own."

"He's never done that before. And he was expecting me."

"Yeah," Mustard said. "Maybe he forgot."

But I knew James hadn't forgotten. He might not have wanted to see me. He might even have left me. But I knew for a fact that James hadn't forgotten me. No matter what, he wouldn't be able to do that.

"Well, I'm real worried about him," I said finally, and I guess Mustard got concerned about him too because he told Barley that we were going off to look for James and to stay awake until he got back.

Ten minutes later, I was sitting behind Mustard on a horse, trotting through the woods. Mustard had the reins in one hand, a lantern in the other, but my hands were empty. Even though I could see the little branches, I didn't stop them from slapping me as they swung past Mustard.

We darted in and out of trees, and I studied the moon, narrow as a claw, the stars that hung prickly above me. Though it was night, the temperature hadn't dropped much, and I was sweating. I could feel the horse sweating beneath my thighs, and I could smell the hot dampness of our bodies. My legs itched from the rough, damp rubbing.

I was almost sure James wasn't swimming, and I tried to concentrate on the shadows the lantern cast, on the horse's breathing and Mustard's. I tried not to notice the fear that felt like it was hugging me too tight. In my mind, I talked to James the way I talked to Jesus—as if he was really there.

"Don't leave me here," I prayed. "Just because the baby ain't in *your* body don't mean you can go. Not without telling me, at least. The least you could've done is told me."

I tried to convince myself that when we got to the pond, we'd find James splashing around, and we'd probably hop in the pond with him and play. I'd have to take off my dress and just swim in my underwear. I'd have to pull up my hair to keep Mamma from noticing. I told myself we'd barely make it back before prayer partners were over, and I tried to feel excited and brave.

But I feared that in spite of Mustard and the horse, I was already completely alone. I didn't want to live at Fire and Brimstone without James.

Just before we got to the pond, I could see another light shining dim through the bushes and trees. Mustard turned the horse in that direction, looked back at me, grinned, and said, "Told you."

"James," I yelled out happy. "Hey, James." And I decided in just that instant that I was going to take off *all* my clothes and dive into the water and not worry about my hair. I'd tell Mamma I went swimming instead of to prayer partners. I'd tell Mamma that I prayed underwater. I decided I might even tell her about the baby, and I decided it wouldn't matter if Mustard saw me and James kissing. I decided I didn't care.

"James, you idiot," Mustard hollered. "What would you have done if the barn'd burned down?"

But nobody answered.

"That's strange," I said.

Mustard stopped the horse near an old broken tree that had fallen into the pond. Though the roots were still partially planted in the ground, the tree sloped down from the bank and gradually disappeared into the water. I knew the boys liked to dive from the trunk even though they'd been warned that they could be caught on limbs underwater. So when I saw the flashlight sitting so still on the tree trunk, abandoned a few feet from the place where water swallowed the old oak, I hopped off the horse right away, climbed onto the tree, and carefully made my way towards the flashlight.

"James," I called out, feeling the panic rush back down to my toes and numb me all over. Mustard waved the lantern around so we could see the surface of the pond, but James wasn't there.

The lantern shook as Mustard bolted towards me, surefooted even though the tree was only a few feet wide, and the light bounced on the water with his steps, making the shadows of other trees appear to wave violently.

By the time he reached me, I had already picked up the piece of rope I found running along the length of the tree and then going under beside the trunk.

"What's the rope for?" I asked. Has this rope always been here?"

"James," he called. "James?"

And I pointed the flashlight to the land-tied end of the

rope and saw that it was knotted around the roots. Then I straddled the log, and pulled from the other way. I could feel the rope giving, then tightening. I caught the rope between my toes and stretched my leg into the pond as far as I could, but the rope was much longer.

Then Mustard grabbed the rope behind me, and we both pulled, and Mustard told me it might just be a sunken boat, and I cried because the other end was too heavy to be the kind of boat you can float in a regular pond and because Mustard was crying too.

We pulled for a while more, but the rope was clearly hung.

"James can hold his breath for a real long time. He's even better at it than Barley," Mustard whispered.

"Should we swim down and try to loosen it?" I asked him.

"Not yet," Mustard said, but his voice sounded like pleading even though he didn't mean for it to.

So we jerked and tugged and fought more with the rope, and leaned backwards until we fell, both of us, off the tree and into the water, knocking the lantern in too. And I sunk like a cinder block. I squinted my eyes shut and rose back up and met Mustard dripping and clutching the tree. To my right, the lantern floated away, and the light was dim from just the flashlight because there was no moon to speak of.

But when we climbed back on and pulled again, the rope wasn't caught anymore. I passed it back to Mustard, grabbing handful after handful of wet rope, and it wasn't as slippery as I thought rope should be, or as light.

Finally we pulled a massive piece of tree out of the water, and as it surfaced, I could see a body tied to it.

"Get the flashlight," I told Mustard. "It might not be him."

But it was James. James and a big chunk of tree tied together like twins joined at the side. The rope was wrapped and knotted around his waist, and then knotted around the middle of the waterlogged tree. They were so twisted together that it looked like they'd grown that way, and a branch thinned narrow in four or five directions over his head.

I stood on the trunk looking down at James, his mouth gaping, and the water captured in my dress dripped down on him. I was suddenly cold and suddenly still, and I didn't hear Mustard say, "Give me the rope," until he'd already pulled it from my hands.

We towed him to the edge of the pond, and then Mustard heaved him onto the grass. I stayed on the bank with James while Mustard rode back to get help. I didn't untie him from the thick piece of tree, or wipe away the algae draped over his ear and neck. I didn't touch him. I held the flashlight on him and studied the way he'd wrapped himself in rope and wood. I wondered if he'd known he would smell like a plant, so fibery, when he was pulled from the pond. I wondered what the rope was for—if he'd worried that no one would find him and he'd sink to the bottom, or if he'd worried that without it, he might change his mind. I imagined him fastening that knot around his waist, so tight it looked elastic around his thin middle. I imagined him swimming down, feeling for the thickest branch. I wondered if he'd died tying knots. I wondered how long it took his lungs to fill.

I held the rope in my hands and watched him, framed with cattails and reeds. And later when I heard voices shouting, voices screaming out as they came towards the pond, the sounds seemed so far away, like how voices from Hell must sound to God, so forgettable.

I'm not sure who cut the rope from his body or who cut the rope from the tree. But when Daddy led me home, I still had it in my hands, twisted around and around.

Some people say you can't change history, but that isn't entirely true. We did it at Fire and Brimstone, and it was easy.

James didn't take his own life. He drowned on a hot night, caught on a root in the bottom of the pond. Nobody ever mentioned that he was tethered to that sunken tree with thick, deliberate knots.

And that was that. At his funeral, with everybody crying and howling so, nobody even blinked when Grandpa Herman said his death was accidental. Nobody minded that he praised James and talked about what a good companion he'd make for the angels. That's what we wanted to hear.

Pammy couldn't stop shaking. She shook for the rest of that summer, and the only thing that made her stop was sitting between my legs and letting me practice on her hair. I learned French braiding after James died. I worked on Pammy's red hair until it looked like something out of a magazine, and even though in the past the adults wouldn't have let us wear our hair in fancy braids, nobody seemed to notice or to care.

Mustard and Barley had a fight and didn't talk to each other for nearly a month. Even though Grandpa Herman made them pray together and hug, they went their separate ways afterwards. Barley stayed in the woods as much as he could, and Mustard just stomped around, his head hung down to hide his strange eyes.

I didn't do much of anything except keep watch over everybody else and study their mouths, the way they dropped down a little more than before. I listened to the quiet. It was quiet all the time. And sometimes when I'd think that things had gotten too quiet, I'd strain my ears and hear sounds that must have been there all along, voices whispering, sewing machines buzzing, tractors thumping across the holes in dirt roads.

Every time I went into Bethany and Olin's house, Bethany grabbed hold of me and cried. But I didn't have any tears to share. I'd just stand there like a post, being something for Bethany to cling to.

I went into James' bedroom right afterwards and sifted through his drawers without asking. I took one of his flannel shirts and wore it all the time, even though it was still summer. When I buttoned it over my dress, it bagged down like my heart, and I liked the way it looked and wouldn't take it off. It had a little bit of smell left in it, and I promised myself that I wouldn't forget that smell.

It was only a couple of weeks after James died that school started again, and even though Mamma tried to get me to take off James' shirt, I wouldn't. I wore it every day, and if anybody made fun of me, I don't remember it.

"Get that thing off and let me wash it," Nanna tried.

"No, ma'am," I said. "I don't want to be without it."

"You can put it right back on."

"It's not that dirty," I claimed.

"But it *was* dirty. It was stained with food I'd spilled, though I hardly ever spilled food before, and it had grease all along one arm from helping Daddy work on a tiller.

"How about if you put on another one of James' shirts. Will you do that? Just until I get this one washed? It's starting to carry an odor, Ninah."

So I agreed. Nanna walked over to Bethany and Olin's to get the clean shirt. I stayed on her couch. And when she handed it to me, I took it to the bathroom to change, even though I had on a perfectly good dress beneath it.

I was too big to sit in Nanna's lap. Way too big. But when she settled in her rocking chair, I went and sat with her, slinging my long legs over the side so it wouldn't put too much weight on her brittle bones.

"My old girl," Nanna said, and patted my back.

"Tell me a story," I begged her.

"I'm tired," Nanna said. "I been working all day, and all you been doing since you got home from school is moping around. You tell *me* a story."

I laughed. "What story do you want to hear?"

"How about the story of the day before James died?" she whispered.

"Why do you want to hear about *that?*" I said, trying to

sound normal but hearing my voice scratching up towards despair.

"Because it's a story I believe you need to tell," she answered.

And I almost told her. I wanted to tell her. But there was so much that came before the words, so much sadness, and it was like my breath was racing down a big flight of stairs, letting itself out one step at a time. Then just when I'd get to the bottom and think I was going to be okay, I'd steal my breath back in one big gulp, and start leaping down again until it was all out of me.

"I'll tell you a story," Nanna said while I cried. "I'll tell you about Liston and Maree Huff. You ever heard of them? They're good people, live out in the country with their family. God-fearing, soul-searching people. The kind of people you'd want to be with except when something goes bad. Because when things go bad, Liston and Maree turn into measuring cups. You know what I mean?"

"No," I wheezed.

"Measuring-cup people always think about quantity. Half a pound of this or a whole cup of that. And for grief, you only get so much—just like you only get so much happiness or so much sickness. They ain't particularly stingy with it, but they just figure half a cup ought to be enough for everybody. So when they're mixing up their cake, they put in just the right amount, and if it comes out not tasting sweet enough for you, then the problem ain't their lack of honey, it's your sweet tooth. But the truth is that that cake might not be sweet enough for them either. And if that's the case, they shovel in forkfuls of bad cake and think about candy while they're eating it, and pretend.

"Everybody's worried about you, Baby," Nanna said. "They just don't know what to do for you. Your mamma and daddy think that if they ignore it, it will go away, all the pain you got in your little heart. They figure that if they don't mention it, then you won't have to feel it. And they don't want to remind you of the thing that makes you hurt."

"I loved him, Nanna," I told her.

"I know, dear."

"No, it was special," I tried.

"Of course it was. And he loved you too."

"Do you know what we did? We let Jesus speak through us. We prayed that Jesus would show us his love through the other person, and it worked."

Nanna rocked me, on and on, patting me almost too hard and letting me stay there even though I must have been hurting her with my weight. I was so tall by then.

"Do you have any idea what made that boy want to leave this world?" she asked me finally.

"No," I lied, and started whimpering again.

"That's okay," Nanna consoled. "You can tell me about it later if you feel like it."

She was just at home with lies as she was with the truth. For that, I was grateful.

But the shirt didn't smell the same after Nanna washed it, so I kept the other one on.

I'm sorry about your friend—James," Ajita Patel told me one day when we were supposed to be dressing out for gym. "Raj told me that he died this summer," she added awkwardly. "That must have been really hard."

"Yeah," I said, privately cursing my eyes for trying to betray me again.

"Is that his shirt?" Ajita asked.

I nodded.

Ajita had dropped her skirt and was working her shorts up over her hips, over her too-white underpants that came all the way up to her waist, the way mine did. She was the only person I knew who wasn't Fire and Brimstone and still wore underpants that came all the way to her waist.

The year before when I'd dressed out, I'd always pulled my shorts up before I took my dress off.

"Are you going to do gym today?"

"No," I told her. "Mr. Groves, he won't let me wear it in there." I held onto the tail of James' shirt and stood there.

"Can you leave it in your locker for just a little while?" she coaxed.

I shook my head and walked away.

I knew I would fail gym. Nothing concerned me less. I spent the hour sitting in the bleachers with a heavy girl who didn't want to take off her clothes for other reasons.

I watched Ajita doing her stretches, her jumping jacks, her sit-ups. I watched the class break into teams and then begin a game of volleyball, the teams rotating so that everybody got to serve.

I wanted to serve. I could have hit that ball so hard

it went through the basketball goal at the far end of the gym.

I didn't think about anything important, sitting there. Just the stale air and the hardness of the bleachers beneath me, like a church pew.

When it was Ajita's turn, she held the ball in her left hand, smacked it with her right fist, and sent it soaring over the net, where somebody else missed and she got to serve again.

If I could have held that ball, I would have put it under my shirt, James' shirt, to see what it would feel like to carry something beneath my clothes besides nettles.

It wasn't long before I knew. Nights, I'd lay flat on my back, wearing just my thin nightgown and James' shirt. I'd lift my neck and peek down to the place where the bones of my pelvis reared up, and I'd look at the place between them, where nothing had ever been but flatness, like the plains, and I could see the beginning of a mountain.

But it wasn't a mountain. It was hardly even a hill. My clothes still fit in the mornings, but by afternoon, I could tell that they were getting too tight.

I tried not to think about James. I figured if everybody else could pretend he'd never existed until the pain let go, I should be able to do that too.

I'd never been able to sleep on my back. I'd always slept on my stomach, like a normal person, but I couldn't do that anymore, not with the breasts that grew and grew and ached with it.

I wanted to talk with Nanna, but I could never get her alone. After school in the pack house, I untied tobacco with the other women, ripping away the string, tossing the cured leaves onto burlap sheets, and hurling the sticks onto the pile to be collected and used again. Even the smell of tobacco, the smell I loved, made me sick, and every motion of my arms irritated my sore chest.

I wanted to talk with Ajita Patel, but then I remembered her little-girl underpants and knew that I couldn't.

There was nobody to talk to, nowhere, without James around.

But Corinthian Lovell was in my classes that year. She'd failed again. I couldn't figure out why she hadn't dropped out of school. She had to be almost seventeen, and she couldn't have been learning much because she only showed up half the time.

She sat at the back during home economics. I decided one day to talk to her. Not to tell her about me or James, but to find out about Ben Harback, to ask if she'd seen him. Or at least that's what I told myself I was doing.

We were on the sewing machines that day. Corinthian, who hadn't brought in a project to work on, was sitting at the back, filing her nails, waiting for the bell to ring so she could leave. I folded up the big skirt I was making before it was time and told the teacher I needed to use the restroom.

Corinthian didn't look at me at all. She never looked at

me. But that day, needing somebody to talk to more than ever, I stood in the doorway, whispered "Corinthian," and motioned her to come out.

She picked up her books unapologetically, waved goodbye to the teacher, and followed me through the door.

"What?" she said disdainfully.

"I need to—ask you something."

"Well?"

I knew there was no time for small talk, so I just blurted out. "I think I'm having a baby, and I don't know what to do."

"What?" she shrieked. "You?"

I looked at the floor.

"Well, goddamn, Ninah—that's your name, isn't it?"

I nodded.

"Well, shit!" she said. "We can't talk about it here. Come on."

"Where are we going?" I asked her, but I was already behind, and she led me out the side door, out into the bus parking lot. She kept looking back at me, breaking into a shocked laugh that made her dimples sink.

"Didn't your boyfriend *die?*" she asked loudly. "I mean, I'm sorry about it and all. But isn't he *dead?*"

"Yeah," I said, and bit my lip.

"Well, is it his? Was it his?"

"I guess so," I muttered.

"You *guess* so? Holy shit. Do your parents know?"

"No," I said. "And they're gonna kill me—if it's true."

"Goddamn, I guess they *might* kill you for that at Fire and Brimstone."

I hadn't meant it. I'd never really thought they might kill me until she said it that way.

"Have you taken the test?" she asked.

"What test?"

"The pregnancy test, dope," she chided, then added, "I'm sorry," because I was crying, and then "It's okay," because I was on her shoulder when she probably didn't even expect it.

She smelled like perfume, sprayed on hard, and I thought she must have squirted it all in one place for it to be so strong. It made me feel like I might throw up, so I backed away.

"Do you have any money?" Corinthian asked me.

"Uh-uh," I said.

"That's okay. We'll figure something out. Come on."

I followed her out to the highway, looking back every few seconds to see if any teachers were chasing us, but I guess they had better things to do. Up ahead, Corinthian was calling out to the air, "Whee, Jesus!" and laughing like I was the biggest joke she'd ever heard.

"You ever cut school before?" she yelled back.

"No," I said.

"Whee, Jesus," she said again.

We didn't have to wait long before a man in a pickup stopped. The first couple of cars had driven by, so Corinthian had yanked the elastic out the bottom of my braid and undone it. All that hair flying loose beside the highway—it was a strange feeling, and pretty soon, I was laughing a little too.

"Take us to Kmart please," Corinthian said to the driver. "If you're going that far."

He smirked and drove along quietly, which was probably a good thing.

Right before he let us out, he said, "You gals want to smoke some?" but Corinthian told him we didn't have time and thanked him.

She knew just where to go in the store. It was so big, with so many things for buying, and I didn't want her to know I'd never been there before.

"I don't have any money," I reminded her.

"You don't need any," she said. "Come on." And she picked up a pregnancy test off the shelf, plucked it away from so many others just like it, and she led me straight into the bathroom where she locked the door.

"You just have to pee on that little stick," she said.

But I'd never even peed in front of another person before—except maybe Pammy at the edge of a tobacco row when nobody else was looking—and even then Pammy looked away.

Corinthian Lovell stared right at me.

"Go ahead," she said. "Pee on it."

But I couldn't.

"Ah, Jesus," she moaned. "You're one of those shy bladder people, ain't you? Just bite your little fingernail. It'll come."

So I did it, blushing, trying not to pee on my hand but doing it anyway.

"Now we'll just leave the little plastic thing in here be-side the commode and pretend to shop. We'll come back and check it in fifteen minutes."

But we didn't have to wait. Before I'd even finished washing my hands, the little sign was turning red.

"Oh, girl," she said. "You're pregnant all right."

I couldn't figure out what I was doing in there with her, in the bathroom of Kmart with a stolen pregnancy test. I already knew I was having a baby. I'd known for two months.

Since the day that James died, Olin hadn't been the same. Bethany couldn't let the mourning hold her down too long—because she had Pammy and Mustard to take care of. But Olin kept sinking deeper and deeper. He wouldn't go into the church after James' funeral. Grandpa Herman said prayers out loud for him, saying he'd slipped into the quick-sand of despair, the quagmire of doubts.

I knew that it worried Grandpa Herman for one of his strongest supporters to stop attending church. I couldn't fig-ure out why Grandpa was so understanding, and then I re-membered that he'd lost a son himself. Grandpa kept saying that he hurt for Olin, but that he wouldn't find peace until he reached back out to Jesus. They talked a lot, Grandpa and Olin, but even Grandpa's presence wasn't enough to penetrate whatever Olin was walking through.

It must have been the thorns. I secretly thought that Olin must be lamenting the way he'd turned James' bed into a briar patch that time he'd soiled it.

I wondered what *his* bed looked like.

Church was totally different without James or Olin or even Ben Harback. Nobody received the gift of tongues. Mamma still held her hands up to God, but I could tell by the way she walked, slow, like an old lady down the church steps, that he hadn't filled them with his love.

I was almost sure that the rapture had come and gone, and with it, God's love had exited Fire and Brimstone for good. It seemed so ironic to me that our tight-knit community, where everybody ate together and prayed together and slept so close we might as well have been in the same bed, hurt so independently. It was the one thing we couldn't do as a group. Everybody felt it differently, and nobody talked.

Except Nanna.

"How long you planning on keeping that secret under your shirt?" she said to me one day while we were canning the last of the tomatoes. It was nearly time for the frost. Wanda and Laura had taken the rest of the mason jars into the kitchen to wash, but I was outside with Nanna, cooking down the red paste.

I didn't even answer her.

"I been thinking about it a lot, Baby, and I swear to you, I don't know what will happen when your blind mamma finds out—or Herman either one. Liston shouldn't be so much of a problem, but your mamma ... Lord, child."

"How did you know?" I whispered.

"I've known for a time. I been waiting for you to tell me, but you're getting as tight-lipped as the rest of them."

"Nanna," I said. "It's not what you think."

"No?" Nanna said. "What you reckon it is then? You swallowed a watermelon seed?"

I knew what I should be feeling was tears, the same tears I'd been coughing down for nearly three months. And the guilt—of breaking the law and letting everybody down and causing James to take his own life. But all I wanted to do was laugh. Not the happy kind of laughing. The kind that comes out sounding like thunder, or a shotgun blast, breaking the day with a big ear-crunching kind of jolt.

Right out loud, I said, "It's Jesus' baby. I'm having Jesus' baby," and then I turned to Laura and Wanda, who were standing on the doorsteps with their mouths dropped open, clean jars in their hands, and I said, "I'm having the child of God."

I *don't know what they took me in the church for. I guess they* thought I wouldn't lie if I was in the church. But they had it all wrong. I didn't set out to lie or anything, but by that time, it didn't matter where I was. Church or no church, truth and lies all looked the same to me by then. It didn't matter where they took me. There was no telling what would come out of my mouth.

Everybody but Olin was there though. Grandpa Herman held me by the arm up at the front while the entire community filled in the first few rows of seats. Everybody sat so close, shoulder to shoulder, with Pammy between Bethany and Wanda, and Mustard between Wanda and Everett, and

Nanna between Everett and Mamma and so on. From the front where I stood, it looked like they were blocking me in, like they were using their bodies to keep me from running away.

Grandpa Herman didn't bother with the fornication sermon. He jumped right in with the questions.

"Does your condition have anything to do with James' untimely death?" he asked me.

Mamma wailed out so loudly that Grandpa said, "Maree, honey, we need to be able to hear the girl's answer."

"No," I said.

"What'd you say?" he scolded.

"No, sir," I corrected.

"Was James the father of this baby growing in your womb?" Grandpa's thumb was trying to break my arm.

"No, sir."

"Are you telling me that you and James were not guilty of fornication?" he bellowed, and I knew that no matter what I said, he wouldn't believe me.

I could see Daddy doubled over, his head on his own knees. Nanna kept her gaze straight ahead, but she didn't look like she was listening. David and Laura both looked into their laps while Everett watched Grandpa and Wanda watched me. But poor Pammy was the one I was worried about most. She had her head buried in Bethany's jacket.

Mamma kept crying and snuffling, but she looked like she had a candle in her head, burning, and I could see it flickering wild behind her eyes.

"No, sir," I answered. "Me and James never fornicated."

"Well, who in God's name have you fornicated with, Ninah?"

I thought it must have been Jesus giving me courage because I had enough courage for two people—or maybe three.

"I've never fornicated with nobody," I claimed.

"And I reckon you're going to tell us next that you ain't with child either," Grandpa Herman proposed. As he talked, he ground his hand harder into my arm.

"I'm with child," I said. "It's Jesus' baby."

"Blasphemy," he shouted, and he slapped me down. "In the Lord's own house!"

Pammy screamed and didn't stop. I was on the floor, and at first all I could see were the boards, little brown rectangles, fitting neatly into each other. I thought I'd like to be just one little wooden rectangle fitted so neatly into the floor. Then Daddy was there, offering me his hand, helping me up, and I could hear Mamma wailing out, joined by Wanda, I think.

There was blood on my face, maybe from my nose. I wasn't sure.

"Sit down, Liston," Grandpa said.

"You will not strike my child again," Daddy spewed. "No leader threatens his people that way."

I looked down, dizzy. Drops of blood fell between pauses, splatting one wooden rectangle of floor. I watched a drop trickle along the board's outline, wishing I could pour myself into the spaces between boards.

"Everett," Grandpa Herman said. "Get your daddy, son."

And Everett staggered over to where Daddy was standing beside me.

"Come on, Daddy," Everett tried, and he put his hand on Daddy's shoulder, but Daddy shook it off.

"She has to be punished, Liston," Grandpa Herman shouted. "The girl is standing up here pregnant, telling us that this unborn child belongs to *Jesus.*"

"I will not leave her," Daddy said. "I ain't opposed to punishments, but I am opposed to violence. Ninah ain't safe up here without me, and I ain't sitting down."

Then Mustard jumped up and said, "I ain't sitting down either!" but before he could get to the front of the church, Everett had caught him and held him off.

"Noooo," Mustard cried, tossing his head like a caged-up horse, "Noooooo," and I thought he was going wild, punching at Everett like it was his fault.

I looked to Nanna, trying to will her to do something, but only her body was there. Her eyes were gone far away. Back to Virginia, I thought. Back to the house where her daddy died.

"Tomorrow morning at eight A.M.," Grandpa Herman said, "Ninah Huff will be dunked for blasphemy. Tonight, there will be no supper."

Daddy held me close to him, walking me back to the house. Mamma didn't come with us. I don't know where she went.

When we got to the house, Olin was there, standing on the doorsteps. He didn't say a thing, but he held the door and kissed me on the head before I went inside.

———

⟡

I *guess all the madness made me stubborn. It might have dazed* my thinking a little bit too because I didn't even notice that there was dried blood on my face until much later when I was sitting in bed and some flecks scabbed onto my blanket.

I figured Grandpa Herman was planning on starving me to death. That'd be one way of getting rid of a baby. If I died from not eating before the baby was born, then the baby'd die too and everything would be settled.

And if that didn't work, maybe he was counting on me catching pneumonia from being dunked and dying that way. Either way, he was planning on killing me.

But I knew I wouldn't die.

I prayed that night. I told God I knew that the child was his and that if he was planning on seeing it grow up and make something of its life, he'd better help me out.

I read in the Bible about Mary and wished there was more to know.

I knew my baby would be born with an invisible ring on its finger, one like I'd given to James. I knew he'd be a special leader for us—one strong enough to tear down Fire and Brimstone and start again—even if nobody could see the ring.

And I fell asleep the way I reckon people fall in love, without even knowing it's happening.

⟡

———

Early that next morning, I woke to the sound of bells ringing. At first they were far away, and then they were right in my ear, Mamma standing there dressed all in black and ringing a bell so close that the sound seeped into my pillow and clanged under my neck. Bethany on the other side of the bed, dressed in gray, moved her wrist like a machine so that the bell hit opposite Mamma's, uneven and terrible instead of beautiful, the way a bell should be.

"Hey," I said, not remembering at first what they were there for.

But then Grandpa Herman yelled, "Silence," and I jumped—because I hadn't known he was in the room.

The bells kept ringing as I stood up and then followed them out, still wearing my nightgown with James' shirt over it, not even putting on my shoes. Outside, everybody was waiting.

We formed a ridiculous parade, walking down the dirt road, that sand so cold on my feet. Mamma and Bethany kept ringing the bells, walking beside me. Grandpa Herman led the way. And behind us, everybody except Olin shuffled along.

It was like walking through a dream.

I wasn't sure if Daddy was there, and I didn't think I was supposed to look behind me, but I did it anyway and saw him with Everett and David. Pammy tried hard to catch my eye, but I wouldn't look at her and only saw her tiny wave after it was too late to wave back.

Grandpa Herman didn't slow down even when we came to the woods. But the straw and sticks and briars hurt my feet. Because I couldn't keep up, he had to shorten his strides.

It wasn't raining just then, but it looked like it might at any minute. I couldn't tell if the dreary sky came from the weather or the earliness. I kept looking at the clouds, waiting for God to rapture me, thinking that maybe I'd had it wrong all along. Maybe I'd be the only one called home when the angel sounded his trumpet. Maybe they'd be left to perish, and I'd live it up in Heaven with Jesus and James and my baby.

In case I was right, I prayed quietly that God would take Daddy too. And Pammy and Mustard and Nanna.

And maybe Mamma and Wanda and the rest of them, but I wasn't sure if I wanted them all up there with me. That'd make Heaven a lot like Fire and Brimstone, and that just didn't seem all that heavenly.

We walked for a long, long time, right along the creek until it widened out at the far end of the property into the pond where James had died. And I knew then that I was being punished for more than blasphemy, but I couldn't let myself think about James. Not just then.

I thought instead about alligators. I knew there were alligators because I'd seen them once before, when we were baptizing Wanda. I decided maybe Grandpa Herman was planning on killing me by dunking me in the water right where the mother alligator had her babies. Because unlike my own mamma, I was almost sure that a mother alligator would raise holy hell when somebody messed with her young.

The bells got louder and louder in my head even though it felt like everybody was far away from me, like they couldn't touch me if they wanted to.

I told myself it'd be like a baptism.

Mercifully, we didn't go to the part of the pond where James had tied his rope and walked out. That would have been too much for Mustard and Pammy and Bethany. We filed along the opposite bank, around dying cattails and withering huckleberry bushes. There was a big upright tree on that side of the pond with limbs thick as washtubs, and somebody had built a stand into it. I'd never noticed the stand before and tried to figure if it was put there for men to sit in while hunting for deer or if it'd been used before for dunkings. The thick plank stretched between two giant limbs that leaned way out over the water.

I'd never seen a dunking in my lifetime. I wasn't even sure what a dunking was.

As I was climbing up the tree's makeshift ladder, with David in front of me and Everett following behind, I tried to recall if I'd seen Nanna in the procession. I couldn't remember seeing her.

I scraped my knees against the bark, reaching high for each wooden slat and pulling myself up, wondering if Everett was looking up my nightgown, if he could help it.

When I got to the top, I followed David out on a limb. I had to straddle it and scoot myself along, and the bark rubbed hard at the inside of my thighs, rubbed the skin off of me, it seemed.

I was glad to have James' shirt. The day was chilly and

damp and so strange. I pretended that the shirt was James,
wrapped around me all the way, and I pretended that I
wasn't alone—even though I knew better.

When I had crawled onto the flimsy board, way up above
the water, I looked down at the people behind me, their
faces so unfamiliar it was like they were somebody else's
family. They were all watching Grandpa Herman tying a
tiny wire cage onto the heavy rope that Everett held from
the top of the tree-ladder. And even though I knew it wasn't
the rope once tied to James, I couldn't help thinking of
it, the way it smelled wet—like an old rug left out in rain.

I could feel the board sag beneath me, not like it was going to give, but like it was thinking about it. I thought
maybe I should jump before they had a chance to do whatever they had planned. I wondered if I'd hit bottom if I
jumped, if I'd break my bones and be in too many pieces to
swim away.

Too bad it wasn't the river. If they'd taken me to the
river, I could have swam underwater until I was far from
them. But in a pond, there was nowhere to go.

Everett made his way along the limb, to the place where
the plank bridged branches. David sat on the branch to my
right, and Everett sat on the branch to my left, and I sat in
the middle, my long, long legs dangling, and I stared down,
stared out at the broken tree and imagined its underwater
arms waiting for something to grab. I stared far beyond the
pond, where the land belonged to someone else.

Everett slid the cage down the plank to me. Fortunately
the plank was sort of wide.

"Toss that rope to David," he said.

So I passed the rope along.

David tied his end of the worn-out rope to his limb. Everett tied his end of the rope to his limb, and then they dropped the cage into the water to make certain that the rope was long enough.

I reminded myself that the James-rope was still coiled up on the floor of my bedroom closet, where I'd hidden it months earlier.

When the cage hit the water, it didn't sink right away. It went down slowly as water passed up through all the holes. It was made of the same wire we used to fence in the chicken coop, heavy wire with square holes almost as big as slices of bread. Then they grabbed the ropes and pulled the cage back up, all the way up to me, where it dripped on my nightgown and chilled my arms.

"Pull it up on the plank," David instructed. "Now balance it, that's good. And open that little flap right there." He pointed. "And crawl in."

"Be careful," Everett said. "Don't fall."

I shook like that spider suspended over the pits of Hell by a thread, the one Grandpa Herman referred to in his sermons ever so often.

"You gotta turn around," Everett told me. "You gotta back in so you can close the door."

It's a miracle I didn't fall off—not that it would have mattered. They'd have made me swim out and climb up to the plank again. But I didn't fall. I trembled as the plank beneath me swayed, but I turned around up there, on my hands and knees, and I backed into the cage so small that I had to squench up like a rock. It was hard for me to find a place for my arm once I'd fastened the hook.

"Ready, boys?" Grandpa Herman called.

"Yeah," one of them yelled, but I was so turned around that I wasn't sure if it was David or Everett.

And maybe it was the fear, because I had plenty of that, or maybe it was the feeling of being captured in the air, because capturing usually happens on the ground when at least you've got the earth to support you, but for whatever reason, everything around me got loud. They were praying down there, voices that didn't sound like voices at all. It sounded like clapping and whistles and moans. And I couldn't tell what was happening because all I could see was the wire and the plank, my face pressed next to that damp wood.

Then Grandpa Herman gave a sermon that I didn't hear like words. I heard it like rain and things blowing in wind, and then I realized that it was raining and the wind was real.

And then I was dropping hard, and I kept my eyes open so I could see the water coming for me, getting closer and closer until it was nothing but a shining, and I fell faster than the cage so that my skin pressed against it, and there was a cold wire barrier like a cross cutting between my nose and my mouth, and I felt like each of my breasts had slipped through a different hole.

When I hit, the water stunned me, not from the temperature but from the hardness of it. I felt like I'd hit a table or a floor, not water, and I didn't even realize I was sinking or that my mouth was full until my ears bubbled.

Before I knew I was under, I could feel myself pulled up, a foot at a time. My backside was in air before my face was.

The praying continued as they raised me, bit by bit, and the water that had been on me dripped off—first like juice, then like seeds.

I wondered if I was as heavy as I felt. I looked out at the fallen tree across the pond and remembered that people weigh more when they're wet. I wondered if David and Everett's arms would give out.

But then I heard, "Let her go," and I fell again.

I tried to cover my face with my hands that time, but I couldn't make them let go of the cage, holding onto it like it was all they knew to grip.

Then underwater, I promised my lungs that I'd take in more air the next time. I let out a little air each time I felt them lifting me, but I couldn't tell how long it would be before I'd find air again. I couldn't tell how deep I was, and I didn't want to open my eyes.

When I was out of the water that time, I managed to tilt my head so that I could look at the congregation, and though I was too far away to see expressions, I could tell that the man who was walking away was Daddy.

I didn't care. It was Nanna I wanted to see, and she was there.

The third time before they dropped me, I sucked in so much air that it hurt, but I let it all out without meaning to when I spanked through the surface.

I mouthed "hebamashundi, hebamashundi," feeling the murkiness saturate my tongue, and that time when they pulled me out I was coughing.

I wondered if they'd stop if I repented. I wondered if I cried out or prayed aloud or begged, if that would be enough.

But I didn't.

Up in the air, the cage rocked and swung. I wondered if they'd stop if I vomited.

Then in the water again, in the dirty water, I decided to breathe. Breathe like James, burst my lungs, and be done with the whole damned thing. I'd breathe he-ba-ma-shun-di, one syllable at a time, and by the time I was through I'd be in Heaven. And I almost did it, too, except I opened my eyes, for one last peek at the things we see alive, and I saw the bottom.

It was brown and soft, and there were pieces of sticks and logs, and there were moving shadows in the distance, maybe of fish, though my splashing kept them from swimming nearby. I wondered if James had opened his eyes.

There were things growing, even in autumn, even underwater, and as I got farther and farther away from them, as David and Everett heaved me up, it seemed like they were a miniature world, underwater, operating by different rules, knowing different things to be true, and thriving all the same.

I decided I couldn't die. Not when I had a baby living in me, depending on me, a baby who could change things. I knew there was something inside me that could imagine a different world and make it so.

Back in the air, suspended like a promise, I listened to them praying, hollering out, and I heard Grandpa Herman yell, "Pull her up another five feet before you drop her again. She ain't getting much impact."

———

But then Nanna said, "She's had enough."

The praying stopped. Everything stopped except the rain and the wind and my strong, strong heart.

"I said pull her up another five feet," Grandpa hollered.

"And *I* said that's *enough*," Nanna spoke.

I dallied over that pond for what seemed like a long time, crouched above the water, closer to Heaven than Grandpa, with all my doubts draining out. And if the rapture had happened right then, if I'd heard the trumpets, I knew that I'd have been the first one to get to Jesus because David and Everett would be slowed down by the trees, but I'd lift right off, and plus, I wasn't as heavy as either of them, though I carried two souls.

———

N*anna put me to bed, and I slept.*

But I wasn't so brave in my dreams. They kept making me cry. First I dreamed I had barbed wire in my chest, coiled around my ribs, and for some reason, my heart was growing bigger and bigger, and my heart couldn't see the barbs waiting there to pierce it. I tried to find someone to unravel the wire and take it out, but everybody I told kept saying, "It's there to keep your heart from swelling up so much. Your heart will see it in time and shrink back down."

Then I dreamed I was dead, but walking around. I kept begging James to bury me, but he'd say, "You ain't dead. Look, you're walking around." But my skin was already falling off, every step was a mile, and nobody would bury me.

Then I dreamed I had the baby, and it was crying and I couldn't make it stop. I tried to feed it, but it wouldn't eat. I shoveled spoonful after spoonful of food into its mouth, but it kept spitting all over the church, covering the pews and the altar and the pulpit with strained vegetables. Finally, I started laughing. There was baby food everywhere, and then the baby started laughing too, hard and like an old, old man, coughing in his laughing, and he said, "It's a joke on you. I'm ninety years old, and I'm not your baby."

Then I dreamed I walked to my bedroom door, opened it, and found Mamma and Daddy in my bed, being carnal. There were candles all over the room, and I could see that there were peppers in the bed with them, all around them, hot peppers, red and green and all over the mattress. But they didn't know that there was another bed up above them, at a forty-five-degree angle from the headboard, and it was about to drop down.

"Daddy," I called.

But he said, "Ninah, get out of here."

I wanted to tell him about the other bed, threatening to drop and crush them there on my sheets. I wanted to tell him that on top of that other bed, Grandpa Herman stood with his bible, preaching crazy about the wages of sin and fornication. They couldn't hear him, but I could see him there in his brown suit, holding up his bible, his other hand over his heart, and Mamma and Daddy holding each other and moving on all those hot peppers without knowing.

"Mamma," I cried.

"Close the door," she said.

And then I was sitting on the doorsteps, crying because Mamma and Daddy were about to die in my bed, and it started snowing. I didn't have on any shoes, so I tried to get up to go inside, but the door was locked.

It was autumn and not cold enough to snow, but the snow was falling everywhere, surprisingly, and I didn't have on any shoes.

So I sat on the doorsteps, and the snow fell over my feet, and I cried because my feet hurt so much. Then my arms got so long I could bang on the door, banging and banging, hoping Mamma and Daddy would hear.

But when the door opened, the ninety-year-old baby was there, and he said in his gravelly voice, "What do you want?"

And then I was standing up and he let me inside. My feet were as red as Grandpa Herman's face, and the baby said, "Did you boil your feet?"

"No," I said. "They got stuck in the snow."

And the ninety-year-old baby who wasn't mine said, "No, you dangled them in the pits of Hell. Your feet are burned. There's no snow here."

I woke up at Nanna's house, and I didn't leave. The spare bedroom and a sitting room were separated from the rest of the house by a swinging door. And that front part of the house became my home. I was left in Grandpa Herman's care, so he could witness to me and read the Bible and try to win me back into Christ's fold. The whole time my stomach grew, I stayed at Nanna's, making baby clothes and sleeping. I didn't eat with everyone else. And I wasn't allowed in the church until the baby was born and dedicated to Christ and until I repented.

I only went into the other part of the house to use the bathroom, and even then, I didn't go when Grandpa Herman was home. Even though I had to pee all the time, I held it—or else I did it in a basin and poured it out the window. I never went to the bathroom when Grandpa Herman was around.

Mamma never came to see me, though sometimes I'd hear her in the next room, talking to Nanna, asking about me and speaking so loudly that I knew she wanted me to hear. She must have been yelling.

"How's Ninah," she'd say.

"Doing good," Nanna'd answer. "I'm sure she'd like to see you."

"I don't want to upset her," Mamma'd answer. "It's too soon."

I found bags and bags of leftover fabric in the closet in the spare bedroom. Nanna went through it with me and said she'd forgot about most of it and that I could make some baby clothes if I wanted. She helped me drag out an old sewing machine that worked just fine once we got the bobbin replaced, and I went to work, cutting out little gowns and blankets and Indian-style pants.

Daddy came to see me almost every day. He never knew what to say, and so he'd talk about the weather.

"It's been cloudy."

"Yes, sir," I'd answer.

"We need the rain."

Sometimes he'd tell me about how Barley had the sweets for Melanie Evans, a younger cousin from the far side of the compound. Or he'd tell me about how Mamma had put on his old trousers while she was painting my bedroom because she didn't want paint to spill on her good dresses.

"Mamma wouldn't wear trousers."

"That's what I thought too," he said. "But she did. Don't tell your grandpa."

I worked at that sewing machine until my eyes got bad, worked late into the nights whenever I couldn't sleep. At first my seams weren't so neat, but they got better and better. I didn't know if it'd be a boy baby or a girl baby, so I made clothes for both. I averaged two or three little outfits a day, only regretting that we didn't wear bright colors, because even if the rest of us wore browns and deep greens, babies should get to wear red and orange and yellow if they felt like it.

Pammy and Mustard and Barley would sit at Nanna's kitchen table and tell her about their grades at school. From the distant wall, I'd listen, though it was always hard to hear Pammy since she said everything as if it were a secret.

"I got an A in gym class," she told Nanna.

"Well, that's great," Nanna praised.

"I can do more sit-ups in one minute than anybody else in my class."

"You're a strong girl."

"Can I have an orange?"

"Go ahead," Nanna would say.

"Can I talk to Ninah?"

"You know your great-grandpa don't allow that."

"But he's in the woods," Pammy'd argue. "Can I?"

"I won't be the one to stop you."

Then Pammy would walk over to the swinging door and say, "Ninah, are you there?"

"Yeah," I'd answer.

"Thank you for that skirt you made me with the little shorts inside," she'd compliment.

"I'm glad you like it. If you'll let Nanna wash it, your mamma won't never know about the shorts."

"I'll wash it in the bathtub," she said. "Barley's got a crush on Melanie."

"That's what Daddy tells me," I'd answer—because really, there was no real news at Fire and Brimstone. The whole time I'd talk to her, I'd rest my head against the door, not hard enough to make it push towards her, but just lightly, hoping that Pammy's head was doing the same thing on the other side.

"Corinthian said to tell you hey."

"Really?"

"Yeah. She asked about you on the bus."

"That's nice."

"She wanted to know how big your belly'd grew, but I told her hardly nobody was allowed to see you, and she rolled her eyes."

"That's just how Corinthian is," I laughed.

"Oh, and Mustard's quit going to church."

"What?"

"He says if Daddy don't have to go, then he don't have to go either."

"Bethany don't make him?"

"She tried, but Daddy said that Mustard could stay home with him. And last Sunday, they went out to check the traps while everybody else was in preaching."

"Bet Grandpa Herman's mad."

"He's about decided they're heathens. Mamma cries about it all the time. She goes over to Granny Maree's— to your house—and they pray for a miracle for the community."

"Hey, Pammy, will you look in your storage closet and see if you find any material y'all don't need? Cause I'm making baby clothes."

"Okay." I heard her getting up.

"And, Pammy, if I write a letter, will you deliver it to somebody at school?"

"Yeah," she said.

"Come back next week," I told her, thinking by then I'd know the right thing to say to Ajita Patel, who I missed more than anybody, almost.

Grandpa Herman would come into the sitting room with me, but we didn't talk about anything but God. He wasn't rude or brutal or anything. But every time, he'd begin with the same question.

"Are you prepared to admit to fornication?"

"No, sir."

"Well, let's go over the Apostle Paul," and then he'd begin Bible study with me, patiently, as if he knew that I'd

come back, sooner or later, come back to Fire and Brimstone in my heart.

"Let us pray," he'd say, and I'd bow my head.

"Heavenly Father, we ask that you help Ninah to admit
to her mistakes, to think about the Scribes and Pharisees
who condemned the prostitute, to think about the prostitute
who admitted to her wicked ways, to think about *Jesus*, who
condemned no repenting sinner. Lord, we ask you to help
Ninah admit to her mistakes so she will be open to Jesus'
love instead of his condemnation."

But I didn't pray with him. I saved prayer for myself, for
sacred times when I could be alone with God and my baby.

All the time that I was growing and my baby was growing within me, all that time that I spent alone, I prayed that
God would show himself to me, would come visit and help
me strangle the lonely.

He came to me in a thousand ways. Sometimes he
came like a lamb for me to cuddle and nurse. Sometimes
he sat on my bed and beat out hymns on the bottoms of my
feet. Sometimes he rode in on the wind, his curly hair long
and thick as mine, blown all over his head so that I was almost sure he was a woman, and he'd pull up my dress and
put his mouth on my stomach and talk to the baby.

Sometimes he came like a thief in the night. Sometimes
he wore lipstick. Sometimes he sent James.

Tell me a story," I said to Nanna. *My sinuses were all stopped*
up even though I didn't think I had a cold. It was after-

noon, and my feet looked plump as unpicked squash. They never looked that way in the mornings.

"All right," Nanna said. "What story do you want this time?"

"Tell me about February—when the baby comes."

"It'll be a cold day," Nanna started. "And you'll wake up hurting."

"Bad?"

"Not at first."

"Worse than period pains?" I asked nervously.

"That's how they'll start."

"Skip ahead," I directed. "Up to the point where it's born." I was sitting in a chair with my feet propped up, embroidering a rabbit on a little smock I'd made, and Nanna was across the room hemming a sheet. She looked tired. Her face had begun to look like an old apple, soft and not shaped quite right.

She stopped sewing but didn't look up.

"What'll happen?" I asked her again.

"Honey, I just don't know."

"Who'll be here?" I tried, and I switched to fishbone stitches because I needed my stitches to be interlocking and secure.

"I don't know."

"You'll be with me, won't you?"

"I reckon so," she said. "Don't know where else I'd be."

"Will it get stuck in me? The way the mare's did?"

"No, Baby," she said. "It'll make its way out."

"Well, what will happen?"

"Ninah, I can't tell you that story because I just don't know how it will be."

There was something sad about her that day. I was scared because she wasn't reassuring me, not hardly at all, and I was scared that if I didn't change the subject, she was going to leave me too. I'd been by myself so much.

"Will you tell me a different story?"

"Maybe," she said, stopping to pick up another spool. "If you'll thread this needle for me, I'll try to think of one for you. I can't hardly see in here. The light's bad."

She hobbled over to where I was sitting, handed me the needle and thread, and then backed out of my way so I could get more light.

"The eye of a needle is like the gateway to Heaven," Nanna said. "Hard to tell who's going to be on a straight enough path to get through it."

But I knew that it took more than being on the straight path. You had to be stiff enough not to bend when you tried to pass through. You had to be careful not to slip to the left or the right and think you were going through the middle all the time. It took me three or four tries before I got that needle threaded, and then I tied it off good so that I wouldn't have to do it again for a while.

"Do you remember your dreams, Nanna? Your pregnant ones?"

She smiled for a second before she spoke. "Oh yes. Before Harold was born, the son that died when Herman was in the war, I had a dream that somebody stole him right out of my belly. I thought I'd woke up with a flat stomach and that I'd give birth during the night without waking up at all, and that somebody had been there to take him away.

"Then with Maree—or it might have been with Ernest—I dreamed that my baby didn't have a face."

"That's scary," I said.

"You don't sleep the same when you're with child. You have all kind of dreams. You having many?"

"Yes, ma'am," I said, and I was about to tell her some when she picked up on a story.

"I was pregnant with Harold before Herman went off to the war. We hadn't known it for too long when they called him away, and then he was up in Pennsylvania for a time in army training before they shipped him overseas.

"I decided I'd go up to see him one time before he left and talked Imogene into going with me. Uncle Ernie carried us all the way to the train in his wagon. And that was bumpy riding as you might expect. Imogene rode up on the seat with Uncle Ernie, and I stretched out in the back because I was sick as a dog, having to lean my head over the side every now and again.

"Me nor Imogene neither one had ever ridden a train before. I remember it was one of the scariest things I'd ever seen, long and stretched out like a great big spine. Most of the cars were for carrying coal, I believe—not people. But we crawled on it and found some seats. Imogene was little for her age, about the size of Pammy, though she was probably fifteen at the time. And she had to carry both our bags because it was all I could do to stand up, I was nauseated so."

I imagined Nanna and Great-Aunt Imogene as me and Pammy, seeing us on a train and wishing we could ride one, even though I knew it'd probably make me sick just then. But I'd have done it if James had been in the army, about to go overseas and waiting to see me.

"That train was rickety and noisy and swayed this way and that. Seemed like I could feel that baby in my belly, sloshing around. But after a while, I didn't feel so sick anymore. I reckon you can get used to anything if you put up with it for long enough," and she paused.

The curtains I'd made for Nanna's sitting room were heavy and kept out most of the light. Even though it was the middle of the afternoon, it felt later, and I yawned.

"So me and Imogene talked for a while, and then she fell asleep, and I just looked out the window, watching all the trees and fields go by, thinking that surely sooner or later, the land would get different and we'd go over a mountain or something. But we didn't. Kept going over rivers though. Once we got up into Virginia, we kept crossing over rivers with big rocks in them, and those rivers up North are a lot wider than the ones we got here. They stretch out so far you'd think they were the sea except for all the rocks.

"Me and Imogene got tired of talking and working on our embroidery which we'd tooken along. There was a man who came around selling things, and Imogene bought a pack of playing cards from him."

"No she didn't," I laughed. We weren't allowed to play cards at Fire and Brimstone—or even touch them if children took them to school. Cards meant gambling, and that was one of the Devil's favorite pastimes. We'd been taught all our lives that touching cards was a quick ticket to Hell.

"Oh yes." Nanna smiled. "Imogene bought us a deck of cards, and we opened them up just giggling. We weren't Fire and Brimstone yet—nobody was. But the Baptists didn't allow cards neither, and young women *especially* weren't allowed to have them. It had to be one of the biggest freedoms I'd ever known, touching them things. Course we didn't know how to play them. So we divided them up by colors and then by numbers, and we studied the pictures of the King and the Queen and the Jack, and I made up a story for Imogene about how we were going to London to meet them."

"I reckon I've sinned in a lot of ways," I teased Nanna. "But I ain't *never* touched no playing cards."

She laughed. "Well, when we got to Pennsylvania, it was a Friday, and Herman was at the station waiting for us, wearing his uniform and hat. He'd shaved his beard off, and I didn't hardly recognize him, but he didn't hardly recognize me either, with my belly so big. Before he'd left, I'd still wore my hair down even though I was married, but after he went off, I started putting my hair up, so I looked different to him too, with my belly big and my hair pinned. He said if it hadn't been for Imogene, he'd have walked right past me."

"What'd you do there?" I asked her.

"He got us a room in somebody's house. Somebody who rented out rooms by the night. And we walked down the streets, all three of us holding hands, but I was in the middle. And Herman had a bag over his shoulder, and Imogene had a bag over hers. It was a big city, Philadelphia, I reckon, or something like that, and there were more people than I'd ever seen, horses everywhere and cars too. We sat on a bench for a long time and watched the people and waved to the soldiers who came by. Seemed like everybody was out shopping even though it weren't Saturday yet. And Pennsylvania had a different smell to it than anywhere else I'd been. Smelled like textiles."

"You didn't tell Grandpa Herman about the playing cards, did you?" I asked.

"Oh child, that's all we did the whole weekend. We sat in that room, me and Herman and Imogene and one of Herman's friends—I've forgot his name, but he was a young married man like Herman who was far from his home—and we played cards all weekend long. Herman had learned some games in the army. One of them was called 'Set-Back,' I believe, and we gambled with pennies from the time we got there until we left. Course we gave everybody their pennies back when the game was over."

My mouth was open by that time, imagining Grandpa Herman happily gambling.

"There weren't but one bed in that room, so me and Imogene slept in it. Herman slept on the floor with his friend. And the next morning Herman woke up early and came and knelt beside the bed and put his hand on my belly, and the youngen moved for him. I remember looking at his face, so surprised and happy, and I could tell he wanted to holler out, but he didn't want to wake up Imogene. He held his hand there for a long time, waiting for it to happen again, and each time, I'd get so tickled, just watching him, that I'd shake the bed a little and make Imogene roll over in her sleep.

"It was one of the sweetest times I remember," Nanna said. "Cause we couldn't even talk for fear of waking them up, so we had to do it with our mouths and our expressions and our hands. I put my hands on his face, at the place where his beard used to be, and I just stroked his face and hoped he knew what I was thinking."

"How long did you stay?" I interrupted. I didn't want to hear what she was going to say next. It made me ache down low for something I wouldn't ever have. Not before the rapture anyway, and I knew that if the rapture hadn't happened yet, it might be a long time coming.

"Oh, we had to leave the next day. Climbed right back on the train and went south. Herman got shipped out that very next week. But that's enough of a story for today. You done made me tired," Nanna said. "I got to get started on supper."

After she left, I imagined riding on a train, moving fast through fields and woods and over big rivers with rocks. I imagined me and Pammy in Philadelphia, sitting on a bench and throwing peanuts at birds, even though I didn't know if they had peanuts or birds either one on the streets of Philadelphia.

But when I imagined us there, James never showed up. We waited at the train for him, we waited in the rented room, we played cards while we waited, and he didn't come.

I kept thinking of that train as Jesus' backbone, wonder-

ing if I could just crawl on it, where it would take me. I
wished so hard.

The tips of my fingers felt minced from so much sewing. At
some point, I took the little outfits out of their stacks and
spread them across the bed, all along the dresser top, then
out in the sitting room on the backs of chairs. There were
so many, all in different sizes. Some had taken whole days
and others had taken half an hour; some had patchwork figures quilted on them, and some were plain, the way the
family'd prefer them to be.

I got tired of sewing, so tired that even early in the
morning, I'd do negligent things like lose my focus as I
slipped the fabric beneath the presser foot and seam right
through the armhole of a garment. Then I'd have to turn it
into a tank top just to salvage it, and I knew that nobody
was allowed to show their shoulders at Fire and Brimstone.
Not even babies.

I decided I didn't want to sew anymore, but I had all
those scraps, whole bags of scraps, brown and green and
black and even some velvet that must have come from making an altar cloth because nobody wore velvet. I tried to
think of what to do with all the scraps that wouldn't hurt
my fingers so much.

One day I was laying back on my bed, and I noticed the
rug on the floor. I started studying it, looking at how the
pieces were woven together and how when the rug-maker
had run out of one piece of cloth, she'd just started in with

another one, and how it didn't really matter when the fabric knotted up. I thought I could do that if I put together a loom. All I'd need was some pieces of wood and some nails.

I started sketching out how a loom would have to look on pieces of notebook paper, holding up the rug, measuring it with my tape measure.

When Daddy came to visit, I said, "When you get a chance, could you bring me some nails and a hammer and some scrap wood from the barn."

He laughed at me.

"What you making?"

"I'm not sure yet."

But he brought it to me, and one morning when Grandpa Herman was gone, I built a little loom.

Nanna came in when she heard the racket I was making, and I told her about my idea.

"Well, you won't be able to use just regular thread on it," she said.

"What can I use?"

"I don't know."

"Nanna, can you get me some tobacco twine?" I asked her.

She brought me back the twine and fishing line too. And some old burlap tobacco sheets that she washed out for me.

So I started weaving. Because my loom was so little, my rugs were little too. At first I couldn't keep the scraps of fabric rolled up tight enough, but after some practice, I got better. I showed one to Daddy, and he said, "Well, that's great, Baby. Cept where you gonna use them little rugs?"

"I'm going to hook them all together later," I told him.

The next time he came, he brought me a bigger loom that he'd built, and it held together better than the one I'd made.

Nanna took the rugs and put them all over her house. By Christmastime, I had made a rug for every house at Fire and Brimstone, and even though we didn't usually give presents, I had one for everybody. Nanna gave them out for me because I missed the family Christmas.

By January, I'd gotten brave again. One Sunday morning when I felt big as the side of the house, when I felt like I'd die if I didn't step outside, I peeked out the window while everybody filed into church. I waited until church had been started for ten minutes or so, and then I left.

I hadn't been out since the day of my dunking. I hadn't seen anybody at all, except for Daddy and Nanna and Grandpa, who visited regularly. I watched Mamma sometimes from the window, and when it was time for the bus, I waved goodbye to Pammy and Mustard. But all they saw was my face.

Just smelling the coldness, the winter smell of firewood smoldering out chimneys and the sound of pine needles half frozen and tinkling in the wind was enough to wake me up.

And all that land, all those fields and trees and all that dirt. It was a happy remembering.

I walked down the road to the chicken coop, wandered inside and spoke to the hens on their nests. Some of them came running towards me, thinking I was going to feed them, and since I didn't want to trick them, I tossed out a handful of scratch for them to snack on.

I went into the stable, sniffing hard at the horseness, stopping at each stall to rub their heads and watch the puffs of their warm breathing clouding up the air as it passed through their nostrils.

I even visited with the pigs. I'd never really understood the pigs and I only stayed there for a minute.

Walking back towards the house, I got carried away by the beauty of the place, the closeness of everybody. I missed being able to walk from house to house, sit down by a fire and be treated like I belonged there.

I remembered the winter before when it had snowed. James had backed out the tractor, and Barley'd tied a rope to the back of it, hooked an old one-man boat to the rope, and we'd all climbed in, everybody except James, who was driving. He'd pulled us through the snow in that boat, and we'd spun wide circles in the middle of the field, laughing and singing Christmas carols even though Christmas was over, bumping into each other every time he turned.

I remembered how later, we all sat on the floor at Grandpa Herman and Nanna's, and Grandpa Herman was in one of his better moods, and he thanked God for the snow and for allowing us to enjoy it so much. Nanna'd made cider, and everybody, children and grown-ups alike, had a cup, and we sung hymns together. Uncle Ernest and Aunt Kate brought out the guitar and banjo, and even though they never got them tuned the same, we didn't mind. Daddy played his harmonica and passed it to David, who blew in it for a while, and passed it to me, and I put it right up to my mouth, not even caring much that it had other people's spit on it, and I played it too until Mustard took it from me.

I got so carried away, remembering all the things I loved about Fire and Brimstone, that I walked right to Mamma and Daddy's house without thinking about it, without remembering that I was pregnant and didn't live there anymore.

When I opened the door, everybody jumped. Olin and Mustard and Daddy, sitting at the table playing cards on a Sunday morning.

"Ninah!" Mustard hollered, and ran up and hugged me before he remembered how old he was and backed away.

Daddy was picking up the cards quick, trying to stuff them back into their little card holder, but some dropped onto the floor.

"Hello, girl," Olin said, and walked up to me and hugged me too. "How have you been?"

He didn't even look at my stomach.

"Good, I guess," I stammered. "I hope it's all right. . . . I didn't mean to interrupt you. . . . I forgot where I lived, I guess."

Then Daddy walked over, shyly, sliding the deck of cards into his back pocket and grinning like he knew he'd been caught.

"Does anybody know you're out?"

"No, sir," I said. "I just needed some air. I thought everybody'd be in church. Why didn't you go?"

"I was feeling a little peak-ed this morning," and he smiled. "You won't tell them what you seen, will you?"

I laughed outright, and they all laughed too. "Long as you don't tell nobody you saw *me*."

"Sit down awhile," Mustard said.

"What time is it?" I asked.

"Twenty minutes till twelve."

"I can only stay for a second," I claimed. "God only knows what they'll do to me if they find out I slipped away."

"You're looking good," Olin said, and then he blushed. "We'll be glad when you're back with us, running around with the rest of the children."

It surprised me to hear him say that. I hadn't thought about what would happen when the baby was born. But one thing I knew for sure was that I didn't feel like a child anymore. I couldn't imagine myself running around with anybody.

"You gassed the tobacco beds yet?" I asked Daddy. We were all a little nervous, and I thought farm talk might be just the thing to ease the mood.

"Did that before Christmas," Daddy told me. "Olin mixed the seeds yesterday."

"Nope. Didn't get around to it. We'll have to do that this afternoon."

"All right," Daddy added.

"If you'll let me stay home from school tomorrow, I'll help you sew them," Mustard promised.

"You going to school," Olin and Daddy both said.

"Supposed to rain around the middle of the next week," I piped in. "At least that's what Grandpa said."

"That's what we're hoping," Daddy claimed. "Beat the

seeds in the ground and we can get the beds covered." Then he glimpsed at his watch, said, "Honey, it's good to see you out, but you got to go. I don't think I can stand to watch you get punished again. All right?"

"Okay," I told him, "but I need to get something first." I hurried to my room, dug around in my closet, and pulled out the rope that had held James to the tree. I wrapped it quickly around my middle and belted the blanket I was wearing as a coat.

They all watched me leaving, and Olin winked at me. "Be seeing you, Ninah," he said.

I *didn't leave the front part of Nanna and Grandpa Herman's* house again until it was nearly time for the baby to be born. I stayed in there and read the letters Pammy snuck me from Ajita Patel and then stuffed them into the inside of my pillow.

Me and Ajita wrote back and forth to one another, but we didn't talk about school. We talked about ideas. She said she didn't think it was right that I'd been shut up that way, but that her family might do the same thing if she was in my condition.

I told her that me and James didn't mean to sin—if we *had* sinned—and she said she understood, that she thought sometimes she'd like to have a boyfriend, but that her family had to pick hers out for her, and that one day when she was older, they'd dress her up and take her to a photographer and make whole heaps of pictures to send out to boys she didn't know, Indian boys who were almost finished with medical school. Then those boys would decide if they wanted her for a wife.

I told her that at Fire and Brimstone, it wasn't much different. We might be allowed to pick out some partners to choose from, but if they didn't have enough religious faith and weren't interested in converting, then Grandpa Herman would chase them off with his shotgun and tell them not to come back.

I guess Pammy had told Ajita that I was making baby clothes because sometimes in her letters, she included pieces of lace. We didn't have lace ourselves, so I treasured the delicate white ruffles. I stitched lace to the bottom of a little pair of trousers and decided that my girl baby could wear pants if she wanted to.

She wrote me again and asked if we married cousins out here, and I told her that we didn't marry close cousins. Then she said that she couldn't marry just any Indian boy, that she'd have to marry a Gujarati—because you're supposed to stick to your own caste. She said Gujaratis were priestly, but that the only Indian boy she knew outside her own family was a Rajasthani, which she explained was sort of like royalty, and she wouldn't mind marrying him, but her family would never allow it, and he wasn't planning on going to medical school anyway. He wanted to be a chef.

That day she sent me some squares of Indian fabric, thin and patterned with tiny flowers. They had a funny smell, like the inside of a cardboard box that'd been full of medicine and one flower, maybe. I didn't use the fabric for clothes because I wanted to keep sniffing it.

I'd sit in my bed for hours, a big white spread thrown over my lap, and I'd read her letters again and again, peeking out the window occasionally to see if the bus was coming, and hoping Pammy would bring me another one. I imagined Pammy bringing Ajita home with her for a visit one day, and though I knew it'd never happen, I thought that if she sat on the other side of that swinging door, I'd stick my hand underneath just enough to touch the fabric of her pants.

I was careful not to let the little loose edges of where she'd ripped the letter out of her notebook litter the bed or the floor. I picked them all up and stuffed them in the pillow too.

Ajita asked me if I'd be coming back to school whenever the baby was born, and I told her that I'd probably stay out until the next school year because Grandpa Herman had refused to allow the county to send their homebound instructor to Fire and Brimstone, and even though he was going to have to go to court over it soon, by the time they got it settled it'd be too late. I told her that I probably wouldn't be in her grade anymore, but she said there were some eighth- and ninth-grade classes combined and maybe.

It was almost time for the baby when Pammy brought my last letter. I could feel a pressure I hadn't felt before. Not a pressure really. It was like whenever I sat up, I felt like I had something between my legs. And when I walked around, my legs didn't want to fit together right. So I was staying off my feet most all the time, and leaning back whenever I could.

In the last letter, Ajita asked me if I was going to take

care of the baby myself or if Mamma would help me and if I thought I'd ever get married one day even though I'd already have a baby.

For that last week before he was born, I tried to figure how to answer Ajita. I knew what to tell her about marrying somebody besides James—I couldn't because I was a widow, even if it wasn't a legal kind of widowhood. But I just didn't know about the rest. The more pregnant I got, the less anybody wanted to talk about what would happen to it. Even Nanna refused to talk about it, and I got an awful feeling that they might knock it in the head like too many girl puppies.

I didn't know of anybody they'd killed before—at least not directly—but I knew that they believed more than anything else in punishing sin, and they thought my baby was sin personified.

The closer it came to time, the more scared I got.

I tried to get Grandpa Herman to give me some kind of indication. One night while we were praying, I asked him if my baby would be born a sinner.

"All babies are born sinners," he claimed.

"But will my baby be more of a sinner than Clyde and Freda's?"

"Well, I don't know about that," he said.

"Do you think you'll be able to love my baby anyway?" I asked him.

"Ninah," he said, "we need to be focusing on the word of God," and then he started up again.

"But wait, Grandpa," I stopped him. "Remember how

when Mary had Baby Jesus, nobody believed he was really
the child of God at first? Remember?"

He raised up his hand like he would strike me, but then
he put it down. "I don't ever want to hear you say something like that again. Do you understand me?" he yelled.
"Your baby is *not* like Jesus. And I just pray to God that the
rapture won't come until you get yourself straight with your
maker, because if it does, you'll be left behind on this pitiful
planet, left to have your limbs cut from your body by Satan's own army, but you won't die. I don't know how we
failed you, but you've got to get your vision directed back
on that cross. Because those soldiers will cut off your fingers
and toes, one by one, and toss them into a great vat of boil-
ing grease, and you'll hear them sizzle as they land there,
but you won't die. They'll cut off your legs and your arms,
and you won't be able to move, but you *won't die*. And the
scorpions will stick their giant tails into your body, will rape
you with their stingers, and you'll wish you could die, but
you won't.

"But Ninah, my child, if you'll just repent. If you'll just
admit that you sinned and that James sinned, and that the
awful burden of that sinfulness caused him to leave this life,
then you can go to Heaven with us all. It won't be long,
Ninah, before Christ returns for his bride. For the Bible says
that he'll come in the blinking of an eye, and if your heart's
not ready, they'll be no hope for your soul, no salvation
when the moon meets the sun."

"No," I said quietly.

"What?" he demanded, and I looked at him only long

enough to see his bushy red eyebrows bump into one another. Then I looked back into my big, big lap.

"No, sir," I said.

He left the room ranting about hardheaded women and
the workings of the Devil.

Nobody came for a long time except Nanna, who still
rubbed my sore muscles and felt my belly but didn't smile.

"Tell me a story," I'd beg her.

"I can't, child."

"Please?"

"No, Ninah. I don't have no stories today."

"You didn't have any yesterday either," I cried. "Or the
day before. What's wrong?"

"I have to leave you now," she said.

And when Daddy came in, he wouldn't look at me. He'd
talk just like normal, about the weather and the new kind of
chickens he'd heard about that grew feathers that fluffed out
like rabbits. But he wouldn't look at me.

"What's gonna happen to me, Daddy?"

"Nothing, Baby."

"I mean after it comes. Are they gonna throw me out of
Fire and Brimstone? Because I don't have any money."

"Ain't nobody gonna hurt you. You're gonna move right
back home with us," he said to his trousers.

"What about the baby?"

"Honey, I can't talk about it. I just don't know."

There was nobody for me to talk to but Jesus, and I got
tired of talking to him all the time. So I talked to the baby.

"I won't let them hurt you," I said. "I'll stay with you
forever, and if you ever sin, you can just say you're sorry

and that will be enough. And you won't have no nettles in your crib either because if anybody puts nettles in your little bed, I'll brush them off. I'll check your crib every day."

I wondered if Daddy had made me a crib the way he'd made one for David and Laura. I thought maybe they'd give that crib to me, even though it was made short and I was taller than most. I didn't figure it would matter much.

I prayed that I'd known enough of Jesus' pain already to be able to handle giving birth.

N anna looked at me strangely when I asked for some pieces of barbed wire and told me that she wouldn't bring it. I tried to convince her that I wanted to use it in a rug, but she called me a liar and said, "Why would anybody walk on a rug with barbed wire in it?"

She had a point.

But Grandpa Herman was delighted to bring me the wire.

"Now you make sure you don't hurt yourself," he said to me. "Cause you can do your penance when the baby's delivered. You be careful where you put it."

I knew he wouldn't mind if I wrapped it around that baby though. All he wanted was to think that I was trying to get close to God again. He didn't care if I got hurt.

But I really *was* making a rug. I knew nobody'd walk on it, but I wanted to make a rug for James.

I bent the barbed wire back and forth until it broke off into strips the right length. Then I cut the rope he'd tied around his waist and that tree to match. And then I took down my hair, combed it out, ran my fingers along the tops of my ears until they met at the back, and I lifted all that top hair up and got it out of the way.

I put a rubber band at the base of my neck to cord off what was left hanging, and then went to work cutting above the rubber band.

It took a long time because my hair was thick. It was more like sawing than cutting. By the time I'd cut just that bottom part off, I had more hair than most people have on their whole heads laying on the floor. Dark brown and more than two feet long. And when I took my other hair down, you couldn't hardly tell the difference.

I worked all night on the rug. Tobacco twine and burlap, barbed wire and rope. I used my hair to weave in a big cross, right in the middle, and the barbed wire outlined it. I shredded up my fingers working on it, and the burlap had little blood stains smeared all over. I wove for most of the night, and I cried a little too. When it was nearly day, when the rooster had already crowed, I tied off the ends and lifted up my rug for James that nobody would ever walk on. I climbed aching into bed, threw the rug across my feet, and slept.

I *woke up late and cramping just a little, and I knew I had* to get out of the house. I didn't ask anybody if I could leave. I just left. And nobody stopped me. Most of the men had taken jobs outside the community for those cold

months, and Grandpa Herman had ridden off to town to
take care of some business. But the women were around.
Most of them were inside, but I walked right past Nanna,
who didn't say a thing. And Wanda was traipsing back from
the henhouse when I passed her on the road. She looked at
me funny, said "hey" and "how you feeling?" but nothing else.

I didn't have a coat big enough to go around me, so I'd
taken the blanket off the bed again, wrapped it around me
like a shawl, and set off for the woods.

I walked out where the boys set their traps and even
checked the traps for them, but they hadn't caught any foxes
that morning. I walked out to the creek, and even though I
was heavy and aching, I crossed it and went to the tree
stand where James killed his first deer.

I tried to climb up the steps, but I didn't have the power.
So I sat down at the base of the tree and remembered James.
So gentle and confused, but so very, very dead.

I thought it might have been better if I'd drowned myself
beside him, in that awful pond. Then we could have been
like those people from great literature who took their lives
for love.

But I just wasn't that brave. I couldn't think of anybody
I loved enough to die for—except maybe the baby, and I
wasn't even sure about that.

I knew I had some time. Nanna had told me the pains
would happen regularly when it was time for the baby, and
I had some pains, but they weren't the kind that took my
breath or the kind you could count with a watch. Sometimes

I closed my eyes and talked myself out of having to use the bathroom, but I figured I had a good while.

So I stayed there, in the woods, listening to the water in the distance dancing over roots and across little sticks and rocks. Listening to the leaves crunch beneath me as I tried to make myself comfortable. I did a little praying, but mostly for the baby—not for me. I prayed that nobody would trick it, or scare it with horrible stories about Revelations and plagues on the earth. I prayed that my baby wouldn't ever have to get up in the night to check the faucet and make sure it still had water.

When it was time to go, I thought about staying. I thought I'd probably be better off alone, just squatting in some pine needles and having my child. And when it was out of me, I'd nurse it with my full breasts, and then I'd carry it over to the pond. We wouldn't have to swim across. We'd just have to walk around it, through some tangles and vines, and then we'd be on somebody else's property, maybe a nice Baptist family who wanted a young girl and her baby to bring up proper.

But I left. I walked back to the house, slowly, my back feeling like somebody was pinching it from the inside, squeezing it so hard it made me grit my teeth.

When I came inside, Nanna was waiting for me and she helped me get to my bed.

"It's coming, ain't it?" Nanna asked me, not happy a bit, not the way I wanted her.

"Yes, ma'am," I said. "I think so."

And when I went to sit down on the edge of the bed, that's when it started pouring out of me, all the water, pouring steady and hard, slippery down my legs, and for a second, I worried that I was having a fish, not a baby.

I soiled the floor and my clothes and the blankets, and I just stood there looking down at it. I tried to stop it, like pee, but it didn't work. My legs would not go back together. I couldn't even slow it down.

"It's all right," Nanna said. "It's expected."

"Uh-oh," I kept saying.

"It's all right," she reassured.

Nanna left me for a while, and when she came back, she brought me something to drink. I think it was alcohol, though I don't know where she got it, and I knew that drinking was a sin, but it seemed like I'd sinned so much already that a little more couldn't hurt.

Then I remembered Ben Harback and the grave, and I said, "Nanna, I don't want to sleep in a grave. Don't give me nothing that will get me in trouble."

But she said, "Hush, child, and drink it."

So I did. I knew that Grandpa called it Satan's own sweet piss, but it wasn't sweet at all. It scalded at my throat and made me feel like if I tried to say something, it'd come out demonic and coughing.

As soon as I finished one cup, she got me another one. But by then, I was having a pain, a real one, worse than barbed wire in my skin, and I said, "Nanna, you gotta tell me a story."

But she said, "Shhhh," and gave me a piece of rubber that came off the back of the washing machine to bite down on.

I was sure I was going to bite that thing in two.

Then it let up for a minute, and I could feel the sweat on me, just like I'd been in a tobacco field in the middle of summer except it was winter and different.

"Uh-oh," I kept saying. "Uh-oh."

"You'll make it through this," Nanna promised. "Most everybody does."

But I was thinking about James' mamma, who had died doing just what I was doing. I was thinking about Dot, the horse, who bled everywhere. I knew I couldn't die because then that baby would be stuck good, and if nobody killed it, it would have to live at Fire and Brimstone forever and wouldn't have me there to whisper in its little ear that rapture or no rapture, it wouldn't be left behind.

I wondered if the rapture happened at just that moment, if the pains would stop, and I almost prayed for it.

But then I got another pain. A bigger one that hurt so much I messed myself without even knowing I was doing it.

"Tell me a *story*," I begged.

"I can't right now," Nanna said. "I got to clean you up."

And I was sorry, in a way, embarrassed in a way, but mostly I just didn't care because I was caught in a wave of hurting that wouldn't break.

Nanna left with the dirty towels and came back with another drink for me. That time I chugged it just to have something to swallow.

The next time when I cried out, Nanna said, "Bite that rubber," so I put it back in my mouth. And I didn't even have to ask for a story because she started telling it on her own.

"When Herman's pappa died, he inherited a lot of land.

More land than one man can handle, I reckon. We were living right here in this house, but not another thing was on this property. It was fields as far as you could see.

"You breathing too fast, Baby. Slow it down. In through your nose and out through your mouth."

I hoped that I wouldn't choke on that piece of rubber. Usually I was adult enough not to choke, but it seemed like I'd lost control of most everything.

"Anyhow, Herman worked all the time, sun-up until sundown. And even though he was right here with me, I felt lonelier than I'd ever felt before. My people was all the way over the swamp, and I didn't hardly ever see them except for on Sundays and Wednesday nights at church."

"It's coming again, Nanna," I panted. "Stop it."

"Here, get you a piece of ice," and she picked up a thick sliver and stuck it in my mouth.

"I had little Ernest already, but having a child ain't always as much company as you think."

"Uh-oh," I muttered through my mouth blocked off with the piece of washing machine and my tongue hanging onto that ice for all it was worth.

"Don't fight it," Nanna said. "Fighting it won't do no good. You might as well dive on in."

"Uh-oh," I said again, in a voice so high that it must not have been mine, the whole world fading to purple, slowly, so that I thought I was going to knot up so tight I strangled myself trying to get little enough to fit through the circle of light. But then it let go.

"Have you another drink," Nanna said, and I did.

"He'd come in nights, and I'd already have the baby

asleep, and I'd be missing him so bad, wanting him to lay down with me for a while—because sometimes when you're lonely enough, you feel like there ain't no way out except having a little bit of another person fill you up—but Herman'd eat and fall right asleep," she told me.

I was trying to listen. I really was. And I wasn't hurting just then. But I was tensing up to get ready for the next round.

"Then in the morning, after all my sweet dreams when I'd been imagining things different, at the time of day when I felt full enough already, he'd wake me up feeling lonely, I reckon. I always figured we must be exact opposites. Cause just when I'd be content, he'd have a need.

"Privately, I hoped there'd be another war. So he'd go off again, and I could take Ernest and go back to my people. I ain't never told nobody that," she added. "Don't you repeat it."

"Uh-oh," I huffed. "Nanna?"

"Breathe," she coached. "In through your nose. Deep. That's good," and paused. "And out through your mouth."

"Nanna?" I called.

"It's okay," she said, and she rubbed me with oil to help my skin get ready to give.

"Tell me a *story*," I hollered.

"Shhhh," she begged. "Bite down."

"So when Herman got the idea for the church, I weren't that disappointed at all. In fact, I was happy. Course I feel guilty about it now, because I didn't care nothing about the religion exactly. I just wanted to have people close by."

It was all I could do not to holler out. The room was

reeling and Nanna was veiled by the anguish of it all. I kept imagining what it must feel like to die—on a cross or in a pond either one.

"Not that story! Tell me about your mamma," I cried, and then coughed, and Nanna gave me another piece of ice.

But then the pain left me. Nanna poured me another drink. We sat there quiet and she rubbed at my stomach and between my legs, and I didn't even care, cause it was Nanna. She ran out for a minute to wet me a cloth to put on my head and to get more ice. But it took her too long, and when she got back I was halfway through my next pain, feeling like I was being torn wide open and leaving my teeth marks in the side of my arm because I'd dropped the piece of rubber and couldn't lean over to get it.

When Nanna saw me, she rushed over and sat beside me on the bed and wiped at my face, glancing occasionally at the clock on the night table.

"Tell me about your *mamma,*" I raved.

"She was pretty," Nanna said quickly. "And she loved being that way. She'd sit in front of her vanity and brush her hair until I was sure it would all come out in her comb."

"No," I moaned, swirling off so far I needed to say something just to make sure I still could. "Tell me about Weston Ward."

"He had hairy arms," Nanna fell in. "And you can tell how good they'll be at loving just by the hair on their arms. My pappa didn't have much, but Weston's arms were like a bear, so he was that much closer to nature, and that much closer to being able to . . ."

"Uh-oh," I interrupted as it peaked. "Uh-oh, uh-oh."

———

233

"Breathe," she said, and I imagined her wiping her face though my own eyes were closed by then. "Breathe deep."

When that one was over, I was crying, more tears than I'd ever had maybe, and I wished James was there so he could see me hurting that way, because I hated him for leaving me to deal with it all alone. But only for a second. Then I wished Jesus could see me too, hurting so much, but he wasn't there either. Nobody was.

Or so I thought. Then I glanced at the window and saw that it was still daytime, though I thought it had to be the middle of the night. And I saw Pammy's little red face, her blue eyes big as plums and peeking in.

I started to holler out and tell her to leave, but then Nanna gave me another drink, and I forgot or just didn't care.

"What was Weston like?" I asked Nanna desperately when I felt the surge begin again.

"He was a sweet man," Nanna said. "And I believe he loved Pappa almost as much as Mamma, except he loved her in another way. It was Pappa he wanted to please though. Helping him out in the store and all. Mamma just latched onto him because he was around."

"I can't do this anymore," I hollered.

"Mamma?" a voice called from the other room, and I knew it was my own mamma, but I didn't care.

"I'll be there in a minute," Nanna hollered back. "Stay out there."

And right in the middle of another pain, she gave me a final swig. I couldn't hardly swallow, and I told Nanna that, but she said, "Drink it. You can't have no more," and so I did.

"Bite that rubber," she instructed. She'd picked it up sometime and washed it off and put it back beside me, but I hadn't even noticed.

"Don't leave me," I begged her.

"You'll be fine," Nanna swore, and kept talking. "It wasn't until I was older that I figured out that Pappa wasn't able to satisfy Mamma anymore, if you know what I mean. And even though she loved my pappa, she had needs that were bigger than that love. I reckon she was just lonely as could be—not having many woman friends and then not knowing how to talk to them about anything except the curtains or what she was making for dinner."

I saw Nanna look over at the window and spot Pammy, who ducked back down as soon as Nanna turned her way.

I was woozy and throbbing all over, but I said, "Let her stay."

Before the next pain happened, Nanna went out to talk with Mamma, and when Nanna came back, she had Mamma and Bethany and Wanda and Laura and Aunt Kate and Great-Aunt Imogene with her too. They didn't all come into the bedroom, but they sat in the sitting room and kept sticking their heads in the door to tell me to hold on.

Then I thought I was screaming, even though I tried not to, but it was just the teakettle from the next room.

Then the pains came again, but I don't remember them. I kept looking at Pammy's big eyes in the window and thinking, "I'll help you feed the chickens tomorrow," because I knew I'd be flat by then.

And then Laura was sitting beside me, dabbing at my face with a cloth and dropping ice into my mouth, and

Mamma was sitting next to my belly, her hand on it low and saying, "It's okay, Ninah. You'll be all right." And I didn't know where Nanna was, until I saw her blurry between my legs, and I thought I might pass out, but she said, "Push," so I did, and the whole rainbow fell down over me, all those colors blazing into each other, slow, and she said, "Push," and I did, and I saw flowers, big azaleas coming at me, and all I wanted to do was bury my head in their middles and swim in like a bee, but she said, "Push," and so I did, and I saw a wooden boat on dark water, and I wanted to get in and float away until the boat turned into James, and she said, "Push," and I did, and I saw James kissing the wound in Jesus' side, and I felt the snip, snip, snip of toenail scissors between my legs, but it didn't even hurt noticeably. It was all so huge by then. And she said, "Push," and I saw the ninety-year-old baby whipping James and Jesus with a wet rope, but neither of them cared, and I didn't either, except that Laura was pushing the hair out of my face, and I said, "No!" and someone cried, someone else, and I don't remember another thing.

I *slept off and on for a long time. I kept waking up, and* Nanna would be there, and I'd say, "Is it okay?"

"I already told you, Baby." Nanna smiled. "He's fine."

"A boy?"

"Yes, child. Rest."

So I'd go back to sleep, dreaming wildly things I couldn't remember when I woke back up.

And then Grandpa Herman came in, and he was grinning, patting me on the head, and he said, "You did it, girl. You gave us the New Messiah," and I thought I must have been dreaming, but it seemed so real.

Later, when I woke up again, Mamma brought me some grits and fed them to me. "He's just beautiful, Ninah," she said somberly.

But I thought I must not be awake really, because my baby was born from sin, so he couldn't possibly be beautiful, and I didn't know what to say.

Wanda came in and brought me a rubber glove filled with ice, and she put it between my legs, and then sat on the bed beside me.

"How you feeling?" she asked me.

"Okay, I reckon. Where's my baby?"

Mamma looked at Wanda, and Wanda looked back at her, and then Mamma reached down and started stroking my face.

"The community decided that it would be best if David and Laura took him to raise. They've been wanting a baby so bad, you know. And you need to get back to school and do things with the other children. So we decided that if David and Laura raised him, you'd be his aunt. And you'd get to see him as much as you wanted and tend him every day. But he'd have two parents, like every child should have."

"Where is he?" I whispered.

"He's with Laura and David," Wanda said. "And oh, Ninah, they love him so much already. When your grandpa handed him to them, they cried and kissed him and prayed over him for an hour."

"I want to see him," I said. "Will you tell Laura to bring him by?"

"That wouldn't be good, honey," Mamma said. "You can see him in a few days when you're feeling better."

I could feel a wetness all over me, coming mostly from my breasts that hurt so much that even breathing was unbearable.

"Can I feed him?" I cried.

"They've got formula for him," Mamma explained. "It'll be best if you just let your breasts dry up."

By that time, the tears were coming hard. "Did they name him already?" I asked them through sniffles.

"Canaan," Wanda said. "Isn't that beautiful? He's the promised land, Ninah. Right here at Fire and Brimstone."

I *got better fast. Nobody believed I was better, but I was, even* though every step made my mouth water with the throbbing. That next morning, early, I hauled my sore self out of bed and wrapped up in a blanket even though I wasn't very fat at all and probably could have fit into a coat if I'd had one, and I wandered out to David and Laura's house.

When I beat on their door, David came to it. As he led me inside, he had tears in his eyes, and he said, "Ninah, I don't think nobody will ever be able to give a gift as nice as the one you gave us," and he hugged me too hard. The watery milk poured out of me, and I could feel it dripping on my belly.

Then Laura came into the room, and she couldn't say anything except, "Oh, Ninah. Oh, Ninah."

And a part of me was glad to have made them so happy, to give them something they couldn't get on their own. But another part of me wanted to run into the back and steal Canaan away, to run for the road with him in my arms. I knew I couldn't run, but I kept imagining it just the same.

"Can I see him?"

"Of course," David said, and smiled to Laura. He put his arm around me and led me down the hall into their bedroom, where the crib Daddy had made was pushed up next to a wall.

He was so tiny. I'd expected him to be bigger, pulling up on the side of the crib or something, because he felt big enough to be walking when he came out. But he was laying there asleep, with the covers pulled up over him, and he had dark hair, already, and thin eyelids so that I could see little red squiggles beneath the skin. I imagined that James must have looked just like that when he was new to this world.

I was surprised to find Grandpa Herman in that room, sitting in a chair next to the crib, just watching him breathe.

Grandpa Herman stood up and gave me his chair and helped me to sit. He put his heavy hand on my shoulder, and we all stood around the short crib, watching Canaan sleep.

"I didn't mean to doubt you, Ninah," Grandpa whispered. "I didn't mean to falsely accuse you of fornication."

"Sir?" I asked, thinking that surely the fornication stuff

had to be done with. It was a baby, after all. A beautiful human child.

"Did you see his little hands, Ninah?" Laura asked me.

"No," I said. "Is something wrong with them?"

"No, Peanut," David said. "They're perfect. Look."

And he pulled back the blanket so I could see. His tiny hands were held together, just like he was praying, peacefully, in his sleep.

I stood up, leaned over the crib, and touched his perfect skin. I touched his fingers, so long already, and examined his fingernails.

But when I tugged at one miniature hand, the other one moved with it. I ran my finger between his fingers, down to his palms, and found that they were seamed together, perfectly, at the heart line.

"How did this happen?" I whispered.

"It's a sign from God." Grandpa Herman beamed. "The world will surely end in this perfect child's lifetime. He's the New Messiah, come to lead his people."

"He was born this way?"

"Of course," Laura answered. "You ain't surprised, are you? You said all along it was Jesus' baby."

"No," I said. "I'm not surprised."

━━◄

I*t didn't take long for everything to make sense to me. I could* understand why Nanna hadn't wanted to talk about what would happen after the baby was born. She knew already that David and Laura would take him.

———

And Daddy knew too.

I began to understand why Mamma wouldn't even come visit. She didn't want to tell me.

Nobody wanted to give the secret away.

I decided the grudges you hold for betrayal might be the very meanest kind. It wasn't that they gave my son to my brother that hurt so much. It was knowing that they'd been talking about it, plotting it, worrying over how I'd react and praying about it behind my back.

And I felt stupid and tricked again. I'd made them Christmas presents.

But all that madness got mixed up once I saw Canaan's hands. It made me wonder if they were planning on killing him all along and decided not to after they saw that he was holy. It made me wonder if he *was* holy, if maybe I really *was* knowing Jesus and not James. Because why else would his hands be that way?

And if Canaan was a sign from God, a New Messiah sent here to lead us, then what did that make me?

It was hard for me not to let the good treatment go to my head. When I left David and Laura's that first day, Barley was working on some kind of little motor just outside. He stopped when he saw me, and I reckon that dragging that blanket behind me, I did look kind of like royalty.

"Wow, Ninah," he said. "All that time I thought you was just an average—well, you know—slut. And come to find out you're chosen by God."

I didn't say anything to him. I didn't know what to say.

"Cause I didn't mean to think bad of you or nothing,"

Barley added, and wiped his hands on the front of his pants. "Can I help you back in the house?"

"Thank you," I said, and took his arm. He directed me to Mamma's house instead of Nanna's though.

"Look here," Bethany said, opening the door for me. "How are you, Ninah?"

"Fine, mostly," I said.

She helped me over to the couch, and I was glad to have her there because I felt a little bit like I was walking with a boat between my legs.

"I believed you all the time," Bethany whispered. "I knew you and James wouldn't do nothing like that."

"Can I get you something to drink?" Mamma asked, and I said "yes," and then "juice."

"Put your feet up," Bethany said. "You hurting?"

"Some. Mostly sore."

"Pammy, get a rubber glove and fill it with ice for Ninah," Bethany instructed, and Pammy, who'd been standing against the wall and looking at me like if she got too close I might shock her with my holy electricity, obliged.

"Maybe by next week I can help you with the chickens again," I told her as she handed it to me.

"You don't have to do that no more," she insisted.

"Well, why not?" I said playfully. "Didn't you miss me?"

"Yeah," she said. "But you're different now."

"She's our same old Ninah," Mamma told Pammy. "Are you ready for school? The bus will be here shortly."

"Yes, ma'am," Pammy said, and left.

"And who'd have thought that we'd have the mother of

the New Messiah right here among us and not even know
it?" Bethany wondered. "My own little sister." She was talking like I'd parted the sea when all I'd done was sinned with
her stepson—or maybe not.

"I want you to see your room," Mamma said. "Do you
feel like walking up the stairs yet? Cause I painted it fresh."

"Maybe I'll wait til tomorrow before I try that. I think I
want to go back to Nanna's and rest awhile."

"That'll be fine," Mamma said. "Here, I'll help you. And
when you feel like it, we'll get Mustard and Barley to move
your things back home."

It wasn't until I was in bed again that I started wondering
where Daddy was. I hadn't seen him since the baby was
born, and he was one of the only people who'd been around
when I was pregnant. It didn't make good sense.

But when I got Nanna alone, instead of asking her about
Daddy, I asked her about Canaan.

"Did you know they were gonna take him from me?"

"I'd caught wind of it," she said tersely.

"Well, why didn't you tell me?" I cried. Seemed like
every time I cried, my breasts hurt more and leaked out
hard to keep my eyes company.

"I didn't know how," Nanna said, holding my head. "I
didn't know what to think about the whole thing. Didn't
know what you'd want or not want. I didn't like the idea,
personally, but you got to think about the greater good, I
reckon. When the idea struck them to give the child to David and Laura, I knew you'd get to be with it and help tend
it—and you'd still be free to finish school. But I thought if

I told you, you'd try to leave Fire and Brimstone, and I reckon it was selfish of me, but I just couldn't imagine being here without you."

"Oh," I said.

We didn't talk for a while. She had her hands at the back of my head where I'd cut the hair away, and I could feel her measuring it and learning of what I'd done, but she didn't mention it at all.

"Nanna, do you think my baby is the New Messiah?"

"I think your baby was born with a simple problem that would have been fixed already if we'd taken you to the hospital where you belonged."

"So you *don't* think I'm—special?"

"You always been special, child," she said. "But one little hinge of skin don't make no baby a messiah."

"What will we do about it?" I asked her.

"Right now, the best thing to do is leave things alone til they settle over. We'll get a doctor to cut his hands apart sooner or later, but I'll have to work on Herman for a while first. I done studied them little hands good, and it wouldn't take but two or three stitches in each one."

That night was my last night at Nanna's. There wasn't much for me to collect. David and Laura had taken all the baby things I'd made, so all that was left was a few garments and my rugs and looms.

I pulled James' rug out of the closet to look at it again, and I thought that the only thing missing, the only thing that would make us a family, me and James and Canaan, even if it was an imaginary family, was the blood from childbirth.

So I placed the rug over my sheet that night and eased myself down onto the edge of it, slipping off my underpants and letting the leftover bleeding stain Canaan onto my hair and James' rope.

~

I *guess everybody was still trying to protect me because nobody* wanted me to know that after Canaan was born, Daddy left Fire and Brimstone and didn't come back for three days.

I kept asking about him, but people'd say, "I believe he's off looking at a man's tobacco beds in Watchesaw," which was a hundred miles away, or, "I think he's gone to help with a revival in Cedar Bluff," which was a hundred miles in the other direction. People told me that they thought Daddy might be scouting for migrant workers or running a load of lumber up to North Carolina. But nobody got their story straight, and everybody seemed so frazzled when I asked that they just said the dumbest things. Mustard won the prize. He said, "I believe Grandpa Liston's in the bathroom, Ninah. That's where he was last time I saw him."

"He must have the drizzling shits then," I told him. "Cause he's been in there for ages."

Mustard put his hand over his mouth, but giggled out anyway. He was helping me pack up my rugs into brown paper sacks, folding them just the way I told him. From the side, I could see the hairs on his face beginning to get fuzzy, though they were still blond.

"What? You never heard nobody say shit before?" I played. "Shit, shit, shit. I'm the new mother of God, and I hereby declare that shit is a word worth using here at Fire and Brimstone."

"Ninah!" he laughed.

"What?"

"You can't make up rules like that. You'll get nettles—or even *dunked* again."

"They'd better not dunk the *mother of God*," I joked.

"You ain't the mother of God," Mustard swore. "You and James did it, and I know cause I watched."

"No you didn't," I moaned, but blushed.

"Did too," Mustard said. "But don't worry. I ain't gonna tell. Cause you deserve to be treated good for a change. How many of these rugs did you make?"

"I don't know. Thirty or so. And I wouldn't say shit to nobody but you," I whispered. "Mustard, where's Daddy?"

"I ain't got no idea," he promised. "Last time I saw him was at the ceremony."

"What ceremony?"

"Where Laura and David stood at the front of the church and Great-Grandpa Herman blessed Canaan and put him in their arms. Grandpa Liston cried so hard he snuffled like a pig. I don't know why exactly—cause Canaan's still his grandson no matter whether he grows up with you or with David and Laura."

"Did you see him leave?"

"No. But Barley said he got in the truck and drove off right afterwards without telling nobody where he was going."

Mustard picked up two bags of rugs and began the haul

to Mamma and Daddy's house. I walked with him, but I
didn't carry anything.

"Do you think he'll come back?"

"Grandma Maree says he will," Mustard answered. "She
said he was just upset and needed a little vacation."

"But he don't have money," I worried.

"He's got a little bit," Mustard confided. "He didn't give
everything he made this winter to Fire and Brimstone. He
saved up just in case."

"In case what?"

"Well, just in case Great-Grandpa Herman didn't want
you to stay here after the baby came."

"How do you know?"

"He's played hooky from church about ever Sunday
with me and Daddy," Mustard allowed. "But nobody else
don't know that, about the money, so don't go around men-
tioning it."

Later it struck me that for everybody to be so upstanding
and honest at Fire and Brimstone, it sure did seem like they
lied a lot, not telling me about what would happen with the
baby, making up tales about where Daddy'd gone. And of
all the people I knew at Fire and Brimstone, sometimes it
seemed like Nanna, who everybody knew to have a past
with lying, lied the least.

The first night that I slept in my old bed, back in Mamma
and Daddy's house, Daddy returned. It was late at night,

and I was already asleep when he came to my bed and sat down.

"Ninah," he called, and I thought at first it must be a dream. "Ninah?"

"Hey," I said, and sat up. There was a nightlight burning orange on the wall behind him, and it lit him up from the back. "Where were you?"

I leaned into him and started hugging him, and even though he put his arms around me too, it didn't seem like he was hugging me back.

"I had to go off for a while," he started. "Had to get some things straight, in my mind . . . ," and I thought he might be crying, so I reached up to touch the skin under his eyes, and he was.

"I'm sorry, Daddy," I said, keeping my thumbs there, pushing the water back.

"Don't need to be," he told me. "You ain't the one."

"What's wrong?" I tried. It seemed like so much could be wrong, like Daddy probably had a hundred things to pick from.

"Do you want to stay here?" he asked me. "At Fire and Brimstone? Cause we can leave, Ninah."

"Who?" I said. "Me and you and Mamma?"

"Me and you," he said. "We can go somewhere else."

"Where?" I asked him.

"I don't know."

"But what about Nanna?" I said. "And the baby? And Mustard and Pammy?"

"I don't know," he echoed.

"I'm not the mother of God, am I, Daddy?"

"Don't matter, Peanut," he said. "You're my heart."

"Don't go away again," I begged him. "If you have to go away again, you've got to tell me—because there's just too much to worry about without having to worry whether you're okay."

"I'm sorry," he said. "Lay back down," and he tucked the covers around me. "I got you a present. A weaving machine. A big one so you can keep making your rugs."

"Really?" I said, sleepy.

"Yeah. It's out at the pack house though."

"Stay with me a minute," I said, and I moved over so he could stretch out.

We rested beside each other for a while, and I held his hand, and it was so cold I knew it must be purple.

"I was over at Ben's," he told me. "Just thinking."

"Did you see the baby?" I asked him.

"Yeah—" he said, and it sounded like the word did a backbend in his throat. "He's a pretty child."

Night after night, I slept poorly. I'd go to my window, imagine Jesus on the cross, but when I saw him, he was dead already, his azaleas withered. I'd climb back into my bed and touch my wet nipples and adjust the flannel pads I kept over them to keep my clothes from getting soaked. My breasts ached like somebody had been wringing them, like towels washed by hand, and even when I did fall asleep, I'd wake up if I rolled to either side.

Night after night, I'd creep out of the house, carefully, so

I wouldn't squeak at the floorboards, and I'd tiptoe through the darkness over to David and Laura's, edge my way behind the bushes that grew up next to their bedroom window, and peek in.

David and Laura slept far apart from each other in the bed. They didn't even touch, and I couldn't imagine why you'd bother to share a bed if you weren't planning on sharing your warmth. I knew that if I had a chance to sleep with James or Jesus or even Canaan, I'd sleep so close that our breathing matched.

I watched them sleeping over and over, sleeping soundly in spite of the baby in their room.

But Canaan wasn't always sleeping. I could see him best—because they left the bathroom light on, and his crib was pushed up next to the wall closest to the bathroom. He rested on his back because his joined palms made it impossible for him to sleep on his stomach. And sometimes when I'd go there, he had his eyes open.

I tried to talk to him in my mind. I told him that of all the people at Fire and Brimstone, we were the only ones sleeping on our backs, the only ones not sleeping. I tried to tell him that when he was older, if he looked out the window after everyone had gone to sleep, he might see me, standing in my window waiting for him.

I tried to tell him about James, about how nice he was, about how good he could shoot, about how much he liked to play even after he was turning into a man. I wanted Canaan to know how soft the skin was at the place where his ear met his face.

I thought my baby Canaan might be praying without ceasing, but there was no way for me to be sure.

➤

Laura and David showed that baby off like he was a fine car they'd bought in an overseas country that nobody'd ever been to except for them.

Canaan was a quiet baby with loud eyes. Even though his eyes had a film over them, it looked like he'd been seeing things for a long time. Sometimes I'd look into his funny dark eyes and imagine that every little sunburst, every little line was a different way of knowing things. Like he could see things in a thousand ways, all at the same time.

He wiggled his arms around some, but no matter what he did, he still looked like he was praying.

He didn't cry. He didn't gurgle or spit hardly at all. It was almost as if he'd been born into this world with a kind of resignation.

And he was heavy in my arms, solid as brownness, which was all he wore even though I'd made him all those outfits. None of my outfits had fit him. I hadn't anticipated the hands.

"He is so *good,*" Mamma would say, holding him in her arms and grinning down on him.

"Yes, ma'am," David said. "He sleeps like a rock, too. We don't hardly ever have to get up with him."

And I started thinking about how hard it would be to be born a messiah. You'd have such a reputation to live up to, and everything you did would be interpreted as a sign. Even if Canaan wasn't a messiah, people still looked to him as if he had all the answers.

"I think he's wet though," Mamma said. "Ninah, you want to go change him?"

"Yes, ma'am," I answered, and took him out of her arms. Mamma was good about giving him to me whenever she could.

"You can use my bed," Mamma said, but I took him upstairs to mine.

I loved the scent of his head, so musky and a little like how I imagined the inside of a heart to smell. It seemed like that smell disappeared a bit more every day, but I sniffed for it anyway and planted light kisses on the soft part of his head, nuzzling my face in his thin hair that stood straight up and didn't cover his whole scalp evenly.

I changed his diaper, and then held him for a long time, just feeling him so real and leaning against my middle. I knew he meant such different things to everybody, but to me, he meant James, and the milk poured out of me while he was in my lap, and my breasts begged and begged.

"Want to see something?" I asked him, and I layed him back, on my pillow so he'd feel soft, and I went to my closet and pulled out the rug I'd made for James.

"Want to feel it?"

I spread the rug out on the bed, picked Canaan up again, and sat the two of us down beside it. "Your real daddy's not here, but maybe you can know him a little bit anyway." With my free hand, I lifted the rug and rubbed the rope part onto the backside of Canaan's praying hands. "That's your daddy," I said, and careful not to let the barbed wire hurt him, just allowing him to feel the lightest scratch, I said, "And that's your daddy too."

⚬

I *didn't go back to school that year, even after I was healed up* from begetting Canaan. I stayed with the women and helped with the household chores, with the garden and even the tobacco beds.

I wore my hair untied, just letting it fling about in the wind and whenever I moved my head. The only person who told me to get it out of my face was Nanna.

"If you don't tie back that hair, I'm going to cut it at the scalp," Nanna threatened. "It looks like Mamma's used to."

"Well, you said she was pretty," I joked.

"And she *was* pretty. But that mess of hair will get you into trouble."

"Let's cut it then," I tempted.

"Herman will have your ass," she said.

"No he won't," I claimed. "Cause I won't let him."

"Oh." Nanna smiled. "Getting brave, ain't you?"

"Yes, ma'am."

"Well, I won't stop you. But I don't know nothing about it."

I needed more materials for my weaving anyway. I was working on a rug just for Canaan. I took the shears and went into the bathroom and clipped at my hair until it all hung evenly at my shoulders. With every strand that fell, I felt lighter.

When I came out of the bathroom, Mamma was working on a cross-stitching for the baby's room.

"Have you used up all the blue thread?" she asked, even though she knew I hadn't been cross-stitching.

"No, ma'am," I answered her, standing there proud and waiting for her reaction.

"Well, I can't find it," she muttered, looking through her sewing kit again.

"I think I'm going out to the barn to work on a new rug for Canaan's room," I told her.

"Okay," she said. "But don't stay out there more than an hour or two cause we'll need some help with the cooking," and then she looked up.

"Ninah!" she said.

"Do you like it?" I asked her, and I swirled around so that it fluffed out before it settled. It might have been the breeziest I'd ever felt.

"It looks . . . real nice," she swallowed, and went right back to work.

Those were times when being the "mother of God" wasn't a bad thing at all. I hurried out to my weaving machine, carrying my hair with me.

~

The week before Grandpa Herman was scheduled to sprinkle Canaan in church, I went to Olin and Mustard and told them I needed their help.

"What is it?" Olin asked me. They were scaling and gutting the fish they'd caught at the river, but they stopped long enough to talk. Olin had a fish scale stuck on the side of his crooked nose and didn't know it.

"Canaan's being sprinkled on Sunday," I said.

"We heard," Mustard answered.

"Well, he's James' baby," I admitted to them outright. "And both of you know that, and I know that—even if nobody else wants to think of him that way. So that makes him your grandson, Olin, and I think you need to be in church when it happens."

He just looked at me for a time.

"I ain't going," Mustard said, and took his knife to another fish.

"I ain't meaning to be disrespectful, Ninah, because I loved James. And I love you. And I love that baby too. But I don't believe I can stand to hear Herman preaching and carrying on over that child. And if I have to hear one more time that he's the New Messiah, I might strangle somebody. That child needs taking to the hospital."

"Please, Olin," I said. "This community's all we got. And Canaan might be a messiah for all we know. Please go to church on Sunday."

"Don't get caught up in this craziness," he snapped. "That's a perfectly normal boy you had, Ninah. All except for his hands, and it's just as easy to say he's patty-caking as he is praying. He ain't no new Jesus, and we don't need another one anyway."

"We need something," I said. "It's like a big split's come in our community, and Canaan might be the one way to get us all back together."

"I ain't believing you're saying that," Mustard barked.

"After all they've done to you, you want things to be the way they used to be? You're crazy."

"No," I said. "That's not what I want at all. But things don't have to be the same for us to all live together and be happy. . . ."

"I ain't going to church," Mustard declared. "And won't nobody make me."

⤚

But on Sunday, he was there, and Olin was and Daddy. I'd talked to Daddy too, told him that we ought to come together for the baby's sake, and he'd nodded.

I sat next to Nanna like always. That day she had some little candies in her purse, and we both ate them while Grandpa Herman talked, and I opened that wrapper right up, realizing for the first time that if I made a little noise, it didn't matter much. Grandpa Herman was making plenty.

David and Laura were sitting on that first pew, holding Canaan, but everybody else was in their regular seats.

"It's good to have our family back together, in the house of the Lord," and Grandpa paused for somebody to say Amen, so Everett did.

And then he went off in his normal way, using some passage from Ezekiel as his preaching point, though I didn't listen that closely.

When it was time for the sermon to be wrapped up, Grandpa Herman started in about sins again, and I knew that he was hoping to see Olin and Daddy and Mustard and probably me all around the altar on our knees when the call was given.

"The good Lord knows all about sinning," he said. "But he's a loving and merciful savior, sending his own son to die on the cross for our shortcomings. This morning, our congregation is filled with those who have lived in sin, who've experienced Satan's temptations firsthand. Liston is back with us. Liston, who turned his back on God, refusing to acknowledge that God continues to speak to us in the present as surely as he spoke to us in the past. God bless him.

"And Olin is here again, thank Jesus. Olin whose own losses seemed so big and so mighty that he forgot that God himself lost a son.

"And young Mustard, who's at that age where he faces the temptations of youth, where he questions everything in ignorance, not realizing that God's word transcends every temptation, every generation.

"And Ninah. Praise God for Ninah. Her struggles with God are her own, and we are not omnipotent enough to judge her heart. But she has returned to Christ's flock after an absence, has brought into this world a tiny child whose hands bear testament to the way that we should live.

"We have Wanda among us, who lived a life of sin and left her people and her wicked ways and came to Fire and Brimstone like the woman at the well, seeking God's sweet love.

"We have others among us who have known lives of sin, and who've turned away from evil to embrace goodness and peace. Leila, my own wife, who you all know and love, whose negligence led to the death of her earthly father and whose lies nearly interfered with the administration of justice, is here with us, living proof that a person can be sinful and repent."

Then in mid-tirade, he broke into prayer, and while he spoke, Mustard gave me a glance that could freeze holy water, and Nanna passed me another piece of candy and shook her weary head.

"God, we just ask that you cover this altar with the bodies and tears of those mentioned. Cover this altar with the hearts of those who have backslidden but want to return to your ways. Lord, I pray that your will might be done here today, and that we might leave this service with a greater sense of your precious love.

"Finally," Grandpa Herman spoke again, when we'd already raised up our hymnbooks and were preparing to sing the altar call. "Finally, we have in our midst today, David and Laura Huff, who have tried unsuccessfully to bring forth a child into this world. Time and time again, their unborn have been snatched away from them, when Jesus saw that in one heart or the other, there was a lack, a sin, a question about their salvation. But now, and praise God for it, the Lord has blessed them with this child, Canaan Huff. It just goes to show that after sinfulness, there is repentance, and after repentance, there is the Lord's great abundance. Won't you come? Won't you fall down on your knees here and ask God into your heart? Or rededicate your life to his service and this community?"

We sang the hymn, everyone together, quietly lifting our voices, our darting, shadowy voices. But no one approached the altar.

"Won't you come?" Grandpa Herman called out. "We have a child in our midst who testifies to the truth of Jesus Christ's imminent return to this earth. A child with hands held in prayer. He's a message sent to us by God in his final days. Won't you come?"

We sang eight verses of the song, but nobody hit the altar. Nobody received tongues. Nobody broke out into prayer. Nobody held us up.

And after the altar call was over, Grandpa called David and Laura up to the front. He blessed some water and lifted Canaan before us. He had to be the most beautiful baby I'd ever seen, and his seamed-up hands looked ludicrous. For a second, I thought I might have sewn him together by accident when I was making all those baby clothes.

"This child comes before God this day as Fire and Brimstone's reminder to prepare for the rapture. This child comes to us as our New Messiah. And who am I to baptize this infant who will be our new leader? A lowly man baptizing ..."

Then Olin stood up and interrupted him. "Preacher Herman," Olin began. "What will become of Canaan nobody knows, not in this room anyway. But in the past, we've baptized infants and sprinkled God's blessings on them because we loved them and we wanted to show our intention of providing them with a childhood filled with the teachings of the Lord. And I believe we should do the same thing for this child, without giving him responsibilities or importance that we haven't given to the other babies of this community."

"*A*-men," Wanda shouted, and I didn't know Wanda had an opinion one way or the other.

"But look at him," Grandpa Herman continued. "Who could doubt the significance of these tiny hands?"

Then Daddy stood up and said, "Let's just ask David and Laura to dedicate this child to God's glory, and leave it be."

There were mutterings all over the congregation. I looked at Nanna, who kept a blank face, and I looked at Pammy, who looked back at me and attempted to wink, though she winked with both eyes.

So the flustered and reddened Grandpa Herman went ahead with the sprinkling in the traditional way, asking David and Laura to commit to bringing Canaan up in the church. After they'd said their prayer, Grandpa dipped his hand in the water and flicked it into Canaan's face.

The baby started crying, and the congregation laughed.

But I didn't think it was so funny. Because Canaan didn't have the freedom to wipe his own face, even if he wanted to.

W*hen I started back to school that next year, I wore James'* trousers. I knew I'd gotten a lot of mileage out of the community's questions about Canaan's holiness, but that didn't stop me. If I had an excuse to be able to wear pants, I wasn't above using it.

Grandpa Herman got mad when he saw me, shouted,

"Deuteronomy twenty-two: five states that 'The woman shall not wear that which pertaineth unto a man . . . for all that do so *are* abominations unto the Lord thy God.' " Then he turned and walked away.

But nobody actually forbid me to zip those pants and walk off the property.

Mamma said, "Well, Ninah!" and kept on washing off butter beans, and Nanna cut her eyes at me sharply, but I could see her trying to hide her smile.

Daddy said I looked real nice, and laughed outright and shook his head.

But Ajita Patel was the one whose compliment meant the most.

"You look so different," she said. "So grown up."

"Do you like my hair?" I asked her.

"I love it," she said. "It's softer," and then she reached right up and ran her brown fingers through it and gave me the shivers. "I had long hair too when I was little. But by the time you reach ninth grade—"

"Eighth," I reminded her. "I'm behind."

She laughed. "Well, by the time you reach eighth grade, you're old enough to decide how you want your hair."

Ajita Patel didn't wear makeup either, and I decided I didn't need it.

"Thanks for all your letters," I told her.

"I would have kept writing," she said. "But after you had the baby, Pammy stopped coming by to pick them up."

"It's okay," I told her. "I wish we had classes together."

"Me too. But we still have lunch. We can meet here every day if you want."

"Okay. I'm making you something."

"Really," she said excited. "What?"

"I can't tell you," I said. "It's gonna be a surprise. It won't be ready for a while."

Once I started going to school again, it got easier to pretend like Canaan was David and Laura's baby. Sometimes I felt guilty about it, but I let it be.

On the bus, Pammy said, "Do you reckon anybody would care if I wore Mustard's britches?"

I told her she might better think on that one for a while.

And one day at home, Wanda came in and said, "You're so good with hair, Ninah. Will you cut mine?"

"Really?" I asked her. "You want to cut your hair?"

"Well, yeah," she laughed. "I mentioned it to Everett, and he said I'd get in trouble, but that he didn't care. And if all I have to do is sleep on nettles for a night or two, well, that's not much of a price to get rid of this heavy mess."

So I pulled out my scissors and chopped Wanda's hair off.

"Not too short," she said, and so I left it falling down the middle of her back.

I liked the way cut hair looked. It didn't need to be short like a man's but cutting it in general made me feel good. Uncut hair doesn't grow even, and it hangs down in the middle longer than on the sides so you always look indecisive, like you don't have an opinion at all.

"What do you think?" Wanda said.

"It's nice," I told her.

And Grandpa Herman didn't even know because Wanda kept her hair up anyway.

———

But on the day I cut Pammy's off, all hell broke loose.

Bethany came storming into the house, pulling Pammy by the ear, saying, "Ninah, did you do this?"

"Yeah," I admitted. "And I think it looks real good on her."

But I'd cut it up to her neck in a bob, like some of the town girls wore theirs. I hadn't meant to do it that short, but I kept getting it uneven, and before I got it straightened out, the back of her neck was showing. Since Pammy was young, she didn't wear her hair up, and there was no way of hiding it.

"Just because *you're* special and were chosen for something special by God don't mean you can go around inflicting the same things on other people," Bethany told me.

Pammy was crying, and I felt awful for cutting it so short. But it looked great. She had shiny red hair that shone more when it wasn't held down so heavy.

And when Grandpa Herman saw it, he threw a fit. Right there at supper, in the middle of the meal when everybody else had already seen and was hoping Grandpa Herman wouldn't.

"Ninah, you might have been given a special gift, but you're still human and prone to sins. And Pammy, you know that you are a regular girl, subject to the rules of this community. Don't you?"

Pammy wept like a plant that's been given too much water, the tears leaking out when there was no place inside left to hold them.

"By the rules of The Church of Fire and Brimstone and God's Almighty Baptizing Wind, I sentence you both to a night in a grave to contemplate the wages of sin," Grandpa roared—and I was shocked, genuinely, because I never would have thought hair-cutting would get the same sentence as drinking.

"David, Everett, Barley, Joshua, Mustard, John," he called to the young men of the church. "Get your shovels."

"Don't worry," I told Pammy. "It's almost dark. They won't have time but to dig one grave, so we'll be together."

"Promise?" Pammy asked.

"Yeah," I said.

But then Wanda stood up and said, "Preacher Herman, I've cut my hair off too," and she undid her bun and her pretty brown hair fell down her back, but only to the middle.

And then Great-Aunt Imogene, who was only a handful of years younger than Grandpa Herman, joined us at the front, laughing and saying, "When I saw how pretty them girls looked, I just decided that there weren't no need in an old woman like me having to carry around a headful. She pulled off the handkerchief she wore on her head, yanked out her bobby pins, and let the gray straggles fall, and they hardly came to her shoulders. But Great-Aunt Imogene kept laughing.

Grandpa Herman stood back, his mouth dropped open like a tailgate, and Nanna broke out laughing, walked up to him, put her arm around him, and said, "Old Man, I believe we need to revise the rule books. They ain't doing no wrong by wearing their hair different than the ways our parents wore theirs. Times change, and we're the only ones resisting it."

But Grandpa Herman pulled away and walked out. He looked like a man who'd been beaten in battle, his wrinkly face pulled and saddened. And I wanted to laugh at him because it was the first time I'd seen him back down. But later that night, all I felt was sorry that he was so hurt, even if the hurting seemed silly.

After school I tended Canaan, giving Laura a break even though Laura wore on my last good nerve. David and Laura were so caught up in their righteous son that they were willing to abide by Grandpa Herman's rules, every one of them, even though so many of us were joyfully carving notches in other people's trees and seeing that nobody cared a bit.

We weren't really doing a thing wrong. We all had a good sense of right and wrong and nobody wanted to do wrong because wrongs just make you have a hard time falling asleep, and we had too much to do to bring on insomnia. But we were living it up at Fire and Brimstone. Some nights Aunt Kate and Uncle Ernest would pull out their guitar and banjo, and after prayers, we'd sit in somebody's living room and sing until the yawning took over.

Mostly we sang Jesus songs, but we didn't bother with the sad ones—like the one where the little girl tells her daddy that he can't be her daddy anymore because the rapture's happened and her daddy's been left behind. We sang about the mansion over the hilltop and flying away to Jesus and about how we were standing on the solid rock.

Happy songs with a good beat that kept us awake and together.

On warm nights, we'd sit outside, and they'd play their music, and we'd make up fake musical groups. We'd sing into the water hose, pretending it was a microphone. And one night when Olin and Mustard were singing a duet, holding that hose between them, Daddy turned the water on and splashed it up in their faces right in the middle of "Just a Little Talk With Jesus." We laughed for an hour about it, and everybody slept good that night.

But there were some who wouldn't participate. Mamma didn't come out too often, although a couple of times she forgot her allegiance and did a solo of "Lily of the Valley" before she remembered. David and Laura never joined us. They claimed that they didn't want Canaan to catch a cold, but we all knew that they didn't want to upset Grandpa.

And it was no wonder. Grandpa Herman treated David and Laura with more respect and attention than anybody else. He still believed completely that Canaan was the son of God, so David and Laura had more responsibility than anybody else and needed more guidance.

Some nights at Singspiration, which was what we called our gatherings, people would talk about little Canaan who, at seven and then eight months old, was beginning to get irritable. He had a hard time holding onto his rattle. He cried whenever Laura dressed him because it took a long time to get his special clothes on. People felt bad because he couldn't crawl, and Wanda said she thought he'd have a hard time learning to walk since he wouldn't have his arms to balance him.

And in the afternoons when I kept him, I played with his hands, thinking if I pulled them hard enough, and if it was God's will, they'd fall apart just the way the little black vine stem had fallen from his navel after he was born.

But it didn't happen like that.

He would sit there with me while I worked on his rug. I'd make him a little pallet on the pack house floor and then sing to him while I wove.

By that time, I'd taken one of James' old flannel shirts and cut it into strips. I was weaving my hair, James' shirt, tobacco twine, and a part of an old altar cloth into a rug for Canaan, but I was working on it slowly, waiting for the right pattern to happen.

I was also working on a rug for Ajita Patel. Canaan's rug was on the weaving machine, but Ajita's was on the loom Daddy built. I wanted hers to be special too. I knew I wanted to use some of the Indian fabric she'd sent to me through Pammy. And I knew I wanted to use some of my hair. But I'd kept Pammy's hair, because it was so vivid, a color that seemed to want to set the world on fire like I did, and I started weaving her hair in Ajita's rug instead.

My fingers wound rope over, under, over, under, and I found myself studying my design and forgetting about Canaan, then periodically remembering him and looking over to see him watching the rafters of the pack house, always looking up. It was dark in there, though I kept the back door open and had a big light hanging overhead. From the corners, old spiderwebs long since deserted draped heavy with dust and sagged. Shreds of cured tobacco leaves and bits of twine and dirt from work boots hid in the deep ridges of the old wooden floor, even though we swept it out. I loved the way the pack house smelled, so musky and tobacco-honeyed and oaty like feed sacks emptied of their grains. I liked having Canaan out there with me so that he could learn to love those smells too. And sometimes I'd roll up pieces of old tobacco leaves and weave them into the rugs as well.

Then when Canaan started whimpering, I'd pick him up and carry him over to the corner where it was dark and there were heaps of burlap tobacco sheets hilled up on the floor, and I'd sit down with him there, holding him close, rocking him and trying to teach him to say Ninah.

"Nigh-Nuh," I'd instruct. "Can you say it? Nigh-Nuh."

He'd look at me and bob his little head against my breasts and shake his arms.

"Nigh-Nuh," I'd tell him again, and I couldn't figure out why he wasn't talking because he was nearly old enough, and at the same time, I was glad he hadn't said anything else, like Mamma, before I'd taught him to say my name. I was glad my name had the same sort of sound as Mamma because at least I could pretend.

I felt a pull in my breasts, with Canaan's face nuzzling there. My milk would not dry up. It'd been eight months, and I still had to pump them out into the sink, and I still had to wear flannel in my bras. Nanna said if I'd quit thinking of Canaan as my own, the milk would go away. But it didn't.

"Are you hungry?" I asked him. "You must be hungry."

He kept nestling in, and I was almost glad that he didn't

have usable fingers because he was doing a fine enough job tugging at my breasts with his praying hands.

"No, Canaan," I told him, and pushed him back like always.

He began to cry, out loud, like his feelings were hurt.

"Shhh," I coaxed.

But it didn't help.

I knew that if Laura or David were there, if Grandpa Herman was, they'd have claimed that his bellowing was a plea to the savior. Anytime Canaan cried, people assumed he was calling to God.

Then one day, when he wouldn't stop tugging at my shirt, when my breasts were leaking, and we were sitting on the tobacco sheets in the darkest corner of the empty pack house, I pulled out my aching breast and let him nurse.

The feeling of lips, even tiny teeth on my lonesome, crusty nipple, pulling at it, dragging from it, smacking and humming as he worked, his seamed hands held up above my breast, the feeling reminded me of times I'd been with James during prayer partners, hoping to not be caught. Canaan tugged and sucked, and I let him, knowing what I was doing had to be wrong because it felt like that milk was being pulled up from between my legs and I heard myself breathing, hoarding that cured tobacco air.

I kept feeding Canaan for a time after that. I couldn't imagine myself denying him that right. But I felt guilty about it, worrying that by that time, my breast milk might be poisonous. He didn't get sick though. He got better and fatter, and he started making the noises that come before words, and he managed to stand up on his own even though he kept falling back down on his diaper.

"You see," Laura said. "If God hadn't meant for his hands to be together, he wouldn't be able to stand up by himself at just ten months. You're a miracle, ain't you, Canaan?" And she tickled the bottoms of his feet and cuddled him tight.

Nobody even tried to tell her that he was simply normal—because to Laura, that would have been like saying he was retarded. And I wanted to shake her until she broke and all the stupidness jingled out because she just couldn't understand that what was normal was miraculous enough.

Nights, in bed, I prayed that God would give me a sign if I should stop nursing him. I wasn't so worried about being caught. It was just that I didn't want to sin. The risk wasn't sleeping in a grave anymore—or the strap or the nettles. It was bigger than that.

I didn't want to hurt Canaan, but I needed to *give* him something. The milk was all I had left.

Nights, I prayed that God would take my milk away or make Canaan stop wanting it if feeding him was a sin. I prayed for a sign until I got one.

One night I woke up to find the moonlight waltzing in and James sitting at the edge of the bed.

"Hey, Ninah," he said, and smiled. I'd always heard that in Heaven, all imperfections disappear. But James still had his broken tooth, after sixteen months in Heaven. And after the shock of seeing him had passed, all I could think about was the feeling of that tooth's slant on my lip. My nipples poured.

"What are you doing here?"

"Just came to tell you you're doing real good," he said.

The moonlight shadowed James like a harmony. My eyes were so heavy, but I was afraid I'd lose him if I blinked.

"Is he God's baby?" I asked him, thinking James would surely know.

"Yeah," he answered. "All babies are."

"But James, you know what I mean."

"It don't matter. Let's go see him." He stood and walked over to the side of the bed where he took my hand and pulled me up. I half-expected to grab air, or to feel his hand cold or dripping wet. But he just felt familiar.

We slipped outside in the frost, crept across the yard. He ducked low, like he didn't want to be seen, and I started giggling because he was there. When he nudged his way be hind the shrubs outside David and Laura's bedroom window, I heard them rustle. It wasn't just me.

We looked inside for a long time. Canaan rocked in his crib until he rolled himself over on his side, looking through the slats of wood towards the window.

"He looks like you," James said.

"No he don't," I protested. "He looks like you."

"You're doing fine," James said again, staring at me, encouraging me. I thought I might cry. I thought he might kiss me, and I think I wanted him to. But he brushed my hair away from my face and let his hand graze my ear, then stay there for a long moment before he moved it. I memorized his touch, knowing somehow that I wouldn't feel him again.

"I have to go," he said.

"Where?"

"I have to leave," he repeated. "I'm going to see my boy first." And then he stepped closer to the house, then looked back one more time. "I hear you when you pray," he said.

For some reason, I felt embarrassed and tried to remember all the things I'd prayed about since James died. I might have closed my eyes for a second, but I don't think so. In the next instant, he was standing by Canaan's crib, and I tensed up all over, thinking that if David or Laura woke up, we'd be in a mess. James knelt by the crib and looked at the baby. A part of me was scared for James to touch him. A part of me didn't want Canaan to miss his touch.

I walked away because I didn't want to know what would happen. I worried for an instant that James might not have been in Heaven at all.

But I didn't go back inside. Because behind the church, I saw Jesus and the cross again. Once more he had the dying azaleas in his hand, and I decided that if I was really awake, if James had really visited me and if Jesus was really crucified in the yard next to the church, I didn't want to miss it.

I headed for Jesus, half-scared that Canaan would be gone the next morning, kidnapped by his ghost-daddy. I told myself I was dreaming. I figured I needed to pray.

But there was something wrong with my sense of distance. The cross was right in front of me, but I walked and walked and couldn't get there.

I started to wonder if James was really James or if James was really Jesus answering me with James' face. Then I wondered if that's all God ever is—somebody who loves you enough to come back from the dead to visit every now and again. Or if that's all other people ever are—different faces of God walking around.

I wondered if it mattered if I was dreaming.

If all things work out in the end, if all things have a purpose, then I wondered if we needed a God at all. I wondered, walking to Jesus. Would I go to him anyway if I thought he did nothing but watch?

A cross, Jesus in a loincloth, the crown of thorns, azaleas, the blood, all right there, watching me. I studied them as I got closer, one at a time. It took me a while to see that this Jesus wasn't nailed to his cross. He was bound to it.

By the time I reached him, he was fading. He was sinking, the cross being swallowed by the earth even though my own feet held steady. I stood so close his toes brushed against my nightgown, slid down between my breasts, his thighs parting them. The virgin on the cross, beaten and humiliated, sliding between my breasts. Don't go, I tried to tell him, but he could only shake his head from side to side. When he opened his mouth, I could see his tooth was chipped in front, maybe from a blow. He sunk so low that his mouth passed across my forehead, nose, scratching me with his thorns, across my mouth, neck. He crossed me at my breasts, dampening his mouth with Canaan's milk, and going lower, lower, until he wasn't there at all. He left me standing at the place where he had been, which is, perhaps, all we can ever ask of our gods.

———

Nanna *always said that Grandpa Herman would die in the* pulpit, preaching himself right into Heaven. I think he would have liked for his life to end that way, so wrought with the power of God that even his muscles and skin couldn't hold him. But that's not what happened.

That next Christmas Eve we were all celebrating. The children of Fire and Brimstone had just put on a play, our standard reenactment of the birth of Christ. And that year I was Mary and Canaan was Baby Jesus. Barley played Joseph, and Mustard was a wise man, and Pammy was a common shepherd, her red bob covered with a belted towel. We'd walked down the aisle of the church one at a time while Aunt Kate and Uncle Ernest played Christmas tunes on their guitar and banjo, and then when we were all on stage, we began singing carols with the whole congregation. Right in the middle, Canaan started crying, and when I picked him up, he nudged my breasts in front of the congregation, but nobody noticed.

Afterwards, we had special Christmas treats in the fellowship hall. We even had a tree, for the very first time, covered with ornaments the youngest children had made in Sunday school, but we didn't have flashing lights on the tree because Grandpa Herman said they were of Satan.

Everybody fixed their plates and settled down at the tables freshly covered with white sheets for the occasion. There were tiny branches from holly trees on each table, and I fingered a red berry until it came loose and rolled free.

After a while, David said, "Grandpa, ain't you gonna read us the Christmas story?" and to everybody's surprise, Grandpa said, "Why don't you do it, son. I believe I'll sit back and listen this time."

There was something about his voice that sounded a tiny bit unfamiliar—like he had a piece of candy stuck in the back of his throat, like he was trying not to cough.

So David went up to the podium, opened his bible, and began to read. People turned their attention to David, but from where I was sitting, it was easier to look at Grandpa Herman. Something about his eyes looked like James' did on the day I said I was pregnant. I didn't think he had anything to be afraid about, but didn't know what would make his eyes so electric.

I looked back down at the holly branch, began to pluck off other berries, and then glanced back at Grandpa. His face was pulling to one side, and his mouth gaped open like a squirrel hole in a tree.

From the front, David's voice rose up. "And the angel said unto them, Fear not: for, behold, I bring you good tidings . . ."

I reached over to Mamma to get her attention. Then right in the middle of the Christmas story and decorations, the nut cake and costumes, Grandpa Herman fell sideways from his chair, knocking into Nanna and thumping them both onto the floor.

Daddy rushed over and pulled Nanna from beneath him.

Other people moved in closer, but I held back, shocked and pressing holly berries into the sheet.

"Everett, get the truck," Daddy hollered. "Do you want to go with us to the hospital, Leila?"

Nanna paled and hobbled off to get her coat.

"You know he wouldn't want to go to the hospital," David tried.

"Do you want him to die?" Daddy said sarcastically, and David, who knew at least to honor his father and mother, shut up.

We all stood around, looking at Grandpa laying there so blank. His eyes were open, but it was like he didn't even know us. Mamma threw a tablecloth over him to hold in his heat and leaned up against the wall with her hand over her mouth.

"Herman?" Daddy called. "Can you hear me?"

"Slap him," Mustard whispered. "Knock him out of it."

But Daddy just shook him. "Herman?"

Our mighty Grandpa was drooling.

Then we heard the horn blowing, and Mamma said, "Ya'll get out of the way," and shooed off the children. There were stains and bits of holly berries all over my fingers and Virgin Mary robe.

Uncle Ernest helped Daddy pick Grandpa up, and Olin supported his back. They had to carry him like a heavy feed sack, and without Olin there, he might have drooped right out of their grip.

That first night Daddy stayed at the hospital with Nanna and Grandpa. When he came home the next day to sleep, he said there were tubes in Grandpa's nose and mouth.

"You know he wouldn't have wanted that," Laura

lamented. "He would have wanted to be left in God's hands—not in the hands of some doctor who has strayed so far from the Bible that he tries to *become* God."

"Just who are you to be judging the doctor?" Olin argued. "Do you even know the doctor's name? Do you know a single thing about that doctor?"

We were all sitting in the fellowship hall. It was Christmas day, and we had a big meal prepared but nobody was eating except for Mustard, who Pammy said would be eating during the rapture, hanging onto that chicken leg even after his clothes fell off.

There were unpoured cups of ice on the counter and unsliced pies on the shelf. All around the room, people were gathered to hear what Daddy had to say about Grandpa's condition.

"And for that matter," Olin attacked again, "why don't you show me one place in the Bible where God says people shouldn't use doctors?"

"Okay, I will," Laura shouted. Then she stormed off, presumably to consult her handbook, though I had my doubts. She yanked up Canaan and took him with her.

"What'd they say, Liston?" Mamma asked, while Daddy took off his coat.

"It's too soon to tell. He's had a major stroke."

"How's Leila?" Great-Aunt Imogene piped in.

"Ornery as a wet setting-hen," Daddy laughed. "She needs some sleep, but I don't reckon she'll be getting none soon. I tried to get her to come home and rest. Told her I'd take her back whenever she wanted to go. But she wouldn't leave."

"Is she in the room with him?" Wanda asked.

"No. He's in intensive care. She's in the waiting room. But the nurses let her go in every hour." Then he turned to Mamma and said, "Will you fix me a plate, honey? I ain't had nothing all day."

"I believe I'll go sit with her," Olin said.

"I'll ride with you," Mamma offered. "Just give me a minute. I want to fix Mamma a plate too. She must be starving."

"Not really," Daddy laughed. "She's been working them snack machines they have at the hospital. She's eat ever kind of sweet thing they sell in them things."

"Well, good," Bethany replied. "She needs to."

Grandpa Herman stayed in the hospital for six days before they let him come home, and even after he got back, he didn't know where he was.

He came home on a Sunday. I half expected him to walk in thumping his bible and giving us all a sermon because we weren't in church.

I went to visit him, and he was sitting in his chair. I leaned over to kiss him, and he kissed me too hard, like he'd missed me or something.

"Herman, that's Ninah," Nanna explained in a way that was almost like scolding.

"My sweet Ninah," he said, and laughed. He didn't have his dentures in, and his breath smelled like cold-sore balm.

When I tried to walk away, he wouldn't let me go. He

held onto my arm with a grip that surprised me, considering
he'd almost died.

"Look, Grandpa," I tried. "Pammy came to visit
you too."

Pammy held back like a cough.

"Ninah, take me home," Grandpa said.

"You *are* home, Grandpa."

"No," he replied, and then he started crying.

"Look," I said. "Pammy's here."

"No," he said, choking on that short word, tears dribbling
down his face so unashamed that it made me feel shamed
for him. "No. Take me home, Ninah," he pleaded.

"Herman, I'm gonna fix you some grits," Nanna said.

And even though Grandpa Herman had always loved
grits, demanding them for breakfast even when that wasn't
what everybody else was eating, he said, "I don't want no
damned grits. I ain't never eat grits in my life." Then he
looked back at me and said, "Take me home."

David said that what Grandpa Herman meant was that he
belonged in Heaven now. He said that "Take me home" was
his way of demanding to be allowed to die.

Laura said we should all go into that church and have a
service because that would be the one thing that would
make Grandpa happy.

So we went. We sang some songs and Everett said a nice
prayer asking for Grandpa's recovery, then amending his request, asking that God's will might be done. But nobody
preached and nobody stayed, even though David wanted us
to have a testimonial time.

Later over black beans and rice, David stood up and said

that he was disappointed in the community, that we should be continuing God's ministry and that everybody who had backslidden at Fire and Brimstone by participating in excessive music or by skipping prayer partners or by private blasphemy should be sleeping on nettles. He claimed the reason such sickness had fallen on Grandpa Herman was our unconfessed sins. He said he was going to dig a grave for anybody who wanted to sleep in it, and he asked for volunteers to help him dig it. By the time he was finished speaking, he had tears.

"I'll help you," Everett offered. "But you won't find me sleeping there because I don't think I've done nothing wrong by saying my prayers when I feel like it and by singing at night."

I rolled my eyes at Pammy, who rolled her eyes back, but that afternoon, I was surprised at how many people had their shovels in the soil. David and Everett and Barley and Jim Langston from the other side and his son Joshua.

I hoped that nobody would sleep there. It was January and so cold. But I watched from my window as Great-Aunt Imogene limped her way across the lawn, slowly bent to the ground until she could sit there, edged her legs against the side of the hole, and then plunked off like a penny out a window.

❦

One afternoon after school, I went to get Canaan to take him with me to the pack house for an hour or so while I worked on Ajita's rug. Laura was making candles at her little stove, and she'd left Canaan in his playpen, unhappily sitting without even a toy.

"Hey," I said. "I just came to get Canaan."

"He can stay here today," she said, without even turning around. "It's too cold for him to be outside."

"He won't *be* outside, Laura. He'll be in the pack house. I took a space heater out there. He'll be as warm there as he will here."

"I don't want him to go."

"Why?"

"He's busy," she claimed.

"Doing what? He can't even play with his toes, for God's sake."

"He's praying. And don't you swear in this house, Ninah Huff, or you won't ever touch my baby again."

"Pardon me," I started, "but I'm the one who *had* him, and you know I wouldn't let him get hurt or cold or anything like that. . . ."

"I think you're a bad influence on him," she said, turning for the first time away from her liquid wax, then returning quickly to her stirring.

"Laura!"

"You heard me. He ain't going today."

"Well, can he go tomorrow? I'd like to spend some time with him."

I was so mad that I thought I might cry. I don't think I was hurt, but I might have been. Mostly I was angry, and the madness clabbered around my vocal cords until I was scared to try to say anything else.

"I don't want to be rude to you, Ninah, but I think

you've strayed from the path of righteousness. And I don't think you appreciate Canaan for what he *is.*"

I know I should have stayed. I should have sat right in her house and played with Canaan there. It would have made Laura uncomfortable, and I didn't wish her anything better. But I had to leave.

In the barn that day, I wept like an orphan, but I finished Ajita's rug. I wove desperately, my fingers flicking and twisting, knotting Pammy's hair and sliding rows of tobacco leaves and twine against it, feeding through strips of flannel and bits of a ripped-up diaper and a torn-away feed sack. I paid no attention to the pattern at all—because I was too busy stewing and mourning and figuring ways to get Canaan back.

But when I was done, I'd crafted an azalea right in the center with Pammy's bright hair that contrasted so wildly with the brownness and paleness of the other fabrics. I thought that maybe azaleas were the flowers on Ajita Patel's Indian pants, and that even if they weren't, she, of all people, might appreciate the uneven blossom I'd sewn.

Inside I felt like kudzu vines running wild. Even winter couldn't kill kudzu. It might turn brownish for a season, but it never died. It grew in spite of cold weather, expanding to mock all natural rules and overrunning everything in its path. Kudzu on a building could grab on so hard that it'd tear the walls away from the foundation. Kudzu on a tree could smother the life out. I felt it twining around my bones, threatening to slip out through my ears and mouth and nose. There was more to it than just Laura not letting me keep Canaan.

There were leaves sprouting just because the community was in shambles, with everybody disagreeing about what to do at Fire and Brimstone. There were vine shoots angling off because I missed James, because nobody could even say he'd killed himself, not even Olin, and because rather than acknowledge that he'd died by his own hand, nobody mentioned him at all. There were buds sprouting because people couldn't make up their minds, because one day Mamma'd be carrying the Fire and Brimstone torch, telling me that she'd been praying for my rededication and the next day she'd be tangoing around the kitchen in a pair of Daddy's overalls and saying she might take herself shopping in town to buy store-bought underwear rather than having to fashion such narrow pieces of elastic.

I feared that the vines would extend from my body at night and stretch so far beyond me that they could wrap themselves around somebody's neck in their sleep. I didn't want to strangle anybody. Not literally anyway.

One day at lunch, Ajita Patel told me that when people came over from India, they had something called culture shock. She said it was hard for the new families to get used to the customs of a whole new society, but that in time, they learned to fit in.

I wondered if we'd ever fit in. It seemed to me that we had the ultimate in culture shock hitting all at once.

Pammy got invited to spend the night at a friend's house, but Bethany said no.

Mustard got invited to go fox hunting with some boys from Mossy Swamp, and Olin said yes. But Olin didn't tell Bethany about it until he'd already dropped Mustard off miles away. When Pammy found out, she came to my house and cried on my bedspread for a long, long time.

On the third afternoon when I wasn't allowed to keep Canaan, I went over to talk to Nanna. I didn't want her to fix anything. I knew she had too much on her mind. But I wanted her to tell me a story that I could make come true.

I walked right in, like always, but what I heard was yelling. It was Grandpa Herman, calling out from the bathroom, "All you damned women. Treating me like a—not treating me like a man. Where's Leila?"

"I'm right here," Nanna said.

"You ain't Leila, you old bitch," he demanded. "Get me Leila."

The bathroom door was closed. I thought maybe I should leave before they knew I was there, but I didn't.

"Please be careful, honey. You gonna cut yourself with that thing. Them blood-thinners you're taking will make you bleed a lot if you cut yourself accidentally."

"Get out of my way," Grandpa hollered. And then I heard the noise of something crashing.

"Where's Leila? Lei-la?"

He wandered out of the bathroom, wearing just his T-shirt. No pants. Not even any underwear. I'd never seen him that way before and didn't know what to do. He had shaved half of his face, even though his own rule book said that men kept beards at Fire and Brimstone. And he was bloody from being nicked by the razor. There was an awful lot of blood for a shaving accident, and something about the half-bare face looked obscene.

"Where you been?" he asked me. "Some old woman told me she was Leila. I thought she'd done something with you."

Grandpa walked up to me, his shriveled privates shaking between his legs, and he threw his arms around me and started kissing my cheek.

I wiggled away. Once he'd opened the door, I could see Nanna in the bathtub in all her clothes, laying back with her legs across the side, stunned.

"Nanna," I called, and ran to her. I had to help her up even though Grandpa was walking off down the hall, bleeding everywhere. Nanna had a knot on her head the size of a small cabbage.

"I'm fine," she assured me. "I'm okay. Where'd Herman go?"

"I don't know," I told her. "You'd better sit down. Here, sit." And I dropped the lid of the toilet to make her a seat.

"No, child. I've got to find Herman."

Nanna staggered quickly away, holding onto the walls.

I followed her, saying, "What'd he *do* to you?"

"He didn't mean it," she said. "He don't even know."

We found Grandpa in bed. She said he was having another little stroke.

"Leila," he said pathetically when she entered the room, "I couldn't find you."

"It's okay. I'm here."

"Some fucking bitch's trying to keep me away from you," he mumbled, his words glued to each other. "Leila, take me home."

"Okay," Nanna promised. "But first you need to go to sleep." She rubbed at his head until he dozed off, still patting his bleeding face to stop the cuts from running.

I stood in the doorway watching, worrying about Nanna, who would never put him in a home. I wondered if maybe David and Laura had been right—that we shouldn't use hospitals because it interfered with God's plans. I thought perhaps the bigger issue was that other people's lives changed for the worse when something interfered with God's plans. I wondered if he'd have died quietly if we hadn't taken him to the hospital, if it would have preserved what dignity he had left.

Later, Nanna made me promise not to tell.

That day's story wasn't the one I was looking for. I was sure that the kudzu had doubled or even tripled since that morning.

⤙

B_y_ March when the tobacco beds were seeded and it was time to begin the garden, Canaan was able to walk around a little. He had a hard time keeping his weight even and fell to one side or the other. And he bruised a lot because he couldn't block his falls with his hands. But he didn't complain about it much, and he'd work himself back up, waver for a moment, then find his balance and run a few feet before he stumbled over his own toes and crashed.

After his strokes, Grandpa Herman didn't remember that Canaan was the New Messiah. On good days, he'd hold Canaan on his knee and say, "Now whose baby is this?" Sometimes he'd tickle him. And sometimes he'd study his hands, pulling at them until Canaan cried.

The family'd been debating all winter who should take over Fire and Brimstone. Daddy and Uncle Ernest jointly took control of the finances. They gave money to each household to buy necessary goods, but apparently they gave out more money than Grandpa Herman ever had. Nearly every person at Fire and Brimstone ended up wearing a new watch. Nobody went about flaunting them, but I began to notice wrists taking on different appearances, black bands and white, faces that blinked and others with long gold hands. Barley got a diving watch, and he hadn't even been swimming since James died.

All of a sudden, people began to realize they preferred red over blue, or flowers over plaids. I thought it was a good thing.

But no new single leader was chosen. We put it off week after week. Mamma said we had to wait because Grandpa might get better, but Mamma was wishing hard and thinking cloudy. Even the doctors couldn't say for sure what his chances of recovery were. Some days, he was almost himself, walking around the community and giving everybody instructions on how to do whatever they were doing—even though his instructions didn't make much sense. But some days he didn't remember even Nanna.

So for the first couple of months of that year, we met in church just like always. Different men took over the sermon, taking turns preparing the scripture. And because Olin's views of Christianity were so different from David's or Everett's, we could never be exactly sure what sort of preaching would be coming our way.

I worried a lot about who would take control. I wished it could be me. I thought to myself that I'd have a good argument, even if it was temporary. If I argued that I was the mother of the Messiah and that I should hold the post until Canaan was old enough to speak his wisdom, I knew it'd keep David from grabbing the reins.

But I was a woman. Not even a woman. Not quite even sixteen years old. I knew I didn't stand a chance.

I thought Nanna would make a good leader, but then she was a woman too. I hoped maybe Daddy would step into the position, but I knew Daddy didn't like those kinds of responsibilities.

I thought maybe we should split the farmland and hire a preacher from outside.

Some Sundays in church, Canaan would holler out during the service, like all babies do, and some people would say, "Amen" or "Hallelujah" while other people would shake their heads. It was hard to know what to believe. And even though we were praying plenty, it was hard to cut through the tension enough to make contact with God. The edginess hovered in our air, and I think that when our prayers hit against it, they bounced off in all kinds of unheavenly directions.

By that time, I'd stopped even trying to get Laura and David to let me take Canaan off alone. They'd let me play with him as long as somebody else was around, but even when I held him during Sunday services, they looked at me suspiciously.

Nanna got mad about it. She started having Bethany or Pammy sit with Grandpa Herman in the afternoons so she could take Canaan for a walk. Then she'd bring him to the pack house and stay with me while I was weaving.

"How are you?" I'd ask her.

"Fair to middling."

"How's Grandpa today?"

"Oh, he's all right, I reckon. I fed him collards for lunch, and he didn't even complain. He hates collards, but he can't taste anything anyway, so I might as well fix what I like."

By that time, we'd stopped eating together at every meal. We only had supper together. Breakfast and lunch were private by then. Private and awfully lonely.

"Does it make you crazy, Nanna? Having to tend him every minute?"

"No," she said somberly. "I took him as husband for better or for worse."

"Do you ever wish he'd just—die."

"Sweet Jesus, child! I don't reckon you know what love's about after all." Then she dropped Canaan from her hip onto the floor and whispered, "I've thought about it. But that ain't my place to decide. And God only gives a body what a body can stand."

Canaan took off across the room, and I ran after him, picked him up, and shook him in the air until he giggled so hard that me and Nanna were both giggling, even though neither of us were happy. The best thing about baby laughter is that it can revive even the sore at heart.

"This here's a nice one," Nanna told me, stroking her hand across the half-finished tapestry. That'd look real pretty on your mamma's living room floor."

I carried Canaan over to the corner, collapsed on the heap of tobacco sheets, and motioned Nanna over to me.

"Come tell us a story," I said.

"Ninah." She smiled. "When you gonna grow up enough to be satisfied with the happenings of the day and not the things of the past?"

"Come on," I pleaded. "For Canaan. Please?"

So Nanna sat down next to us, and I leaned Canaan up against my lap and nestled underneath Nanna's arm. She patted me, and I gently rocked Canaan, and in the afternoon haze passing in through the window, light descended downwards, and we could see the dust twirling and dizzying through the air.

"What story you want to hear?"

"The one about the day she killed him."

"Why don't you tell it? You know it better than I do by now."

I situated Canaan in my arms and encouraged his yawns with my swaying. "You were coloring your paper dolls, right? And you'd just had supper. What'd you have for supper anyway?"

"Corn bread and ham," Nanna answered.

"Really?"

"Maybe. I don't know."

"So you were coloring, and your mamma was in the back with your daddy."

"My pappa," she corrected. "I called him Pappa." But I already knew that. It was just a mistake.

"And then you heard the gun go off. What'd it sound like?"

She considered for a minute. "Like a tractor tire blowing out."

"And then you kept coloring, waiting for something else to happen, but nothing did for a long time. You waited and waited and scribbled redness on all your dolls."

"And then Weston Ward stopped by," Nanna took over. "I reckon probably he had helped Mamma to plan the murder, although nobody ever prosecuted him."

"Do you hate him now?" I asked her.

"For what? For loving my mamma so much that she decided to get rid of Pappa?"

"Yeah."

"Or for ruining my childhood by taking me away from both Mamma *and* Pappa?"

"Yeah."

"Well, I don't like to harbor hatred in my heart, but there might be a little bit there for him."

"And what about your mamma? Do you hate her too? Even a little bit?"

Nanna pondered, ran her fingers at the back of my neck where the hairs just began, pinching and feeling with her bony loving hands.

"Grudges are bad things, Ninah," she said at last. "There's only so much room in one heart. You can fill it up with love or you can fill it with resentment. But every bit of resentment you hold takes space away from the love. And the resentment don't do no good noway, but look what love can do."

I watched the rectangles of light on the wooden floor, narrow in all the darkness but bright enough to make up for being so small.

"Like with you," Nanna continued. "If you'd wanted to, you could have been so mad about this baby going to live with David and Laura that you built up spite inside rather than goodness. But then you'd be so busy feeling angry that you wouldn't be able to appreciate what he feels like in your arms, sleeping that way."

"No," I disagreed. "I can do both at the same time. I can love him and still feel mad."

"Well, sometimes you got to hold onto a little bit of rage." Nanna nodded. "You got to have something to spit out. It's what wakes you up in the morning. It's what keeps you breathing. But if you keep too much of it, it will sour everything else around."

"Do you have some rage towards Grandpa?"

"A little bit," she admitted. "Just a tad. But mostly it's love. Except on mornings when he pisses the bed."

I could tell she was trying to lighten the subject, so I let her.

"Does he really do that?"

"I put some plastic over the mattress. I tell him not to worry about it."

Then Nanna kissed my head and took Canaan out of my arms, swaddling him in her own coat. "I better get this child back home before Laura comes after us with the butcher knife."

When she walked through the light in the doorway, she sent the airborne dust cascading in whole new places.

⟜

I *don't know exactly how long it was afterwards that Grandpa* Herman wandered away one day, but it was still late winter or maybe the earliest, earliest part of spring. The men hadn't even quit their winter jobs.

The women had decided to replace all the curtains in the church, so they'd set up sewing machines in the back of the fellowship hall and placed the supper tables so that they could cut out cloth on them. It was a community-wide endeavor, and I think that everybody hoped that the new curtains would restore something Fire and Brimstone had lost but no one could name.

And the children were all at school.

The way Nanna tells it, she was sitting in her house with Grandpa Herman. He was having a particularly good day and had already been out for a brief walk before he came inside to rest. She fed him his lunch and stayed there until he dozed off in his chair.

Since Grandpa usually slept for a couple of hours in the afternoons, Nanna slipped out the house, careful not to disturb him, and walked the short distance to the fellowship hall. She had grown so lonely, it seemed, and the times she spent away from Grandpa were the times when she resur-

rected her spirit. She told me every now and then that it was
hard to see a good man sink to Grandpa Herman's place.
Grandpa had become as unpredictable as weather, a star that
flickered on somebody else's whim.

Nanna didn't stay there long. She put the pins in the bottom of one curtain so that Wanda could hem it. And she put
on some water, waited for it to heat, and then made hot water with honey for everyone working. As soon as she'd had
her cup, she headed back home, just to be on the safe side.

But when she got there, Grandpa was gone. She didn't
panic at first. He was having a good day, and she knew he'd
probably just gone out for a stroll around the fields. She
checked to make sure he'd taken his coat, and he had.

So she went to the fellowship hall, but none of the
women had seen him. Great-Aunt Imogene told her not
to worry, that he'd probably gone to check on the cows.
But Mamma put down her scissors and went to help
Nanna look.

They didn't find him.

They checked to make sure he hadn't taken his truck.
Nanna'd had to hide the keys from him, and she worried at
first that Grandpa Herman might have found them and tried
to drive away. But the keys were still hidden. The truck was
still parked.

There were a lot of fields at Fire and Brimstone, and
when he didn't turn up nearby, Mamma went back to the
fellowship hall and rounded up the rest of the women to
help scout the place.

Laura took Grandpa Herman's truck and went to get
the men.

———

By the time we got off the bus and made it to the houses, the men were looking too. Everybody was in a tizzy, and I walked up to Nanna and layed my head against her chest. She wrapped her arms around me, and I could hear her heart racing like somebody dancing in Sunday shoes across a hardwood floor.

"Now, Herman's all right," Daddy said. "We'll find him. Has anybody started supper? Cause we gonna need to eat tonight, and Herman will be hungry when he gets back. Leila, will you make us a pound cake?"

Everybody knew that Daddy was just trying to get us distracted, to get us all working and not worrying so hard. But I could see concern in his folded shoulders.

"I don't know, Liston," Nanna answered weakly.

"Please, Nanna," Pammy tried. "We'll find him."

So Nanna went with Aunt Kate and Great-Aunt Imogene and Laura to the kitchen, and the rest of us set out to find Grandpa.

"Everett and Olin's done gone off in one truck," Daddy said. "David, why don't you take another one, and Mustard, you go with him. Barley, go check the barn, and Ninah, you and Pammy take the henhouse and the pigpen." He kept talking until he'd sent every person somewhere, and then Daddy and Mamma went off on their own.

It was Bethany who turned up the first clue.

"The tractor's missing," she hollered. "Hey, the tractor's gone."

"The John Deere's in the garden," Barley hollered back.

"No," Bethany shouted. "The old one. It's gone."

We followed the tire tracks to the edges of a field, then

around the back side to a tiny pond not even big enough for fishing. It was left right there.

When people heard the news, they began surveying the woods all around it, but at night time, nobody had found a trace of Grandpa Herman.

Over supper, we collected flashlights, and everybody warmed up with soup and bread. Then Everett said that there was no need for anybody else to get lost and that only the men should go out after dark because they knew the woods, and besides, if Grandpa came back, he'd need some people to greet him.

"That's craziness," Nanna argued. "And I'm going looking."

"Now, Mamma," Uncle Ernest said, "you won't do us a bit of good out there. Please don't make us have to worry about you too. Just stay here and wait with the women."

Then I thought that Nanna was going to cry because her lips began to tremble, and the little blue place on her bottom lip jumped like a flea. She said, "I can't figure out how we didn't hear him crank that tractor."

"The barn's a ways away," Mustard said. "It ain't your fault, Nanna."

"A big old noise like a tractor cranking though. You'd think we would have heard that."

"We were running all them sewing machines," Mamma mourned.

We sat up all night waiting for the men to come back with Grandpa, but they didn't. Then it started raining, hard, and when Nanna heard the drops hitting against the tin roof, her lips quivered so violently that she had to bite down on them to keep them from wiggling right off her face. But she didn't cry.

I thought I knew what she felt like. I imagined her feeling just the way I did when James died. It wasn't that crying was shameful or unexpected. It wasn't that crying made you look little or weak. It was just that one tear that broke away from an eye held that tight was enough to bring down a floodwall. Who could ever know the pressure behind it, or how big that flood might be? And what if the water kept coming and coming forever?

Around ten o'clock, the younger boys came home, soggy and cold. Mamma fed them, and Bethany sent them all to sleep at her house.

"You need some sleep, Nanna," Bethany said.

"I can't sleep," Nanna snapped. "I'm going out there to look for him."

"No, Leila," Great-Aunt Imogene tried. "You know old women can't see at night, even with a flashlight."

I was holding Canaan, and Laura wasn't even trying to take him away. It seemed like all the rules and all the problems of the community had been suspended temporarily, and I got to play with him all that night and kiss his head as much as I wanted and follow him around that great room as he ran. I got to feed him and watch the way he opened his mouth when the spoon approached. I was the one who got to rock him to sleep. I only felt the tinest bit guilty for taking pleasure in such a troubled time.

"I think the best thing we can do is hold a prayer meeting," Laura said.

"That's the best idea I've heard all day," Mamma replied, placing her hand on Laura's shoulder.

So we sat in a circle and began calling out to Christ. Everybody prayed, together, aloud, and most people cried. Occasionally, there'd be a break, and then they'd start up again.

But during one break, Nanna spoke up and said, "Children, I believe I'm going to get in my bed and do my praying there."

"Do you want me to go with you?" Mamma volunteered.

"No. You stay here. Maybe Ninah will come sleep with me."

"Go with her, Ninah," Mamma instructed, even though I was already on my feet.

"Now, y'all come get me if you hear anything," Nanna demanded. "Don't let me sleep if you hear any news."

"We won't," Wanda said, and kissed her cheek.

"Any news at all," Nanna whispered.

We *walked right in Nanna's back door, and I was about to* take off my shoes when Nanna pulled out a flashlight and threw me some long johns to put on under my clothes. "We're going looking," she said.

I knew from her tone that there was no need to try and change her mind. I didn't want to anyway.

Five minutes later, we stole out the front door, walking quickly down the dirt road and keeping our eyes primed for headlights in the distance.

"Where are we going?" I asked her.

"To the place where we dunked you," she said carefully.

"Do you think he's there?" I asked. I wondered if she was afraid he'd drowned himself. Just the thought chilled me.

"I don't know."

She was almost running. I had to hustle just to keep up.

When we came to the woods, we turned on the flashlight and made our way through the branches. I went first so I could hold back branches for her and strip down the spiderwebs with my face so they wouldn't cross hers. But I don't think Nanna noticed any of that.

I hoped the batteries in the flashlight were good. We needed the light. The moon was hidden by all the clouds, and the rain felt like a million mosquito bites against my skin.

When we got to the creek, I shined the light on the water, looking for a narrow place to cross, but Nanna never slowed down. She walked right through the water, and I ran behind her, then ahead.

When we came to the clearing where James had killed his first deer, I talked her into stopping to catch her breath. My own lungs were stinging, and I had to spit to make way for the air I was gulping.

But not long afterwards, Nanna was walking again, and we didn't stop until we came to the broken tree that stretched out over the pond.

Nanna took the flashlight, pulled herself onto the trunk, and stepped out over the water. "Herman?" she hollered. "Old Man, you've been out here long enough. You've scared us good, and it's time to go home." When she said "home," her voice caught halfway and squeaked with the loss.

"Nanna, he'll be okay," I promised her stupidly.

"Now you don't know that, do you, young lady?"

"No, ma'am," I admitted.

"Well, then hush."

She swung the flashlight left and right, studying the reeds, the surface of the pond. But I was searching for rope. Even after Nanna got down and we walked along the bank, rope was all I could think about.

"Do you reckon we could see any better from the dunking plank?" she asked as we approached the giant tree.

I couldn't imagine climbing to that place again.

"Maybe," I said. "I'll go."

"We'll both go," Nanna insisted, and she walked over to the makeshift ladder and began her climb.

I had the flashlight then, holding it straight up so Nanna could see where to put her hands. I worried so hard that she'd fall, and if she did, I wanted to be there to catch her. But she was steady and moving like someone so determined that I knew that even if she was marching to her death, she was sure it was what she wanted to do.

When she reached the top, she straddled the thick branch and scooted her way along.

I couldn't help feeling that sick fear of heights. I couldn't help remembering the only other time I'd been in that tree, and I sensed again and again that everything inside my rib cage was dropping from within its frame. My heart, my lungs, my stomach and liver and gallbladder, all dropping.

The only thing that convinced me it couldn't happen was the thought of all that kudzu tangled inside.

And then we were on the plank, side by side. Nanna took the flashlight and waved it across the water and land.

"Did you see that?" she said, when she noted a movement.

"Turtle," I replied.

The rain had cut to a drizzle, but I was soaked and shivering, listening to my teeth tapping out the fear and coldness I couldn't admit. Because the leaves hadn't grown on the trees yet, there was nothing to protect us from the wetness, even up high. In the quiet, I let myself remember for just a second the horrible swishing of a branch being pulled through water.

"The night I first loved Herman," Nanna said finally, "I knew there was more to God than praying and singing songs and going to preaching."

She turned off the light, and we sat completely in darkness, suspended above the pond like someone about to be punished. I thought maybe we were being punished already. I worried that she might jump.

"I knew after holding him and kissing that way, kissing so hard that one person's breathing was enough for two, I knew one of the reasons why my mamma killed my pappa, and at the same time, I knew I'd found out what God was about."

I put my hand on her legs to be sure that if she moved, I'd have a grip on her, and even if I couldn't keep her up there with me, I could go down too. He-ba-ma-shun-di and splash.

"I remember the day he began Fire and Brimstone. He'd been planning it for a time, and he couldn't think of the right name. He came bustling into the kitchen one day and said, 'The Church of Fire and Brimstone and God's Almighty Baptizing Wind,' and then he broke out laughing, and I fixed him some grits, and I watched him eat, just staring at his speckled skin and his laughing eyes. All along I wanted to call it 'God's Wind.' I thought 'God's Wind' was enough. But it was Herman's project."

Nanna chuckled to herself. "Crazy old man. Always coming up with a plan, a way to do something different. Something that ain't never been done before."

After a time, the wind started passing right through me, not even shuddering me, and though I couldn't feel my feet anymore, it didn't seem to matter. I thought we might be ghosts already, or that that's what we'd always been.

"I have loved that man more than anything," Nanna muttered, more to herself than to me. "I've wondered a lot of times when this day would come."

The night seemed to be holding its breath. For a while there, with Nanna saying so much and me not having a word worth its air, I thought for sure that the darkness was going to suffocate itself, blacking us out with it.

"And you know what else?" Nanna choked, then shook her head. "My mamma killed Pappa because she was always *wishing*, always wishing for more than she had. Wishing for another chance, another story to tell. But even Weston Ward wouldn't have been enough. Even if he'd given her the moon, she would have been wishing for a star to go along with it. . . ."

"It ain't so bad to wish for things," I told her.

"I reckon me and Mamma have more in common than I'd like to admit. Never satisfied with what the good Lord puts down before us." She reached over and touched my thigh. I think her hand was pressing hard, but I was too chilled to feel it.

"But you've always known that, haven't you?" Nanna continued. "That's why you want me to keep telling the story. You wish for more than anybody I know, but you better be careful. That's all I got to say."

I forced myself to breathe, deep, to keep from dying with the night. The only thing I understood was that God's will or not—Nanna wanted Grandpa back. But at least she was honest about it. At least she wasn't afraid to say she'd like her tale to have a happier ending.

"Nanna," I said, "you don't know how this is going to wind up."

"No," she answered. "But things are going to change now. From here on out. That much I *do* know."

I don't quite remember how we got down. I think it was Nanna who held the light, and I groped around in the darkness, feeling my way. But I wasn't worried about falling anymore. For some reason, maybe just exhaustion, I trusted my hands and the tree.

⌐

Back at Nanna's we dried off with heavy towels, and Nanna got us both dry clothes. I wore one of her dresses and a sweater, and I didn't even mind looking like an old woman.

We sat by her wood stove long enough to burn the chill out, though it never quite left my feet.

I didn't know what to say to her. I wanted to comfort her, but I also understood that sorrow's a silent place. It seemed like I could see Nanna shriveling behind her eyes. The force that made her eyes shine was backing up, getting farther and farther away.

"Are you okay?" I asked her finally.

It took her a minute to figure out I'd posed a question. She looked at me, her eyes like unplugged sockets, and replied, "Put on your shoes."

I followed her onto the porch, hurrying to button my coat. "We should get started on breakfast," I said. "The men will be back soon."

"I want to take one more look," Nanna replied. So we headed back out to the woods.

The foliage and weeds dried themselves against our ankles. It had rained so hard during the night that even after daylight came, it looked like the darkness had stuck to the ground. And as much as I loved Nanna, the only place I wanted to be was in the fellowship hall, preferably drinking something hot and holding Canaan.

Nanna marched across land we'd covered before. I could see the footprints of others in the muddy mulch. She took us in circles around the same piece of land and didn't seem to notice we weren't getting anywhere.

I kept trying to take the lead, but Nanna'd step out in front. It was almost as if she was assuring herself that I couldn't see her face.

"We're not going to find him out here," I said after a while.

Nanna stopped walking, turned back to me, her hair pushed out of its bun by the rain and splatted against the sides of her neck. "If you don't want to be out here," she snapped, "then go your ass back to the church."

I was surprised to hear her talk that way to *me*. But the thing that made me think I might cry was watching her stand with her hand against a tree and seeing a fat drop of water fall from a pine bough and land on her forehead. Nanna looked so insulted, as if the rain had hit her on purpose, and she slapped the drop away like a tick or a spider, put her hands over her face, and wandered off.

"I don't want to leave you," I yelled.

"If you've given up on Herman, you've left me already," she called back without turning around.

"Nanna," I begged, catching up. Then I held onto her, wishing I had a rocking chair so I could soothe her proper. "It's okay, Nanna. It's okay."

And when she couldn't stop, when I felt her shuddering so hard I worried I wouldn't be able to keep her bones from separating and slipping from my hands, I said, "We don't have time for this right now, Nanna. Come on."

She followed me.

We crossed the creek, and only a few minutes later, we heard a voice call out—David's—and then Nanna raced towards him. By the time I got there, David was kneeling on the ground, lifting up Grandpa Herman's khaki pants, dark flannel shirt, and camouflage jacket.

As others gathered around and more voices called from far echoes, "Did you find him?" Nanna reached down and gathered Grandpa's boxer shorts, socks, and shoes.

"Oh, Lord," Everett said. "Did y'all see this?" He motioned to the ground beneath a bush where a bottle of Coca-Cola sat upright, half-full. There was a pack of Nabs beside it, with two uneaten and a soggy one bitten in two.

We stood together at daybreak, not feeling the light at all. We stood so silently that breathing sounded like shouting. And then David said it.

"He was raptured. It was the rapture."

"Hush, David," Daddy whispered. But other voices were already launching, and I couldn't tell one from another. It was as if the voices were struggling to hoist each other into Heaven—hoping to at least get their voices there if their bodies had missed the call.

"Oh dear Jesus" overlapped by "Help us, Heavenly Father," tumbling across "The Rapture? When?" The voices called from behind trees. The voices puffed and panted. The voices blasted into the morning, "Save us, Jesus."

"No way," I said out loud. "Stop it!"

"It was the *rapture*," David repeated, then began crying, then praying. "We've been left behind. Jesus, don't tell me we've been left behind."

I turned to Barley, who held his mouth open—like he was trying to keep it from moving. I could see him filling up, rising like a thermometer, and I knew it would only be a matter of time before the top blew off.

"I don't believe it," Barley yelled out. "Great-Grandpa got raptured?" He shook his head as if to throw the idea away, then took off running. "I've got to tell them," he called back, his voice cluttered with fear.

"Hold on, now," Daddy shouted, but Barley was gone. David stood up and took off running after him. Then Joshua and the others, screaming, crying out to trees, "Lord, forgive us. Lord, don't leave us here."

"Do you think it's true, Daddy?" Everett asked. His chin rigored beneath his beard, and then he ran behind them, forgetting who he was.

It all happened so fast and felt so slow.

"Y'all get back here right now," Nanna hollered. "We got to keep *looking.*"

But nobody came back for her.

"Come on, Leila," Daddy said. "My truck's over here." And he offered her his arm and hustled her away. I ran behind, then ahead of them. I hopped into the truck bed. They climbed inside. And Daddy drove us home.

◄

I*t seemed like a long ride back, though we got there just as the* others were running into the yard. Uncle Ernest's truck clanked behind us, then halted to park. I didn't know what to think. There's something about fear that gets in your blood and thickens everything up. I didn't feel much of anything. I knew that Fire and Brimstone had been consumed, but I was scared not to stick with them for fear of having nothing to hold onto at all.

David was the first through the door, then Barley and Daddy and Nanna and me.

The women were sitting at the table, eating toast and eager for news.

"We found his clothes," David shouted. "We found all his clothes."

"Well, did you find *him?*" somebody asked.

"Don't you see?" David said. "It was the rapture. He's been raptured."

"What?" Mamma said.

Then Barley screamed out, "We've been left behind."

Everybody was quiet for a second, and then Mamma broke into tears and began to hold onto Laura, who had started to scream.

"We got left behind?" Pammy said, and then she began crying too. "Why'd we get left behind?"

"God, have mercy," Olin said, and then Mustard, who had just come in with John and some younger boys, took off running, hollering, "Nooooo" so loudly that his voice graveled.

"We ain't missed the rapture," Daddy said, but in his voice, I could tell that he wasn't quite sure himself. "I *know* we ain't *all* missed it. Do you think Herman would have been the *only* one taken?"

But three-quarters of the people were already on their knees, sobbing out to Jesus, hollering and begging.

"It was the storm last night," Wanda called. "That must have been when it happened." And then she began praying too.

Some people broke into tongues. Some people screamed and begged God to reconsider. I stood looking at Daddy and Nanna, who were as perplexed as I was. "That's bull-shit," I said. "Ain't been no rapture."

"He was the only one," Laura yelled, "the only one who tried to get you to repent. And it's *your* sinfulness that tainted this community, Ninah, and kept us from being resurrected."

"It's not the rapture," I defended. "Look." And I ran to the faucet and turned on the water to show her that it wasn't running blood. But I was grateful for the clearness when it came.

"That won't happen until later," she wailed. "It's *your* sinfulness that's kept us here," and she ran to me and grabbed my head and began pulling my hair, shaking me by my hair until Nanna hauled off and slapped her into the floor where she collapsed and began her prayers again.

I thought it must have been the long night and the stress, the worry and uncertainty that had made them all so strange.

Outside, I could hear Mustard roaring "Noooooo," and Bethany shrieking out to Jesus, demanding that our family be taken, even if we were to be taken late.

"You can't be taken late, Beth," Olin bellowed. "But maybe it weren't the rapture. We should pray."

"Help usssss," Pammy implored, her short red hair shaking across her terrified face.

"Good God, y'all," Uncle Ernest tried. "All these clothes mean is that Daddy took them off. Maybe he got hot or something. . . . We need to get back out there and keep looking."

"That's right," Nanna demanded.

"It's no use," Aunt Kate moaned. "The lamb has called the roll, and we've been left behind. How long will the potatoes keep if we put them in the cellar? Six months? A year? Oh, Jesus . . ."

That's when I remembered Canaan. I knew that if God had really called his special children home, Canaan would be gone. But I didn't know where he'd been sleeping. I tried to listen for his cries, because surely in all that noise, he'd be awake. But I couldn't hear him for all the voices lifting off, voices like sirens, voices mourning and cursing and hating. All those voices so heavy and afraid. I worried that the walls and floorboards wouldn't be able to hold them.

I wandered to the back of the room, stepping around the praying bodies. As new people would come in, someone would say, "Gabriel blew his trumpet last night. The rapture's happened, and we've been left here for the years of tribulation." The doorway became a heap of bodies, falling one into another and repenting. Daddy stood in the kitchen holding Nanna, both of them watching amazed.

Mamma stood up and wiped her strained eyes. "It's okay," she said. "We've got to slow down. We've got to think logical. This don't make good sense." But then Bethany wailed out, and when Mamma touched her, it was like she was consumed again in the horrible dejection.

"Maree," Daddy called. "Maree!"

But she didn't pay him any attention. She was too far gone.

I couldn't stop watching the praying bodies. I saw them

all as paper dolls, cut from the same brown sack. What one did, the rest had to do. It was almost as if they thought with one great misshapen mind.

It was almost as if Nanna and Daddy were the dolls on the end, with one hand attached and one hand free, trying desperately to yank the others up.

But I wasn't attached to anybody, and Canaan was only attached to himself. I knew I had to find him.

Canaan was against the wall on his pallet, yelling like someone about to be sacrificed, though nobody had noticed. I picked him up and held onto him, too tired and too stunned to try to interrupt their shouting.

I tried to remember if Canaan was really holy. I checked his finger to see if the invisible ring was there, but I couldn't feel it. I couldn't feel my invisible ring either.

I tried to remember if invisible meant the same thing as imaginary. My mind was so dulled, and the clamor was so impossible to penetrate. I held Canaan to my chest, and as he cried, he sucked at my nipple through Nanna's dress.

I remembered that on the resurrection day, the graves were supposed to open and the dead were to rise in Christ's name. But when I looked out the window, all the graves looked normal, and I began to feel relieved.

Fire and Brimstone had turned into a mob. I thought they might all be insane. I thought I must be dreaming, and I knew I'd better wake up quick.

But then Grandpa Herman walked up to the door, looked in at us like we were all crazy. He stood there naked as the day he was born, puzzled and muddy and with sprigs of hair standing up all over his head.

"Leila," he hollered. "What in the hell's going on?"

It took a while for everybody to hush. The silence rode through like a wind gust that passes slow, leaving a few leaves to rustle after it's gone.

"Baby," Nanna said. "Where you been?"

Everybody looked up at him, standing there without his clothes. There was snuffling and choked-back coughs throughout the room.

"The store," he explained—like it was the most natural thing in the world. "I went to get you a moon pie." And he held it out, smushed and dirty but still in its wrapper. "The brown ones you liked when we was courtin. Is that marshmallow inside or something else?"

"Herman," Nanna said, and somebody handed her a coat, and she wrapped it around him and layed down his hair with her palm.

"Fix him some breakfast," she demanded.

"Praise Jesus," somebody called, then "Hallelujah."

"It was a warning," Laura shouted. "We've been given another chance to get our lives right." Her eyes looked possessed. I wasn't sure that I could be a good mother, but I couldn't leave Canaan with her.

"I want to be the new leader," David cried. "God's calling me to do it. I want to lead our people back to God." As he spoke, he shook one leg like he had something down his pants.

"What makes you think we ever strayed away?" Daddy asked him.

"We've been given the biggest *sign* we could ever see,"

David preached. "And *praise* his name, we've been given a second chance to repent, to do all in our power necessary to make our hearts right with God."

"David," Mamma said. "We were wrong. We were wrong. We're just scared. Sit down."

But the fighting began again. Mustard, who had to be close to splattering, began to curse David and Laura and even Olin for scaring him to death, and he said that there wasn't going to be any rapture.

People broke out into prayers, and other people grabbed them by the hair and lifted their heads up and said, "Listen! We were *wrong*. Herman's *back.*"

I huddled Canaan next to me and walked right out the room, without anybody paying us any attention at all.

A*ll the way to the pack house, I could hear them yelling. The* voices vibrated in my head, and I kept telling Canaan, "You don't have to hear this. You don't have to listen."

I was glad it was still early. I was glad we were out before daytime had a chance to shove the early up into the clouds.

"You don't have to think about it," I told him. "You don't have to dream about it. You don't have to live this way, and I'm sure as *hell* tired of it."

By the time I climbed the rickety steps and made my way into the pack house, Canaan wasn't crying anymore. But he was shaken and scared, and if he'd been able to use his hands, I knew he would have been grasping for me. Because everybody needs something to hold onto besides themselves every now and then.

"Nobody's gonna take you away from me again. You want to see your daddy?" I asked him. "You want to go to Heaven right now so we don't have to live like this?"

I kept a pair of scissors in the pack house to clip my twine and fabric with. I found them and tested them against my hands. They weren't so sharp, but I thought they'd do the trick.

I wanted to do it fast. First to him, and then to me. I wished I could do it to us both at the same time, but I only had one pair of scissors, and I'd need my spare hand to hold him still.

I took Canaan and the scissors and settled down on the tobacco sheets. The door was cracked, so there was a bit of light, but I didn't want it to be bright enough for him to see me. I didn't want him to think I'd hurt him for the sake of pain. Not ever.

A part of me wanted to hurry. But a part of me wanted to do it slow, the way I imagined James had done it, securing that knot around his middle. I wondered what thoughts had gone through his head that day. I wondered if he'd wished for a pocketknife in those last moments underwater. I wondered if he'd had more nerve than I did.

I thought about Nanna's mamma, pointing that gun at her husband's back. I tried to imagine her pulling the trigger without a second thought, but I knew that wasn't how it happened. She'd kept him there, frightened, at gunpoint, pondering what she was doing.

I wondered if she did it for love, if James did it for love, if I was about to do it for love or if it was really something else.

"Sit here," I told Canaan. "I'll be right back."

I went to my stack of rugs and took the James rug and the Canaan rug. I put Canaan's rug beneath us and James' rug at our back. To finish telling both stories. After we were gone.

Then I held Canaan's hands in mine, my big, big hands covering his small ones completely, and I hummed to him for a minute. I thought that if I could make him fall asleep, it'd be easier.

He didn't sleep. I didn't know how much time I had left. I listened for the voices calling out, but all I could hear was my own memories, Grandpa Herman shouting, "There shall be weeping and wailing and gnashing of teeth," and Nanna saying, "Sometimes you got to hold onto a little bit of rage," and James saying, "You're doing real good. I can hear you when you pray."

When I picked up the scissors, they seemed to act without me, in spite of me, and before I knew what I was doing, I had placed them between his palms and snipped, snipped, snipped his hands apart.

He cried out so loudly that I knew I couldn't hurt him any worse. He screamed and buried himself in my lap, his hollering mouth at the center of Nanna's dress, between my breasts, so deafening that I knew it was killing the kudzu in there and his little hands shaking on both sides, free and moving, spilling bits of blood all around us, flicking them onto my wet face.

"Canaan," I sung to him. "It's okay." I don't know how long I held him like that before I put him down to find something to act as a bandage.

He stood up, and when he teetered, he used his hands to shove himself back up. Then he ran around the pack house squealing, shaking his hands maniacally and splashing the slightest bleeding over the walls and the floor, bleeding from both palms.

I thought he was crying, but by the time I caught him and began to bandage his hands with the leftover flannel from my weaving, I realized his squeals weren't of pain or terror or anything bad. He was laughing. I could hardly hold him still enough to tie the strips around his little palms that were about to clot on their own.

Then I let him run about, in his baby way so that his little legs moved from side to side, stepping awkwardly. I let him flick his hands. I let him slap his own round face.

"You are so goddamned beautiful," I told him, and even though I was crying, I understood something new. Something about connections. Somehow, I knew that splitting his hands was like severing a vine, like killing the vine about to strangle *not* somebody else but me. *Me.*

I remembered Corinthian's words that I'd misunderstood all along. "Whee, Jesus," she'd said. But it wasn't a curse at all. It was a prayer, and not a frightened one. It was a prayer praising freedom.

I picked him up, and he held on. He held one of my breasts in one bandaged hand and a fistful of my hair in the other.

"Whee, Jesus," I said, and I kissed his face, his mouth,

his head. Then I adjusted him on my hip and began the
slow walk back.

⤙

When *I've used up all my rags and lies, rope and hair, fabric*
and love, when I'm out of twine and my loom is broken and
there's still a story in me, that's when I unknot and begin
the unraveling.

My rugs are never finished. I use the same materials to
make them over and over again, featuring something new
each time and hearing a different tale. But sometimes they
speak the most wisely when they are heaps of fibers on the
pack house floor, intermingled and waiting.

If I sit with them silent for long enough, they will talk.
Just listening, I can give them tongues. They will speak like
prophets.

AFTERWORD

While I was writing this book, I was auditing a course in medieval history at Virginia Commonwealth University. The professor, Dr. Catherine Mooney, gave the class a bibliography of law codes and penitentials, and I found myself curious about the rules and punishments in different medieval societies. I pursued the subject in my studies, and I included variations of these medieval beliefs in *The Rapture of Canaan*. The laws from Grandpa Herman's handbook did not come from any single source, but many were influenced by my readings in the following:

The Burgundian Code: Book of Constitutions or Law of Gundobad: Additional Enactments, trans. Katherine Fischer Drew. Philadelphia: University of Pennsylvania Press, 1972.

AFTERWORD

The Irish Penitentials, ed. Ludwig Bieler. Dublin: Scriptores Latini Hiberniae, 1963.

The Lombard Laws, ed. Katherine Fischer Drew. Philadelphia: University of Pennsylvania Press, 1973.

The Medieval Handbooks of Penance, ed. John Thomas McNeil and Helena Gamer. New York: Columbia University Press, 1938.

Payer, Pierre J. *Sex and the Penitentials: The Development of a Sexual Code, 550–1150.* Toronto: University of Toronto Press, 1984.

Readings in Medieval History, ed. Patrick J. Geary. Peterborough, Canada: Broadview Press, 1989.